THE BRANDING OF A CHILD

First Novel in the Branded series

ELDON REED

ISBN: 1491209909
ISBN 13: 9781491209905
Library of Congress Control Number: 2013914159
CreateSpace Independent Publishing Platform
North Charleston, South Carolina

To my sweet mother-in-law,

Rosemary Hopper,

a voracious reader and inspiration to all.

ACKNOWLEDGEMENTS:

I'd like to thank a new friend of mine, Jamie Albee Lopez, who also lived on this same ranch, many years later. Jamie has shared her memories of that special part of the world with me. I am thankful you did, Jamie. It was, indeed, a very special place.

I'd also like to thank the readers of my first published novel, *Indebted*, for encouraging me to continue writing stories from the deepest parts of my soul. They are the reason writers keep doing what they love.

EVERY CHILD IS A STORY YET TO BE TOLD.

CHAPTER 1

At exactly 10:45 p.m., five-year-old Brandon Hall bolted upright in bed after the ear-splitting boom that came from his parents' room. He'd been used to hearing them argue after he was put to bed, but this was something else. With both ears covered, the booming echo lingered. Then he heard hurried footsteps tramping up the stairway.

He waited.

His mother's scream from down the hall caused Brandon's small body to quiver. He jumped out of bed and was met at the door by his mom. Denise grabbed him up in her arms and carried him downstairs, picked up the phone in the kitchen and dialed nine-one-one.

Brandon's father was perceived to be a good man in the community. Friends and acquaintances believed he had it all—tall, handsome, a beautiful home, a drop-dead gorgeous wife. They lived in a multistory ocean front home in Longport, New Jersey. Country club membership, new luxury cars, fancy restaurants—and maxed out credit cards—were part of their lifestyle.

The Smith & Wesson .357 was confiscated by the Longport Police Department. The body of Brandon's father was gurneyed away by a St John ambulance. Brandon clung to his mother. Still trembling, he buried his head up against her warm body.

For the first five years of his life, Brandon had been left with baby sitters almost daily and introduced to what would become his closest friend—the thirty-two inch flat-screen TV sitting on top of the Brazilian rosewood chest of drawers in his closed-door bedroom. He had been toted off to preschool with little or no parental training from home. His father was not a dad, just an occasional occupant of the house and legal mate to Brandon's mother.

A female police officer came into the kitchen where she found Denise holding her son. "Mrs. Hall, I'll need to ask you a few questions."

"Look, I'm in no mood to talk to you now."

"Well, I'm afraid we must talk."

Brandon was sniveling and clutching his mother. Denise rocked him back and forth in her arms as she sat on the ladder back chair next to the kitchen table.

The officer was in no hurry.

Denise ran her hand over her forehead and her fingers through her salon-crimped blood-red hair. "Lady, I said I'm in no mood to talk. My husband has just plugged his head full of lead. I have no way to make a living for me and my son, and that's a notice of foreclosure on the table where your elbow is perched."

"I can feel your pain, Mrs. Hall, but I do need to ask you a few questions."

"Make it quick, because I'm getting outta this house. I can't stand to stay here tonight in the same bed where my chicken husband blew his brains out."

"Yes, I can understand that." The officer pulled out a small recorder from her bag. "It'll just take a couple of minutes. Then you can go."

Denise came back to the house the next morning to get a change of clothes to take back to the motel where she and Brandon had spent the night. The phone rang. It was a girlfriend from Oklahoma where Denise had dropped out of high school. She'd heard the news from her mother who also lived in New Jersey.

After a few words of condolence from her friend, Denise could no longer hold back the tears. "I don't know what I'm gonna do. The house has gone into foreclosure, we owe more than the thing's worth, and I've got debts up to my eyeballs. I hate this town. I have no friends here."

There was an awkward silence.

Denise sucked in air, slowly exhaling. "I was simply known as the beautiful, but silent wife of Clinton Hall." She bit her French manicured nail. "Yeah, Clinton Hall—the big casino executive!"

"Well you sure had us all fooled. We were envious of you." Another awkward pause. "So you were sort of like… a trophy wife."

"You said that right. And now I feel like a very tarnished and broken trophy, ready for the trash."

"Hon, I remember you had a sister; where is she?"

"My goody two-shoes sister lives in L.A.—and we're not speaking." The nail biting continued. "I have no place to go. I'm hangin' by my eyelids!"

"Why don't you move back here to Oklahoma City? You went to school here, so I know you'd have a few friends. Besides, you've got me, and I'm here."

A distant gaze accompanied her thought. "You know, I might do just that. This is sure not my home. I've gotta get out of here."

With the little cash Denise managed to hold onto, she bought a thirty-year-old, twelve by sixty-foot, two-bedroom trailer in much need of repair in an older part of Oklahoma City. Her new neighborhood was about as opposite as it could be from the one in her New Jersey Shore home. Her lifestyle was about to be drastically altered, and more importantly, Brandon's life was to undergo a radical change that she could never have anticipated.

CHAPTER 2

Desperate for money to pay the bills, Denise sat at the little kitchen table, in the run-down trailer, circling jobs from the help-wanted ads in the *Daily Oklahoman*. She looked up at her beautiful child, golden blonde hair, unrivaled by anything coming out of a bottle. "Brandon, Mama's gotta get you a haircut. I can barely see those crystal-blue eyes."

"That's okay. You can't a…afford it." He ducked his head, and the blonde bangs fell down past the tip of his nose.

There was a familiar voice at the door. "Denise, you home?"

"Girlfriend, just open it and come on in."

"Hey, thought I might catch you home."

Denise offered her friend the other fifties style chrome dining chair.

"What are you doing? Searching the paper for jobs?"

"Looks like I don't have a choice. Bills have gotta be paid and we've gotta eat."

Her friend probed, "What happened to Brewer? He take off and leave you empty-handed?"

"No, I ran him off."

"What! You two just got married less than six weeks ago." She scooted her chair up closer. "And I know he loved Brandon. So what happened?"

Denise looked over at her son playing with a toy that someone had discarded out by the dumpster. It broke her heart that he had nothing else to play with. Soon, soon, she promised herself. Things would be different.

"Brandon, honey, why don't you take that and go outside to play? Mamma needs to talk to her friend."

With Brandon out of ear shot, Denise revealed the truth about her recent marriage to Brewer. "Yeah, that's just it, see, I think he *loved* him a little too much. I don't really have proof, but when I confronted him and threatened to call the cops, he packed up and left within the hour."

"You don't mean..."

"Yep. I mean, if he wasn't guilty, why'd he agree to move out so quickly?"

"You talk to Brandon about it?"

"No, I didn't know what to say to him. But he's been wetting the bed again, and reverting to baby talk a lot—and you know that's not like him. I swear the kid's got English down better than I do—and I don't think he got that from his dad either."

"Then you did the right thing, girl. You don't need Brewer, no matter how much money the old goat was bringing in." She stared at Denise. "Besides, he was twice your age. I know you were lonely–but honey–you can do better than that."

"Hey, I just thought of something. I remember seeing a help-wanted sign on the marquis at one of the motels just off I-40 on the west side of the city..."

"When were you even over in that part of town anyway?"

"Don't ask."

"Denise, that's a long drive over..."

"Well, I'm desperate. Without a high school diploma my employment options are pretty stinking limited."

"Yeah, probably minimum wage."

"I know it won't pay the bills, but I've got no choice. I've gotta have some income.

∽

Denise applied the next day and was hired on the spot. Once again, Brandon was left from time to time with a number of impromptu sitters, from neighborhood teens to out-of-work adult women—and men. But most of the time he was left alone.

The motel laundry room, hot and humid with no air conditioning, is where she met Bryce Collier. He was a full two inches shorter than her, a scrawny worm of a man, his body ravished by years of illicit drug use. But he had mastered the art of flirting, using just the right words and facial expressions to seduce.

"Hey sweet thang, you're way too pretty to be workin' in a place like this."

Before she could think of a reply, he was pulling out a pack of Marlboros and offered her one. "Wanna take a smoke break with me?" He leaned over close. "I'm lovin' that gorgeous red hair of yours."

After their shift was over, Denise picked up her purse and headed for the door. Brice cornered her again. "Hey, babe, you wanna hit the happy hour with me down at Jake's Place. I'll buy you a drink."

Denise was standing next to the wall, ready to walk out. "Where is this Jake's Place?"

Bryce's palm was on the wall above her shoulder, his face inches from hers. "It's just over on Portland, not far from here." He brought his hand down and let it rest on her shoulder. "Come on, babe, let's go. I'm buyin'."

"I guess I could call my neighbor to come over and watch my son for a while, but I'll need to be back in a couple of hours."

Brandon's *sitter* for the evening turned out to be the twenty-one inch black and white TV on the living room floor. At nine-thirty that evening, he fell asleep—alone.

One week later, her supervisor approached her. "Denise, I'm happy with the way you've caught on and are pulling your share of the work load, but your friend—what's his name, Bryce?—is a different story. The motel's not paying him to chit chat with you. You should ignore him. I'll have a talk... I'm not sure why I hired him in the first place."

"Bryce is Bryce. I can't shut him up, but I won't let him affect my work."

It was a matter of days before Bryce had moved up—up from the old boxy Bronco he'd called home to the trailer he now shared with Denise. She'd felt sorry for him and invited him to stay with her until he could get a place of his own. Six months and three jobs later, Bryce Collier was still there.

When he wasn't drinking, Bryce could be quite a Casanova. But get a few beers in him, and he'd turn into a number one führer within the hour. More than once Denise had asked him to move out, but the real truth was, she couldn't pay the bills on her paycheck alone.

At a hundred and ten pounds, Denise picked her way up the wobbly narrow metal steps of her trailer, yanked open the warped door, and saw Bryce sprawled out on the recently acquired shabby sofa someone had discarded and set out by the park dumpster. The seven empty amber colored bottles on the floor by the couch foretold what was still to come. It was too early for him to be home from work, so she asked him what happened.

With speech a little slurred he mumbled, "I got canned."

Denise knew it was best to stay clear of him when he came in drunk, so she sat down at the tiny kitchen table, picked up the paperback mystery she had started reading earlier and said no more to him.

She had read only a few pages when he pulled himself up out of the sagging sofa, staggered over and snatched the book out of her hands, "Ain't you got nuthin' better to do than set around readin' your stupid books?"

She stood and got up in his face, "What would you rather I be doing, Bryce Collier?"

She could see the bulging vein in his neck. She tried to step back, but his fist was faster. Her left eye socket took the hit. She went down, and Bryce stumbled out the door.

One week later, the neighbor next door came over and sat down by Denise on the old once blue lawn chairs. "Sweetie, your eye has turned from black to blue and now to green. You still got that scrawny little beast livin' with you?"

"Yep, he's still here. Come inside for a minute."

"There's almost no food in the house. He promised some of his final paycheck to buy groceries, but I've yet to see any of it. I suspect he drank the grocery money." Denise stood there staring into the mostly empty cupboard—one can of chicken noodle soup and a partial bag of stale Doritos. She opened the avocado green fridge. "Look at this. One gallon container of milk with maybe a cup left, a package of questionable bologna, ketchup, and three very limp carrots."

"Honey, why don't I bring a few things over? I don't have much either, but I can share what little I have."

She stood there, about to cry, when Bryce appeared in the doorway, "Hey babe, can you give me a hand with these groceries?"

Denise scrambled down the teetering steps and out to his old white Bronco, opened the tail gate and saw a dozen or more bags of groceries. She grabbed two of the heavy ones and met him coming out of the house, "Where did you get all this?"

He gave her a flirtatious wink. "I got it at the grocery store, silly."

"What I meant was where did you get the money to buy all of this?"

"I got a job." Bryce gave her a quick peck on the cheek.

She stood back a bit, smirked. "You got a job. And you got paid after one day of work?"

"No, babe, I start work tomorrow. I had a few bucks left from my last paycheck, so I went ahead and bought groceries. I knew we were out."

She could read him like a book. "When you left this morning you told me you didn't have any money." She walked to the bottom tread of the wobbly metal steps. "So I guess that means you made a sale."

"Shut up, Denise!"

She set the bags down and hurried back out to the Bronco for more. She reached inside the cargo area and was picking up another bag when she felt two arms wrapping around her waist. She looked down at the hands. "Brandon! How about giving me a hand with these?"

Brandon picked up two bags and fell in behind his mother as she climbed the steep little metal steps. "After school I went to a friend's house three blocks down. We played video games in his room 'til his mom came home. She said I'd have to leave, so that is when I walked home."

It was a Wednesday. Denise was working late. With a biker's convention in town, the motel had been booked solid, which meant the mountain of laundry had to be finished and ready for the next day. She was training a new girl, and most everyone was getting overtime.

Bryce was in between jobs again, so he was home when Brandon came in from school. With one leg slung over the top of the couch and the other dangling down to the floor, he glanced up at Brandon and stuttered, "Brandon, son, come and take this tr... trash out to the dempster. Your mother will be home any minute, and she won't be happy with you sack...slacking off on your job."

Brandon looked over at the overfilled trash can, then back at Bryce. "I took it out this morning before school. How'd it get so full?"

"Boy, don't you smart mouth me. Get over there and do your job like you were told."

Brandon pulled the heavy bag out of the pink plastic garbage can, tied the strings and dragged the bag, with bottles clanking, across the living room floor.

"Pick up that bag, son! You don't drag it across the floor."

He managed to pick it up long enough to get out the door. Then he dragged it down the steps and out to the dumpster, all the way hoping it didn't break open and spill out. He climbed on an old kitchen chair someone had thrown out and heaved the bag of clanking bottles over the side of the smelly dumpster. Back on the sidewalk he sat down and played with the neighbor's dog, taking his time before going back in the house.

As soon as he walked in the door, Bryce staggered over with a belt in his hand. "Boy, I told you not to drag that trash on the floor like that."

"I didn't! Only after I got outside. It was too heavy for me."

The bully was back. "Bend over, you little –––." The belt slashed Brandon's side, then his bottom. "This will teach you to sass me! Now drop them pants!"

"No... no...no!"

"I said drop um NOW!"

Brandon obeyed, and Bryce swung hard. The end of the belt wrapped around and hit his private parts. Brandon screamed! The belt kept coming, once tearing into his upper arm as well.

"Now, are you gonna sass me anymore?"

"No sir. I won't." Brandon grabbed at his bare leg; then he pulled back his hand, saw the blood, and pulled his jeans up.

When Denise came home from work she could see that Bryce had been drinking again. She also noticed the whelps on Brandon's right arm. "What have you done to my son?"

"Your *son* needs to learn a little re… respect around this house."

Denise knew it was the alcohol talking. She also knew she had to get Brandon out of the house. "Okay, but one of Brandon's friends has invited him over for a sleep-over. I'll be back in a little."

She hurried Brandon out the door before Bryce's temper erupted again. And she knew it would. On her way out to her car she said under her breath, "I'm gonna kill that son-of-a- ——! Come on, Brandon, get in."

He looked up at her. "Mom, where are we going?"

"I don't know. Doesn't one of your friends live over on Cherry Street?"

"Um, Christopher does. You think I could stay with him tonight?"

"We'll see if you can. How much farther is it?

"I think it's down in the next block."

Denise rolled through the stop sign. "Which house is it?"

"It's the brown one with the bike on the driveway."

She pulled up to the curb, got out and opened the door for Brandon. Seat belts were apparently optional in Denise's new world. After she had knocked on the front door, a middle-aged lady appeared.

"Are you Christopher's mother?"

"I'm his grandmother. Has he done something wrong?"

"No, Brandon was just wondering if he and Christopher could hang out for a while."

"Well, I suppose so. I'm sure Chris would like that."

Denise was stepping inside the door. "I'm sorry. I didn't get your name—"

Just as the lady started to answer, Denise butted in. "I'm Denise Brewer, and this is my son, Brandon. There are no other kids his age in our area, and he was hoping Christopher was home."

"Yes, he's in the back yard now with his dog, Dancer. I'm sure he'll be glad to see Brandon." She glanced at the watch on her wrist. "What time can I expect you to call for him?"

"I'll try to get back over about seven-thirty. Is that okay?"

"Sure, we'll see you then."

Instead of going straight home, Denise stopped and picked up a couple of burgers, fries and two Cokes. She parked her old Pinto wagon on the gravel drive next to Bryce's Bronco and carried the bag of fast food inside. Bryce appeared to be passed out on the couch. Rather than wake the little banty rooster, she went ahead, ate her burger and took her Coke outside to sit down in one of the rusty lawn chairs. Her neighbor saw her there, came out and sat down beside her.

A half hour passed, and Bryce stumbled to the door. "Denise, you just got one burger for me! And the fries are stone cold."

"Bryce, you were sleeping. I didn't want to disturb you."

"Well you shoulda woke me up. No one likes cold burgers and especially cold fries."

Denise looked at her neighbor and rolled her own brown eyes. "Excuse me. It looks like Daddy Grizzly needs some TLC."

She hurried back up the metal steps, yanked on the warped door and stepped in. Bryce was right there in her face. "Denise, where were you? You shoulda been home by four."

"I had to work over. Every room was rented, so that means the laundry was piled sky high. I'm surprised you even knew what time it was."

"Look, I don't like you showing up here at just any time."

"Showing up here at just any time! Look, Daddy Warbucks, you forget this is *my house*, not yours. I can show up at my house any time I want."

"You did this last week too. I'm startin' to think you're seeing someone else. Who is it, Denise?" Standing directly in front of her, he placed his hands on her shoulders, and gave her a bit of a shove backward. "Come on Denise, fess up!"

"Bryce, there is no one else—but I'm starting to think I should find someone!"

That remark earned her a hard slap on her right ear. Then she saw his fist, tried to dodge, but it caught her right eye. She managed to back away, ran into the bathroom and locked the door. After looking in the mirror and seeing the swelling starting around her eye, she took a couple of aspirins and wandered back to the kitchen to get some ice.

He walked over, pushed her away and shoved at the freezer door. It bounced back. With both his palms he forced it shut. He then turned toward her, grabbed both of her arms and shook her back and forth, then side to side, like a dog shaking its prey. "Denise, fess up and tell me right now who you've been sleepin' with."

She caught her breath and swallowed hard. "I have not been sleeping with anyone else. If I'm late getting home, it's because I worked overtime. You should appreciate that, seeing how you don't even have a job yourself."

He bristled and shoved her delicate frame backward. She fell with her head slamming into the kitchen window. The single-pane glass cracked and a large triangular piece sliced downward. Had it not been for the plastic mini-blinds, her head would have been lacerated by the large shard. She managed to pull herself up and sat down at the kitchen table.

An hour later Bryce came to her, apologized, and played his charm card again. "Hey babe, sorry I accused you. I'll put on some soft music, make you a cup of that fancy tea you like, and you and I can kick back and relax. Tomorrow evening I'll have dinner ready for you when you get in." Denise knew that was a lie, but she liked the idea of the soft music and relaxing. Brandon was forgotten.

CHAPTER 3

Kirk and Katie Childers sat at the breakfast table in what they called the big room. In the center of the room a massive wagon-wheel chandelier hung over a farmhouse type dining table. At the far end of the room was a colossal river rock fireplace, reaching upward to the twenty-foot vaulted ceiling.

Kirk carefully set down his over-full mug of morning coffee, sat down across the table from his pretty little wife of five years. "So, all the paper work is complete now?"

"Yes, I hand delivered it to the DFS office yesterday. The lady told me we had completed everything, and we might be getting a call soon for them to do a home study."

"So I guess they wanna make sure we don't have a path out to the toilet, the roof doesn't leak, and," he grinned, "you know how to cook."

"One look at you, and they can see I know how to cook."

"Of course, that's why I married you."

"Oh really?"

He winked, "Well, that and you wash my socks."

Katie picked up the dish towel on the table next to her and slung it toward his face. "Okay big guy, you'd better come up with better reasons than that if you expect to keep feeding that six-foot-two frame of yours and putting on clean socks."

He reached over and kissed her. "Hey, you wanna go for a ride this morning?"

"I thought you were going to the Johnson's farm auction."

"Naw, I'd rather go for a ride with my favorite chef and washer woman."

"Get outta here!"

Kirk blew her a kiss on his way out. "I'll do the milking, saddle up our rides and be back in an hour—maybe an hour and a half tops."

CHAPTER 4

Even though they had finished their evening meal, Christopher's grandmother made a quick sandwich for Brandon. When Denise didn't show up by bedtime, she pulled out a trundle bed for him and noticed the raised whelps on his arm.

She tucked him in, but the next morning, when Denise had still not picked him up, she called the Oklahoma Department of Family Services.

A caseworker showed up within the hour. "I'm Betty Sawyer. I am a caseworker for the Department of Family Services. Is the child still here?"

"Yes, I thought you should see this boy before I send him back to school. His mother dropped him off yesterday afternoon. She agreed to pick him up about seven-thirty but never did. I discovered the whelps on his arm last night as I was putting him to bed. He said his mother's boyfriend whipped him. He told me that those on his arm didn't hurt as much as the ones under his pants."

The caseworker asked about Brandon's family. "You said his mother dropped him off yesterday?"

"Yes, that's correct."

"Do you know where he lives?"

"No, I don't even know this family. I believe she said her name was Denise. Brandon should be able to tell you more. I think he lives in that trailer park over on Elm Street."

"Let's go ahead and bring in Brandon. I want to question him a bit and take a look at his injuries."

Brandon slowly walked in the living room and ducked his head. "I'm supposed to be in school now. I will be in trouble."

Mrs. Sawyer assured him that he wouldn't be in trouble; then asked if she could see all of his injuries. He pulled his pants down just low enough for Betty to see the deep wounds. She looked at Christopher's grandmother. "This is not good. I am going to take this child and try to find out where he lives and who his mother is. In the meantime, if she calls for him, give her my card and ask her to contact me."

"Oh, I hope I did the right thing by calling you."

"Trust me; this child does not need any more beatings like he has just suffered. The boy will be with me until I can find a temporary home for him."

Brandon agreed to go with Mrs. Sawyer. He got in her car, buckled up when the caseworker reminded him, then showed her where he lived. "My name is Brandon Hall, but my mother's name is Denise Brewer."

As they pulled up to the trailer that he pointed out, Betty told him to stay in her car while she went to the door. She stepped up on the unbalanced metal steps, and without a railing to steady her, she quickly reached for the loose door knob. She knocked, and then knocked again. There were no vehicles in the driveway. No one answered the door. When she got back in her car, Brandon spoke up. "My mom is probably at work. I don't know where Bryce is."

"Where does your mother work?"

"She works at a motel. She does their laundry."

"Do you know which motel?"

"No, it's a long ways from here. I think she said it was on the other side of town. Are you going to take me to school now? 'Cause if I miss school, I'll get another whipping from Bryce."

"Honey, you don't need to worry about that. I'll see that you get back in school, and you won't have to worry about getting more whippings from Bryce."

Denise worked late again. She knew Bryce wouldn't have dinner ready as he had promised. Remembering Brandon's favorite fast food was Taco Bell, she entered the drive-up lane, waited in line, and a few minutes later drove out with a sack of bean burritos and hard shell tacos to take home. She hoped Christopher's grandmother wasn't angry for her not picking him up the previous night as she had agreed, but Brandon was a good kid, and she knew he wouldn't be any trouble. The grandmother opened the door.

Running her hand through her stringy blood-red hair, Denise blurted out, "I'm so sorry. I hope Brandon wasn't too much trouble. My mother had a heart attack and I had to take her to the hospital."

"Really?" The gray haired lady's face showed doubt. "How is your mother doing now?"

"Well, they found out it wasn't a heart attack. She's back home now."

The grandmother—fifty-eight years wise—dipped her head, peaked over her large plastic bi-focal glasses. "Lady, your son is not here." She handed her Betty Sawyer's card. "You should give this woman a call."

Denise glanced at the card. "You called DFS to come pick up my child?"

"That is precisely what I did. The child has multiple wounds on his body. He says your boyfriend whipped him."

"I think you just didn't want to be bothered with him, so you called DFS!" She turned, and while running back to the beat up old Pinto yelled an obscenity. "I thought I could trust you!"

It was after six. Denise assumed the DFS offices wouldn't be open, so she called the caseworker's cell number listed on the card. "This is Denise Brewer. I want to know where my child is."

"Ms. Brewer, you seemed to not be concerned where your child was last night."

"I—"

"As I understand it, you left him overnight with a total stranger, telling her you would be back to pick him up by seven-thirty yesterday evening."

"Look, I told that lady I had to take my father to the hospital and couldn't get back over." She twirled a strand of her hair. "I had to be at work by seven this morning."

"Miss Brewer, you should work at getting your stories straight—"

"What have you done with my son?"

Betty held the phone out from her ear, lowering the volume. "Okay, Miss Brewer, this is the way it is. Brandon has severe wounds to his body. He claims your boyfriend whipped him with a belt. Believe me, this was no ordinary swat on the bottom. The boy was forced to drop his pants. Your boyfriend slashed him repeatedly. He is being treated for multiple wounds and he will remain in protective custody until further notice."

"Are you telling me that I can't even see my son?"

"At this time, no, you cannot." She paused. "I'll need a way to contact you. Is this number you are calling from a good way to reach you?"

Denise fouled her next comment with a string of obscenities, "I think this was a set up. That old woman didn't want to be bothered with my son, so she called you to come get him. I think I see a lawsuit here!"

"Is this a number where I can reach you?"

"Yes, you can reach me here in the evenings. I work at the Lamplighter Inn just off I-40 on the west side of the city. If you need to reach me during the day, you can call there. I still say the whole thing was a set up."

"Okay, Denise, I'll be back in touch with you. But for now, Brandon is being cared for, and his wounds are being treated."

CHAPTER 5

"Hello, Childers Ranch; this is Katie."

"Mrs. Childers, this is Betty Sawyer with the Department of Family Services. I believe you and your husband applied to be part of our foster parenting program."

"Yes, that's right. We finished the evening classes, got our certificate, and now we're ready to receive a child into our home."

"May I call you Katie?"

"Of course, and my husband is Kirk."

"Katie, this is a little unusual. The Department rules call for an in-home visit prior to placing a child in your home, but all of our homes are at capacity and we have a seven-year-old boy that needs to be placed now."

Katie's excitement spilled through the phone, "Oh, yes! That would be great. We live on a big ranch. So that will be perfect for a little boy."

"Katie, you do understand that this placement will be temporary. He will only be with you until his family situation can be resolved."

"Yes, that's fine. We understand it might be for just a short time. You see, we have no children of our own. We feel that fostering is right for us now."

"Would it be possible for me to bring him out this afternoon? I'll just do the in-home study when I bring him out."

"Yes, that would be great. Do you know how to find us?"

"I have your address and a GPS. If I have trouble, I'll call you. Would five o'clock be okay?"

"That would be fine, Betty. We'll see you then."

Katie hung up the phone, hoping Kirk would come to the house soon. She went back to the room they had already prepared. Since she hadn't known beforehand if they might be getting a boy or a girl, she had tried to keep the room pretty neutral—no pink frilly stuff, but no footballs or western décor.

She took a long look at the special room where she and Kirk had spent many hours working. With a unisex theme in mind, they had transformed the plain white walls into a colorful and youthful gallery. She found pictures of happy-faced children, framed each one and planned to eventually replace the unknown faces with those of the children she and Kirk would foster. Kirk had built a bookcase to hold all of the books she had been collecting. They painted the room a subtle shade of yellow with a border of various breeds of dogs. There were toys for different ages. Some were given to them by friends and relatives, but they had bought a few themselves.

Kirk opened the back door and walked into the mudroom. Katie was there, reaching up to kiss him. "We are getting a little seven-year-old boy at five o'clock today!"

"That's great. What's his name?"

"I was so excited that I forgot to ask. The caseworker—I think her name is Betty—wants us both to be here. She said DFS normally would come for a home visit prior to placing a child, but they had no place to put this little boy. All the foster homes in the metro area were full. I think she'll be inspecting our home and us. I just hope we meet her standards."

Kirk reached down, hugged his wife, and said, "Honey, we'll have no problem with that. We've been preparing for a couple of months now." He grinned. "The room is ready and we've got food in the house. What more could a kid want?"

"I'm afraid we won't know what to do tonight. I've never had a seven-year-old boy to entertain all evening."

"Katie, you're making too big a deal of it. We'll just play it by ear. If he wants to talk, you're good at that. If he just wants to be alone, I can handle that." He placed his cracked and callused hands on her shoulders. "Besides, remember, you are a teacher. You've entertained seven-year-olds before."

"Remember our rules," she said, "in bed by eight, eat all our meals together, pray with him at bedtime—"

"Katie, it's like I said, we've gotta play it by ear. A seven-year-old should be able to stay up till nine or ten. We just need to make sure he gets enough sleep, that's all."

"You're right. But right now, I want to bake some cookies to have when he gets here."

As she was all but skipping back to the kitchen, he hollered, "Make 'em chocolate chip. I'll help him eat 'em." He headed back to the door. "Hey, call me when he gets here. Right now, I need to check on a couple of cows that are about to calve. I just came by first to sneak a kiss from my beautiful wife." He winked at her. "Couldn't do that with a regular job, uh?"

Kirk jumped on the ATV, with Old Chubby following. When he found the two heifers he could see they were having trouble with birthing. He did what he could but decided he should call the veterinarian. Between the veterinarian and Kirk, they were able to save both calves. Kirk thanked the vet, got back on his ATV and rode to the milk barn. It was a little early for milking, but the three dairy cows must have heard the ATV pull up to the barn and went inside without being coaxed.

"Come on, Chubby, you know dogs aren't allowed in the milk barn." It didn't take long to milk the three Jerseys, but separating the cream did. Of course after separating the cream, the equipment had to be washed and ready for the next use. It was almost five, so he headed back to the ranch house. Chubby again followed him the half mile back to the big rock house hidden in the trees.

As he always did, Kirk pulled off his well-seasoned and fertilized boots before going in the back door. He was greeted by a wonderful aroma of chocolate chip cookies fresh out of the oven. In his sock feet, he sneaked into the kitchen and was reaching for a cookie when he heard a scolding voice.

"Don't you even think of it!"

"What! Come on. They're warm and fresh."

"I thought we should wait till they get here."

"I saw a car pull through the front gate as I was riding in." With a mouthful of cookie, he said, "Maybe that's them. I'm gonna go put on a clean shirt. This one smells a little like Jersey cows—or maybe an export product of Jersey cows."

Katie had just finished putting on a fresh pot of coffee. Kirk was walking into the kitchen, fumbling with the last button on his clean flannel shirt when they heard the knock at the door. He was first to get there and open it.

"You must be Kirk," Betty Sawyer said.

"Yes." He turned. "And this is my wife Katie. And who do we have here?"

Betty put her hand on Brandon's shoulder, "This is Brandon." Brandon showed his bashful side and turned in toward the caseworker. "Brandon, say hello to Mr. and Mrs. Childers."

The boy remained silent, trying to hide behind Betty.

Katie stooped down to Brandon's height. "Brandon, I've just pulled some chocolate chip cookies out of the oven. Come on in. Let's see if they are any good."

To the right of the front door was the big farm kitchen, where the air was still scented with the wonderful cookie aroma. Kirk looked down at the frail little boy, still hiding his face in the caseworker's side. "I was able to sneak one earlier, even though Miss Katie thought I should wait. Let's go sit at the kitchen table and see if you can eat more than I can."

Betty looked over the large open room. "Your house is amazing. I love the high ceilings and the big wagon wheel chandelier over the dining table."

"Thank you," Kirk said. We enjoy it. The walls are solid rock—no wood framework— just rock on the inside as well as another layer of rock on the exterior." He then peeked behind the caseworker toward Brandon. "So, Brandon, have you ever been on a ranch?"

Brandon shook his head no but still was trying to hide his face.

"Brandon saw the horses when we came through the gate. Do you ride them?"

"You bet. Dandy and Lilly are very tame and like to be ridden." Kirk ducked his head toward Brandon's face. "Would you like to ride sometime? I'll buy you a helmet."

Brandon was still hiding his face but gave an affirmative shake of the head. He hadn't picked up his cookie.

Katie tried to get him talking. "Would you like a glass of milk to go with your cookie?

This time he turned toward her with a whisper. "Yes. Thank you." His lips barely moved.

Katie poured a glass of milk for him and brought the coffee pot to the table. She set the glass in front of Brandon. "This is fresh milk, straight from our dairy cows. It is very rich, even though some of the cream has been taken off."

Betty picked up the coffee mug in front of her. "I have told Brandon that he is a very lucky boy. He gets to have a vacation on a big ranch. He will probably see a lot of cows, some horses, and other farm animals. Not very many kids from his neighborhood will ever have that opportunity."

Brandon looked up. His eyes had brightened. "And I saw a dog just outside the door."

"Yep. That would have been Old Chubby." Kirk smiled. "He'll love for you to play with him. He hasn't had any little boys to romp around with, so he's gonna be glad you're here."

"Does he fart?"

"Brandon!" The caseworker held her hands to either side of her face.

Kirk was unfazed. "Yes, Brandon, I'm sure he does, but he does that outside. Did you know that isn't a very nice word to use in public? Maybe you could just say stink instead."

"I had a dog once and he let a stink. Mom fed him some leftover beans one time, and the whole house stunk for two days. She didn't ever do that again."

Katie looked at Betty and whispered, "At least we got him talking."

Kirk got up and poured Brandon more milk. He slid his chair over closer to him, turned it around and straddled it with his arms resting on the chair back. "Brandon, would you want to help me feed the horses later today?"

"Can we feed them now?"

"First, let's go have a look at your room. When Mrs. Sawyer is ready to head back to the city, we can go feed them then. Okay?"

Brandon laid his cookie down, took a drink of milk and said, "Let's go see my room now. I've never had my own room."

"Well you do now, buddy." Kirk took Brandon's hand and the other two followed them back to the newly decorated room.

As he peeked into the room Brandon mouthed the word, "Wow!" He looked up at Kirk. "This is really cool. This is my room?"

"As long as you are staying here with us, yes, it will be your room."

"Will Mom come and stay here too?"

Betty quickly jumped in. "Brandon, your mother will be working on some things. She can't come, but you will get to see her from time to time."

"What is her tie to tie?"

Betty laughed. "No, I said from time to time. That means you will have short visits with her every week or so."

"Oh."

Betty Sawyer looked around the colorful room. "This is amazing. Have you just decorated it recently?"

"Yes, but it wasn't easy decorating for a child when we didn't know the sex or age." Katie's eyes were fixed on the wall of pictures.

"Well you've done a great job here. I love those happy children's faces in frames on the wall, and I see all of the children's books."

"Yes, after our family and friends learned about our new fostering adventure, they gave us some of the books. We did buy a few ourselves, but again, it was tough deciding on books to buy when I didn't know what ages we would be fostering. So there is a wide range, all the way from toddler to teen." She touched the distinctive grain of the wood. "Oh, and Kirk made this bookcase."

"That is beautiful. Is it oak?"

"Yes—red oak, I think—he enjoys woodworking when he has time. Kirk and I both think books are so important in a child's life. I was a kindergarten teacher—well, I did teach second grade one year. Then we moved out here. Ranch life has become a full-time job for me."

Betty looked at Kirk. "Would you like to take Brandon and introduce him to Dandy and Lilly now?"

"Come on Brandon. Let's go see what the horses have to say." He opened the fridge and grabbed a few carrots. "You can feed these to Dandy. Lilly doesn't seem to like them, but Dandy eats them like they're Christmas candy."

After they were out the door, Betty told Katie about Brandon's injuries.

"I saw the whelps on his arm."

"Oh, honey, that is nothing. He has deep cuts below his waist. He had been made to drop his pants and was whipped with a belt on his bare skin. I have some medication for him in the car that I'll need to get for you before I leave. He has a few stitches where the skin was laid open by the belt."

"Oh, you are kidding!"

"Brandon doesn't like pulling his pants down to have the cream applied to the cuts. You might want to try having Kirk be with him and see if Brandon will apply the medication himself. He is a brave little guy that has been hurt deeply. I'm not allowed to disclose the exact details of his past to you, but I can say that we have learned about several traumatic events in his life. I suspect that Brandon will have nightmares. He may have times that he will be sad and depressed. He loves his mom, but I have explained to him that she needs some time to work on some things before he can live with her again."

"Kirk is going to be good for Brandon. Every kid should be so lucky to have a father like him."

"Yes, I can see that already, and I think this ranch will be good for Brandon. He needs a little time away from the neighborhood he was in. Like I told him, it will be a nice vacation." The roar of the ATV engine starting up was heard. "Is that a four-wheeler I hear out there?"

"Yes," Katie said, "that's a big help on a ranch this size."

"I have to tell you that Brandon must wear a helmet anytime he rides on the four-wheeler."

"Oh, yes, that's one thing we forgot. I'll run into town and buy one this evening, because Kirk will be taking him all over this ranch on that ATV."

"Come with me to my car. I'll give you that medication, along with the few clothes that are Brandon's. His mother couldn't find much— one pair of jeans and two shirts. I'll need to get you an authorization form to purchase clothing for him. It's not much, but we do have a clothing allowance."

CHAPTER 6

After Betty Sawyer got in her car, she checked the messages on her cell phone—one from the office and one from Denise Brewer. She returned the two calls before she pulled out onto the highway. The one from the office was just saying that Denise Brewer had called and wanted to talk to Betty. When she returned Denise's call, her ear was filled with obscene language and uncontrolled anger. Betty listened until Denise's repertoire of obscenities ran out. Then she calmly replied, "Denise, Brandon is where he needs to be. He is fine. His injuries are being treated and, as I told you earlier, he will remain in the custody of the Department until you can make arrangements to evict your boyfriend from the house. I'm sure you don't want your son beaten again like that."

Denise's crass language turned to tears. "I know you're right. I just keep thinking Bryce will change...."

"Denise, men that beat women and children never change. Get him out of your house and out of your life, then we will see about returning Brandon to you."

"Mrs. Sawyer, you don't understand. That isn't going to be easy."

"Denise, you will have to do it. You invited him into your home; now you must get rid of him. I can assure you, we will not return Brandon to endure more beatings."

Betty made another trip out to the ranch to take the clothing voucher to Katie. As she drove in past the endless line of white fences she saw Kirk with Brandon in front of him on the brown horse.

Brandon was wearing a helmet and holding on to the saddle horn. She stopped the car, got out and ambled over to the fence. She pulled out her cell phone and asked them both to pose for a picture. After she had snapped it, Brandon leaned down toward Betty. "Can I see?"

"I don't know how much you can see in this bright sunlight, but here." She reached over the fence and held the phone up for Kirk to take.

Brandon looked at the picture and grinned big. "I want my mom to see this."

"I'll make sure your mom gets a copy. You guys enjoy your ride." She took the phone and flipped it closed. "Is Katie up at the house?"

"Yeah, she's probably behind it working in her little garden." Kirk clucked and Dandy carried his passengers off in the direction dictated to him by the reins in Kirk's hand.

Betty got back in her car and drove the half mile country lane, bordered on each side by white wooden fences, to the big rock house sheltered by towering sycamores and silver leaf maples. She got out, walked around to the back, and saw Katie down on her knees, pulling weeds around the tomato plants. "Katie, you've got quite a nice little garden here."

"Oh. Hi. I thought I heard a car pull up, but I didn't know you were standing there." She pulled off her flower printed garden gloves. "I don't put out a big garden, but I like to have a few fresh vegetables during season."

"I don't want to interrupt you. I just brought the clothing voucher. I saw Brandon and Kirk on the brown horse. Is Brandon opening up a bit more now?"

Katie brushed at a bit of dirt on the knees of her pants. "Let's go in the house. I can do this later. Brandon is doing great. He is a fantastic little guy. Kirk took him to the barber shop this morning for a much needed haircut. He seems to have ditched that bashfulness and replaced it with hundreds of questions about the ranch.

"Betty, it is amazing to see how he has turned on the smiles. When you brought him out I was afraid he would always be introverted and sad, but he's acting like a different little boy now. I think he's really going to take to this ranch life. Kirk and I can both see this is a very special little guy."

They sat down at the kitchen table. Betty took Katie's hand. "Katie, what you are seeing now is the honeymoon period. He may revert back to an unhappy state of mind. He'll miss his mother and want to go back. A supervised visit can be arranged later, but right now, I want him to get comfortable here with you and Kirk."

"I am so proud of the way Kirk has taken him under his wing. So far, the two of them have been inseparable—and Brandon loves it."

"Katie, we caseworkers are overworked. There are not enough of us for the caseloads we have, but I still want to be kept informed. I need to know when he has a change in disposition. You can expect a little sadness when he doesn't get to visit his mother soon, but if you detect a severe despondency, please let me know. You have my cell number. I'll call you back as soon as I get the chance."

"What happens if he needs medical treatment?"

"Use the form letter I gave you earlier for authorization. I'll get a Medicaid card for him out to you as soon as possible. I was glad to see him wearing the helmet. You and I both could be in big trouble if he got thrown from the horse or the ATV without a helmet." She pulled out her cell phone, flipped it open, and tapped to retrieve her saved images. She handed the open phone to Katie. "I took a picture of them on that brown horse as I came in. I'll make a couple of copies, one for Brandon's mother and the other one for him."

As Betty started out the front door, Kirk and Brandon came in the back. Brandon ran into the kitchen. "Don't forget to send that picture to my mom."

"Brandon, you can count on it. I'll get her a copy. Right now, though, I have to go back to the office. I have another case and have no idea where I can place him."

"You can send him here."

"That is very nice of you to offer, Brandon, but I'm not allowed to do that."

Kirk and Katie had been told that they could only have one child in their home at a time for the first six months. After that, the number would depend on available sleeping arrangements in the foster home.

"Well when someone changes the rules, you can bring him here. I start back to school tomorrow and he could ride with me on the bus."

"I'll remember that. You do your best in school so we'll all be proud of you. Okay?"

"Miss Betty, I'm real smart. You'll see—I will make hundreds on all my tests."

"You do that, Brandon. I'll see you later."

That afternoon, Katie drove to the school to enroll Brandon so he could start Monday morning.

CHAPTER 7

Kirk was acquainted with the school bus driver that was assigned to the route running by the ranch. Even though it was Sunday afternoon, he went ahead and called the driver at his home to let him know Brandon would be riding. "I'll have him up by the ranch gate at seven-fifty."

The driver told Kirk that he'd been informed Friday afternoon and would be ready for the pick up Monday morning.

Luther was a small town three miles northeast from the ranch, just off the Turner Turnpike. The school had a total enrollment of two hundred fifty-six students. That was for all grades, kindergarten through twelfth. There were advantages to living the rural life. It was close enough, but minus a lot of the problems of the big city. Drugs and alcohol among the students was pretty rare. Of course there were a few high school students that could be seen out in the parking lot with cigarettes, and any school has its pranksters. For the most part, the faculty at Luther Independent School was able to concentrate on teaching instead of disciplining.

At seven-fifty, Monday morning, Kirk was waiting with Brandon up by the ranch gate for the bus. "Did you ride a school bus in Oklahoma City?"

"No, I just walked."

"How far was it?"

"I don't know, but I had to cross a busy street. We had a guard lady that stopped the cars while we crossed."

"Well you're gonna like riding the bus here. Mr. Simpson is a good bus—oh, here he comes now. Hop out buddy. I'll be right here to pick you up this afternoon."

Kirk watched as Brandon climbed in the bus. *How could anyone whip a kid like that?* He was already falling in love with him, and no wonder, Brandon followed him every step he took.

Katie was anxiously waiting when Kirk got back to the house, "How did it go?"

"He did fine. He said he's never ridden a bus. He had to walk to school in the city. He was ready and waiting for Mr. Simpson to open the door. He marched right up, and I drove away."

"How did his wounds look this morning?"

"They seemed to be healing up as they should, but he's gonna have to have those stitches removed in about a week. Will DFS allow us to remove them, or should we take him in to the clinic in town?"

"I don't know. That's something I need to ask Betty."

"You know, Katie, I'm really falling for this kid. He is a real joy to have around."

"Yes, he seems to want to be with you every minute of the day. Maybe he sees you as the dad he never had. Just remember though, we will have to say goodbye to him at some point. So don't allow yourself to get hurt. We talked about this you know."

"Honey, with a little boy like Brandon, how could we not get hurt? How could we not love him just so we can protect our own emotions? The kid is starved for love. I'm not going to turn him away just so I won't get hurt when he leaves."

She took Kirk's hand. "I know. I know. But just remember, he will leave us one day, and you have to be strong and not let it get to you."

"Well, it will get to me. I can already see that. But until then, I'm gonna give that little guy all the love I can. I want him to know what it's like to have a good home and loving parents."

Kirk waited up by the gate for the afternoon school bus. He thought about what Katie had said about not getting hurt when Brandon leaves. *But I would rather be the one to get hurt than Brandon. He needs what I can give. Sure it'll be tough when he leaves, but I'm the adult; he's the child.* As he waited for the bus he determined to make the little guy his buddy. *He needs that. I should be able to handle the consequences.*

Kirk had gotten out of his pickup and was standing there waiting. Brandon must have been sitting in the first row, because he exited about as soon as the door opened. "How'd my little buddy do?" Kirk asked Mr. Simpson.

"Kirk, I could use a whole bus load like him. See you tomorrow."

With the short drive back to the ranch house, Brandon talked non-stop. "I have a nice teacher; I think she likes me."

"Oh yeah? Tell me about her."

"She is very pretty. Her name is Miss Bates, and she introduced me to the class. She even got my name right."

"So tell me what you had for lunch."

"Oh it was pretty yucky. I hate green beans, and the mashed potatoes tasted like glue."

"You should try the cafeteria lunch one more day. If you don't like it, Katie can fix you a lunch bucket."

"Can she do that tomorrow? I've never had a lunch bucket."

"Well, buddy, we're just gonna have to ask her about that. I'm not in the habit of making decisions for her."

They were coming close to the ranch house. "Kirk, my cuts down here are stinging."

"I know you applied the medication on them this morning. Do you want me to take a look?"

"Would you? It's stinging really bad."

"Let's go in and see what Miss Katie is up to, and then we'll go to your room where I can take a look."

Inside the house, the sweet smell of fresh bread being pulled from the oven welcomed the guys. Katie asked if Brandon would like to have a piece of warm bread with butter and jelly.

"It smells good, but Kirk is going to look at my cuts. They're stinging."

The two of them went to Brandon's room. When they came back, Kirk whispered to Katie, "Honey, I think we need to take him into the clinic. His cuts look like a solid piece of raw meat. I think he may have wet his pants a bit, and that caused his wounds to inflame. It looks pretty bad."

He went back to Brandon, "Hey buddy, I need you to stay here with Miss Katie while I go milk."

"But I need to help you."

"Well you are a big help, but you need to just lie here in your bed or go to the big room and sit in a chair. Your wounds are not looking very good. The more you move around, the more they are going to hurt. I can handle the milking today. You just rest up. Okay?"

"I guess." Brandon turned his head to the pillow.

Kirk looked on the shelf and found a book. "Here, does this look like a book you'd like to read?" It was titled *Frog and Toad Together* by Arnold Lobel.

Brandon looked up, took it, and thumbed through a bit of the book. "This is a baby book. Don't you have anything more my age?"

"Okay, let's see. Here are two books that are supposed to be for ten year olds. They may be too hard for you."

"No, they won't be too hard for me. I'm real smart."

Kirk grinned. "I'll go get you a piece of that warm bread with butter and jelly. You can eat it here in your room."

While Kirk was getting the bread, Katie walked into Brandon's room. She picked up *Frog and Toad Together*, sat down on the bed beside him. "Brandon, I know you consider this to be a baby book—too easy for you—but I'd like for you to read the first two pages to me."

Brandon hesitated before taking the book from Katie. "I have a sore throat now; can we do it later."

"Brandon, if you have a sore throat, it would be just as hard for you to read the more difficult books as it would be for you to read an easy one. Go ahead, give it a shot."

Brandon opened to the first page, hesitated again and grabbed his throat. "Miss Katie, I have a sore throat."

"Open up wide; let me take a look."

Brandon turned to the side, ducked his head in the pillow and started to cry. Kirk came in with the buttered bread and jelly. "Hey, buddy, what's wrong?"

Katie rolled her eyes. "Brandon thinks he has a sore throat and can't read now."

Kirk picked up her drift and sat down on the other side of the bed. "Do you have a sore throat, or is it something else?"

Brandon's face was still hidden, and he shook his head from side to side.

Miss Katie and I have always found that we have to be honest with each other. If I were to tell her a fib, it would always come back on me, and I'd have to tell three more to try to cover for that first one. Are you sure reading is easy for you? We know how to help you get fast at reading. We'll talk about it a little later. Your bread is getting cold, but can I get a big hug before you dig into it?"

"I'm glad you didn't force the issue," Katie said to Kirk, just outside the room. "He knows he can't read well. The fib is just a part of his culture. He sees nothing wrong with covering his embarrassment with a fib. I'll have a talk with his teacher and see where he is on reading."

"Good idea."

CHAPTER 8

Denise managed to find a time when Bryce hadn't been drinking to sit down for a talk about her son. "Bryce, the caseworker came for a visit today. DFS is refusing to let me have Brandon back as long as you are still living here. You are going to have to get out if I ever have a chance of getting my son back."

"It's pretty bad when a man can't even discipline his own—"

Denise cut him off promptly. "Bryce, he is not *your* son. You had no right to whip him like you did. I want you out of this house by tomorrow."

"Why, so you can move in that toy boy you been seein'?"

"Get out! I don't need your kind."

Denise left the house to run some errands. When she returned Bryce was gone—so were the TV, DVD player, and forty-five bucks in the Mason jar she'd been saving for emergencies.

With Bryce out of the house, Denise tried to call Betty Sawyer at DFS. She was told that Ms. Sawyer was in court and wouldn't be available until the next day.

"Have her call the motel and have me paged first thing tomorrow morning. She's got the number." The sarcasm in her voice was unmistakable.

That evening she went to Brandon's room to clean it up a bit. She found his report card in the closet behind some toys. It was in a sealed envelope along with a note requesting a parent-teacher conference. Without looking at his grades, she tossed them both in the trash.

In her recent visit to Denise's trailer, Betty Sawyer had not only insisted that Bryce get out of the house, she had pointed out several home repairs that had to be made. The broken glass was still propped up by the plastic blinds. A few smaller shards were on the floor beneath the window. She had also mentioned the dangerous metal steps at the front door that had no railing. There were exposed electrical wires hanging from the ceiling in the living room where a light fixture had once hung.

After her day in court, Betty played the message. She didn't try to return Denise's call; three other cases were more urgent. Another child had to be removed from her home immediately, and she had no place for her. The child's situation was so critical that Betty decided to pick her up and have her stay in her own home for the night, hoping something would open up. The TV ads for more foster parents had not drawn the prospects they had hoped for.

It was after five when she found a few minutes to return the call. Denise's irritation came over the phone line, loud and clear. "Look, I called you yesterday, and you're just now getting back with me?"

Betty held the phone out from her ear.

"Bryce is out of the house now, so you can return my son."

"Hold on, Denise! Brandon is doing fine where he is. I want to see if Bryce *stays* out of the house. Have you corrected any of the safety issues around your house that we talked about?"

"The broken glass is gone and I am going to redecorate Brandon's room."

"Denise, redecorating the room is of little importance. The front steps are dangerous with no railing. And as I told you, those exposed wires in the living room ceiling must be removed or repaired—"

"I can fix that before you can even get over here—"

"I want Brandon to remain where he is for at least two more weeks. I will call you for a visit to make sure the safety issues have been taken care of."

"Look, my son needs to be back in school. His education is my first concern."

"Denise, Brandon *is* in school, and your first concern should be his safety. You say that Bryce is out of the house—good. Is he out permanently? Give me a couple of weeks at least, and I'll call you for another in-home visit."

"I promise you, I'll have all of those issues taken care of by the time you call me back for a visit."

"Good, I'll see you…" But mid-sentence, Denise had slammed the phone down.

Betty had to make a visit to one of her foster homes in the same area as Kirk and Katie. She pulled over to the side of the road and called to see how Brandon was doing.

"Katie. Hi, this is Betty Sawyer. I thought I'd call to see how Brandon is doing. Are those wounds healing up like they should?"

"Betty, they are not. We suspect that he may have wet his pants a bit. It looks like that has infected the cuts. As soon as he got off the bus yesterday, I put him to bed. The more he moved around, the more irritated the wounds became. I took him to the little clinic in town this morning, and Dr. Chandler gave us an antibiotic ointment that is supposed to be better than what he had before. He told us to keep Brandon out of school and in bed or in a chair for a couple of days to give his wounds a chance to heal a bit before he did much walking around."

"Katie, I'm in your area. Would it be okay if I drop by for a few minutes?"

"Sure, Kirk and one of his helpers are doctoring the heard, but I'm here."

When she arrived, the front door was open, and Katie hollered for her to come on in.

She entered the large room. "What's cooking? It smells heavenly."

"Oh, I'm making chicken pot pie. It's Kirk's favorite."

"You make your own from scratch?"

Katie pulled a large Corning dish from the oven and set it on the old well-worn butcher block table in the middle of the room. The crust was golden brown, and the wonderful aroma was steaming up through the happy face vents she'd cut into the uncooked crust. "Normally I would use one of our hens that have quit laying, but this one came from the market in town. There are carrots, onion, new potatoes, green peas, and red peppers under that golden blanket of crust."

"Well, I want to see our little guy."

"He's in his room *reading* some books. I noticed he is only reading the ones with a lot of pictures. Just go on back, I'll join you in a minute or two."

Betty found Brandon's door open. "Hey, big guy, what are you doing?"

"Hi, Miss Betty. I didn't know you were here."

"I just got here; Katie and I were talking in the kitchen."

"Look at all of these books I've read this morning. I'm a fast reader."

"Well, I guess you are! How are your cuts on your leg healing up?"

"Oh, Dr. Chandler said I will be all well tomorrow and I can go back to school."

"Is that so?"

Katie peeked in the room. "Brandon, you should get that story straight, don't you think?"

Brandon looked down at his book and mumbled. "He said I would be well soon and could go back to school then."

"That's more like the story I heard from Dr. Chandler." Katie grinned. "Thank you for clearing that up for us."

Betty stepped out of the room and motioned for Katie to follow. Katie pulled out two chairs at the big farm table under that wagon wheel chandelier.

"I think we talked about the possibility of Brandon digressing after he's been here awhile. His wetting his pants and stretching the truth is part of that behavior modification we talked about. The little guy has gone through a lot in his short lifetime. The pendulum will swing even farther away before settling down toward the middle." Betty started to get up. "If you experience any worse problems and feel you need help—or just someone to talk to—please call me. If it is too severe, we'll get professional help involved."

"Thanks, Betty; I'll call you if I need to. If you can stay just a few minutes more, Kirk will be in, and we can have some of that chicken pot pie."

"Thanks, but I've gotta go. They keep us all running now days. We need at least ten more caseworkers."

CHAPTER 9

It was three days before Kirk felt like Brandon might be okay to go back to school. The wounds were healing up pretty well, and he had not wet his pants anymore. Kirk took him for a horseback ride. Dandy was gentle and provided a smooth ride. Dandy had placed first in the National Morgan Horse Competition last October in Oklahoma City. The horse was sensitive to Kirk's commands and very trustworthy. They rode down to the large pond about a quarter mile east of the milk barn. Kirk got off and led Dandy around the pond. He handed Brandon the reins and told him to just hold them and let Dandy wander as he pleased.

Brandon's eyes lit up like two halogen lamps, and a big grin spread across his face. "I need a hat, Kirk."

"Yes, you do, buddy. I'll get you one later, but for now you can wear mine."

With the oversize hat propped up by Brandon's ears and the big grin escaping underneath, Kirk took out his cell phone and snapped a picture, then another. Kirk asked him if his wounds were hurting him and stressed that it was very important to tell him if they were. Even though Dandy was delivering a gentle ride, he wanted to make sure the saddle didn't rub and open up those awful slashes he had received

Kirk climbed back on and dropped the reins over the saddle horn, "Come on Dandy, let's go back to the house. You know the way."

The aroma from the pot pie Katie had just pulled out of the oven was wafting through the open kitchen window. "Hey buddy, something sure smells good. Let's check it out." He got off, laid the reins over the yard fence and then helped Brandon down.

Brandon ran ahead and met Katie at the door. Excitement was in his eyes. "Miss Katie, I rode Dandy all by myself! He's a big horse, but I can handle him just fine."

"Really?"

Brandon's hand shot up with an index finger pointing straight up as if a new thought had just sprouted. "After I get my hat that Kirk promised, I'm gonna ride Dandy over to my mom's house to see her."

Kirk frowned. "Whoa! Dandy doesn't go off this ranch, and neither do you unless we are with you."

"Where did you two ride this morning?"

"We rode down to this big lake. We rode all the way around it and then back here."

Kirk laughed. "Well that *lake* is really just a farm pond. But you're right, it is pretty big."

Katie turned and whispered to Kirk. "You probably should check out his wounds and make sure the ride didn't open them up."

"Come on, man. Let's go see if that saddle was too rough on you."

"Oh, it wasn't too rough. I could handle it just fine."

"Just the same, let's go look and make sure they're still healing up the way they are supposed to."

When they came back in, Katie asked how it looked. "I guess he gets to go back to school tomorrow." He moved a little closer to Katie and cupped his mouth. "I'm gonna head on down to the milk barn."

Brandon was all ears. "Wait for me; I'm coming too."

"Sorry, Brandon, that horseback ride was all you need to do today. You've got to be ready to go to school in the morning."

⸝⸍

The next week Katie scheduled a visit with Brandon's second grade teacher. It was much as she expected. Miss Bates told her that he was too far behind for her to promote him to third grade for the next term. "He isn't even reading at first grade level, and he is having trouble accepting his own inadequacies—so he lies a lot. I believe he can overcome some of these problems. You're an elementary teacher. That should be a real advantage for him. It'll require a lot of your time." The teacher looked down at Brandon's folder. "I believe this little guy has been blessed with a good deal of intelligence. If he can conquer reading now, he stands a good chance of being a very good student in the later grades."

"I agree with everything you've said. My problem is that Brandon is a foster child. I have no way of knowing how long he will be with us. If he is returned to his mother prior to school starting again in the fall, she may insist on him moving on to third grade."

"Katie, since you are in agreement with me, I'll recommend retaining Brandon. His school record will follow him, and at that point it's out of our hands. But at least we'll have it on record that he isn't ready for third grade. His reading inabilities are holding him back in all areas."

"Good, let's do that."

"By the way, I thought you might be interested in knowing what Brandon told the class."

"Oh I can imagine."

"Brandon says that he has a million-dollar stud horse, and he rode him to Oklahoma City to see his friend, Christopher."

"A million dollars, uh? To Oklahoma City? The kid has a colorful imagination."

CHAPTER 10

In the past two weeks Betty Sawyer had received multiple calls from Denise Brewer. Most of the calls went to voice mail, which she promptly deleted. She did, however, take the last call and then wished she hadn't.

Without any greeting, Denise blurted out, "Okay, here's the deal. I've made those repairs you asked me to. Bryce is still not living here, so when can I expect you to come out for that home visit?"

Betty wanted to say in about in about twelve years, but thought she'd go out and see what Denise had done. "I can be out there tomorrow afternoon. You get home around four?"

"I will unless I have to work over."

"Call me if you do. Otherwise I'll see you about four-thirty tomorrow."

Betty's day started in court. Then she tried to catch up on her voice mail and e-mail. By noon she had learned she had four siblings to place immediately. Two homes had opened up but she had no choice but separate the children because neither home could accommodate all four. At two o'clock Denise called her cell to tell her she couldn't be home till after five.

"Well, that's all a part of the job. I didn't know I signed on for twenty-four hour duty, but I guess I'll see you a little after five."

At six o'clock she pulled into Denise's driveway. As she was getting out of the car she looked over at the broken window. The shards of glass were now lying on the ground under the window, as if they had just been pushed out of the frame and ignored. In place of the glass a piece of cardboard had been cut and fit neatly in the metal frame. She started toward the front steps. A two by four board was toe-nailed into the siding on each side of the door, slanting down to another two by four standing almost vertical, propping up the *rails.*

Denise opened the door. "I'm sorry I couldn't be here when we agreed, but I had a flat on the way home. A nice guy came by and fixed it for me, so I just now got home. I hope you didn't have to wait long for me."

Betty stared at her and said, "Denise, I don't know what you are talking about. Your car was already here when I pulled up."

"Oh, I guess I was. You must think I'm crazy. I'm so excited that I can finally get my son back."

"Hold on. There are some things we need to discuss. How about we sit at your kitchen table?" She looked up at the living room ceiling where the wires had been exposed. A piece of quarter inch splintered plywood had been nailed—or rather, glued to the Styrofoam ceiling over the electrical box. As she started to sit down at the little kitchen table she looked at the smaller pieces of glass from the broken window—now swept into a corner. "Denise we have to talk about the *repairs* you have done here. Did you do this yourself?"

"I didn't have anyone to call on, so I had to do them myself."

Betty went over each item and told Denise what she would have to do to correct each. "You can start by sweeping up those pieces of glass over there in the corner and put them in the trash." She got up and went back to the bedrooms and bath. "Denise, I'd like for you to spend your next day off cleaning your house front to back. I'm not too picky about housekeeping—not much of a housekeeper myself—but you know this house needs some of your attention." Dirty laundry covered most of the floor of the smaller bedroom. There was no bed in the room other than a thin foam mattress, covered by a blood-stained sheet, on the filthy carpet.

Denise stood with her arms folded in front of her. "Look, some of us don't make the kind of money you do. We can't afford to hire carpenters and have the carpets shampooed."

"You know you can do better than this and still not be out any money. It's a matter of cleaning and tidying up. It would make a big difference in the appearance of your home. But now, I need to go. I have another home visit before I can go to my own house."

She opened the door, stepped out onto the first step, and touched the top of the unstable rails with her fingertips for balance. The door slammed shut behind her with a string of obscenities filtering through the thin walls.

CHAPTER 11

Although Brandon said he would have rather been with Kirk, Katie thought she needed to spend time with him reading. She was glad she had bought the boxed set of four of the Magic Tree House books by Mary Pope Osborne, *Dinosaurs before Dark, The Knight at Dawn, Mummies in the Morning, and Pirates Past Noon.* Brandon was able to read some, but had to have help with the more difficult words.

Kirk popped in to check on his little buddy. With an excited expression on his face, Brandon looked up at his new father figure. "I liked the part where Jack crawled out of the secret tunnel and fell into the moat!"

"See, reading can be a lot of fun." Kirk said. "You get to travel to magical places and meet interesting people."

Katie pulled another book off the shelf, *Arthur's Honey Bear* by Lillian Hoban. She knew the story. It could be analogous to his own home situation. In the story, Arthur gave up his Honey Bear, but later was able to have visits with him. Deciding the book hit too close to home, she returned it to the shelf and picked up *Happy Birthday Moon* by Frank Asch. She knew Brandon should be able to read that one with no help from her, and it wouldn't remind him that he had been away from his mother.

It was Saturday. Kirk planned to muck out the stalls. While he was doing that, he thought he'd let Brandon feed the hogs. He opened the feed sack and filled a bucket of shorts; then he added water. He handed it off to Brandon to feed to the two hogs. This is called shorts."

"Are you kidding? They eat *shorts?*" Brandon bent over and stared into the bucket.

Kirk doubled over laughing. "Yeah, shorts are a little bit like hominy—mostly corn. We mix it with water and this fattens them up.

"How do I feed it to them?"

"Just climb up on their fence and dump the stuff in the pig trough below. Do not go in the pen!"

Kirk went back to mucking the stalls. A few minutes later he heard Brandon scream. He threw down the shovel and ran to the pen. Brandon was inside with an old sow rooting at him. He fell down, and the sow kept at him. He managed to get up to head back to the fence when the old sow nudged his bottom and Brandon went face down in the manure laden mud. Every time he tried to stand on his feet, the sow would knock him down in the mud again. Kirk vaulted the fence with one jump and grabbed him. He boot-kicked the old sow, grabbed Brandon, and sat him on the fence while he climbed over. Brandon was encrusted with a mixture of mud and pig manure. He started to cry. "Don't whip me, please! I won't do it again."

Kirk held Brandon out away from him and started to laugh. "I don't believe in whipping. I think you learned your lesson." He took a finger and wiped the yucky stuff away from Brandon's eyes. "I think we might need a picture about now." Kirk started to reach for his cell phone to snap a priceless picture.

"NO!" Brandon wiped the manure from his open lips with the back of his hand. "I don't want a picture. I want this nasty stuff off of me."

Kirk took him to the barn, grabbed a garden hose, and rinsed off most of the sludge. "Brandon, those old hogs are dangerous. They are capable of killing and eating someone like you. That's why I told you not to go in the pen. Always stand up on the outside of the fence and just throw it over to the trough below."

"Okay."

"Now, we need to get you back to the house so you can get a shower."

Kirk followed him through the back door. Katie was there and giggled! "Brandon! Did you fall in the pond?"

He refused to answer, so Kirk volunteered. "No, he fell in the pig pen. He was going to feed the hogs, and rather than pour the grain into the pig trough from atop the fence like I told him, he decided he could feed them better from inside the pen."

Katie laughed. "I'll bet you don't do that again, uh?"

"I'm sorry." His head ducked down and he ran toward the bathroom.

Kirk followed his little buddy to the shower and threw him a towel and clean underwear. "That's okay, Brandon. Sometimes we only learn by making mistakes." He closed the door and grinned. "I still think that would have made a great picture!"

The next week Katie got a call from Betty. "Katie, I think it is time we allowed Brandon to visit his mother. Could you bring him to our office Wednesday at four-thirty?"

"Yes, I can do that. Will you be there also?"

"No, I can't, but there will be other staff members present. I've made arrangements for Denise to be there. She's a bit undependable, but I stressed to her that she must be on time. You do understand that you are not to allow her to take Brandon out of your sight."

"Yes, that shouldn't be a problem."

Kirk told Katie he couldn't go with her. If I did the milking before going, it would be too early, and afterward would be too late."

Katie thought it was best to not tell Brandon about a visit with his mother until Wednesday after school. She picked him up at three-fifteen and they drove the thirty miles to the DFS offices, arriving there about four-twenty. It was a multi-storied building, but Betty had given her directions as to where the meeting was to take place. Katie and Brandon sat down at a table in a small room where they had been directed. She brought a couple of books to keep him occupied and to show his mother how well he was reading now, but Brandon was too excited about seeing his mom to look at the books. At four-forty he asked, "When is my mom gonna be here?"

"It should be any minute now."

Denise had not showed up by five o'clock and the offices were closing. They were told they would have to leave. Brandon started to cry. "Where is my mom?"

"Brandon, I don't know. She may have had some kind of trouble. She would be here if she could."

They left the room and were entering the elevator. Brandon was sobbing uncontrollably. Katie tried to comfort him, but he was still sniffling when they exited the building. Just as Katie unlocked the doors to her pickup, a slender woman with long red curly hair came running over and was yelling. "Brandon! Wait! Don't leave."

Brandon saw her and darted toward her. Katie caught up with him and grabbed his hand. "That's my mom." He was pulling Katie forward.

Denise kept running until she finally reached them. She reached out and grabbed Brandon. "Oh Brandon! Mamma's so glad to get to see you." Then she stepped back, looked at him, and changed her tone. "Who peeled your head? You look awful!"

Katie, still holding on to Brandon's hand, said, "I take it you are Denise Brewer."

Denise ignored her comment and ran her fingers through Brandon's hair; then she looked up at Katie. "Who gave you permission to whack my son's hair off like this?"

Katie told her Brandon had needed a haircut to enter school.

"I am Brandon's mother, and I say when his hair gets cut. He looks ridiculous!"

Katie stared at her in disbelief and then found some words. "Denise, you were supposed to be here at four-thirty. What happened?"

"I tried to get here but I had car trouble." She grabbed Brandon's hand. "Brandon, come on, Mamma's gonna go buy you a Happy Meal."

Katie held tight to the boy's hand. "Denise, I have been instructed to not allow him out of my sight. He is not going anywhere with you."

Denise reached around Brandon, pulling him away from Katie's grasp and started toward the direction she came from. Katie caught up with her and tried to remove him from her grip. Denise held on and raced forward.

"Denise, you can't do that. Stop right now!"

"This is my son and I can do what I ---- well please with him. Now you just get the ---out of my way!"

Katie pulled out her phone and dialed nine-one-one. Just as the operator answered, a man jumped out of his car and sprinted toward Denise. He reached her from behind, wrapped his muscular arms around her and said, "Let go of the boy, NOW!" She refused. He tightened his hold on her. "I said let go of the boy!"

"This is my son. I will not let go."

"You *will* let go, or I'll hold you 'til the cops get here."

Denise turned loose, and Katie quickly reached out and took his hand. "Brandon, honey, you will have to come with me this time."

"But I wanted to go with my mom to get a Happy Meal."

The man was still holding Denise. "Lady, where is your car?"

She pointed to an older Bronco and he escorted her to it. "Now get in, and if you try that again, you will be arrested. Do you understand me?"

Denise mouthed another obscenity at him, and he shoved her inside the Bronco. "Now get on out of here."

He came over to Katie. "Are you okay?"

"Yes, I'm okay. Who are you?"

"My name is Bob. I'm a caseworker for DFS. I was just getting ready to pull out of the parking lot when I saw what was happening. Is this Brandon?"

"Yes, and I'm sorry he had to witness that. Let me get him in the pickup so we can talk."

"These kids witness a lot of things they shouldn't have to. Your caseworker, Betty Sawyer, asked me to hang around for a bit to make sure everything went okay with your visit. Wasn't the mother supposed to be here at four-thirty?"

"Yes, we were here a little before four-thirty and waited. When she didn't show by five, we had to leave the building. That's when she showed up in the parking lot. Should I report this to Betty?"

"No, I'll discuss this with her, and a report will be filed. If this happens again, we'll notify the police. She'll be facing attempted kidnapping."

"I can see Brandon is crying. I need to go to him. Thanks for your help. I don't know what I would have done without you."

"I'm glad I was here."

After she climbed in the pickup truck, she felt herself shaking. *What if Denise had gotten away with Brandon?* She wasn't thinking of the consequences for Denise, but she began to realize how she and Kirk would feel without him.

CHAPTER 12

When Katie got home she relayed the events at the DFS parking lot to Kirk. Even then, she felt herself trembling a bit. Kirk wrapped his arms around her. "Next time, I'm going with you. The cows will have to wait."

School had been dismissed for the summer and she was determined to get Brandon to reading at second grade level. Brandon insisted that he needed to help Kirk, so the major reading sessions were moved to evenings after the ranch chores were done. Most of the books she had accumulated were a bit too difficult for Brandon, so she found a used book store in the city and brought back a shopping bag full that were more on his level. The little town of Luther had no public library, so buying the books was about her only option.

The first book Katie found was *Once Upon a Time* by Niki Daly. It's the story of Sarie, a South African girl who loved to learn but hated to be called on to read aloud in class. Often the other kids made fun of her because she was such a poor reader. With the help of her aunt and a kind classmate, Sarie gained confidence, and reading became easier for her. Katie found a book of poetry by Shel Silverstein. It was above his reading level, but he loved for her to read the poems to him. That helped to stretch his vocabulary.

After reading with him in the big room, Kirk and Katie both accompanied Brandon to his bedroom, where prayers were always a part of the bedtime scene. Katie had started this the first night Brandon was in their home, and then Kirk joined. They had taught Brandon to talk to God in his own way. Whatever he wanted to tell God or ask Him was okay. Sometimes Brandon's prayers were a bit sad, especially when he was missing his mother. Then there were times that Kirk and Katie fought to keep from laughing at what he was saying. The night after the pig pen incident Brandon prayed, "God, make those pigs take a shower before supper." Another night he said, "God, see if you can get Kirk to marry my mom so she can live here." Neither Kirk nor Katie could withhold their laughter on that one.

"Brandon, where does that leave me?" Katie said.

Brandon had a puzzled look on his face. "I guess I prayed wrong that time."

Katie agreed with him, "Yes, you may have. Just remember I'm the one that makes those good chocolate chip cookies for you."

It was Memorial Day weekend and Kirk had promised Brandon a trip to the zoo. "Have you ever been to the zoo?"

"No, my mom promised to take me, but that was when she had a new boyfriend. He wanted her to stay home with him."

"Let's see if Miss Katie is ready."

"Can I wear my hat that you bought me?"

"If you wear yours, I'll wear mine too."

When they got to the zoo, Kirk let Katie and Brandon out near the gate while he parked the truck. The nearest spot was in the far corner of the parking lot. He got out; locked the doors, and jogged back across the huge parking lot, finally reaching the gate.

Brandon pointed to Kirk's head. "Kirk, you forgot your hat."

He felt the top of his head, "You're right; what should I do?"

"You should go back and get it."

"But that's a long way back to the truck."

"It doesn't matter. You promised you'd wear yours if I wore mine."

"Okay, buddy. A promise is a promise. I'll be back here in a minute." *Man, I'm getting my exercise today!*

Inside the gate Brandon had already started the I-wants. First he wanted popcorn, and then he wanted a snow cone. Ice cream came next, then nachos.

Kirk put his hand on Brandon's shoulder. "Hey, we talked about this while we were still in the truck. You can have one thing now and one thing just before we leave. Remember?"

Brandon gave him a sheepish look. "Yeah, I remember, but I thought you wouldn't."

"You'll see that I don't forget much, Brandon."

"Well you forgot your hat."

"Yep, now you know I'm not perfect, uh?"

"Yeah, and you've got your hat on backwards."

"I thought you wouldn't notice," Kirk said.

"I notice everything."

"Okay, Mr. Perfect, let's go see what the bears are up to."

"Then can we come back here to the monkeys?"

Kirk started to answer, but then Brandon suddenly ducked behind him and grabbed hold of the back of his shirt. "Hey, buddy, what's wrong?"

"Get me out of here!"

Katie turned toward Kirk with a puzzled look.

"Brandon, what is wrong?" He felt the squeeze on his shirt as Brandon tightened his grip.

"Get me out of here now…"

"Why?"

Still hiding behind Kirk, Brandon's voice was just a whisper. "Bryce is standing over there with my mom. I don't want him to see me."

Kirk looked in that direction, turned toward Brandon, and knelt down on one knee, blocking Brandon from view.

"Can we just leave?"

"If that's what you want."

"Let's go now!"

Kirk took his hand and Katie followed them out through the gates.

"Do you think they saw us?" Katie said.

"I don't know. I didn't want to turn around and look."

Brandon was whimpering. Kirk again knelt down on one knee in front of him. "It's okay, buddy. I don't think they saw us. Come on, let's go climb in the truck."

After he was buckled in, Brandon was still whimpering and trembling.

Katie was looking at him in her visor mirror. "Since Brandon didn't get his last treat at the zoo, why don't we stop at McDonalds and get him a Happy Meal?"

"Is that okay, Brandon?"

Brandon said nothing, barely shaking his head yes. The sniffles continued.

"Kirk, why don't you pull over and let me get in the back seat with him. He needs one of us next to him right now."

Kirk stopped and let her get in the back seat of the truck. He turned and saw Katie looking at Brandon, her face mirroring her compassion.

"Honey, it's going to be alright." She reached her arm around the little boy. "I know that scared you, but we won't let Bryce come near you."

CHAPTER 13

Katie got a call from Betty Sawyer asking if she would be home. "I have some clothing for Brandon. I'm not far from you. I can be there in about ten minutes."

Betty arrived with two paper grocery sacks full of clothes. "These aren't new. They are passed down from foster child to foster child. She pulled out several pairs of jeans, two button-up shirts with collars that would be good for Sunday, and several tee shirts. The second sack had a pair of swim trunks, denim shorts, and about a dozen pairs of socks. "I think most of this will fit him. If it doesn't, just hang on to it, because you may have a child later that it does fit."

"I bought him a few things with the clothing allowance but everything is so expensive I wasn't able to get much. I was thinking about finding a second-hand store. This is great."

Betty changed the subject. "I heard about the attempted abduction the other day. I'm sorry I couldn't be there. Bob said he was about to leave when he saw what was happening with Denise. That must have been very upsetting to Brandon."

"Oh it was. I'm not sure Brandon has recovered yet. We took him to the zoo yesterday. Brandon spotted his mother with Bryce and was terrifi—"

"Did you say with Bryce?"

"Yes, Denise and Bryce were standing over by a concession stand. Brandon got behind Kirk and said, 'Get me out of here.' I couldn't understand why he would want to leave so soon. Then he told us that Bryce was there, along with Denise."

"She's not even supposed to be with Bryce."

"Brandon was shaking and sobbing. We left immediately, hoping they didn't see us. But Kirk and I both wonder if Brandon will ever overcome his fear of that man."

"Katie, Bob told me he was sure Denise got into a white Bronco the other day in the parking lot. Did you get a look at the vehicle she got in?"

"Yes, Bob was right. It was a white Bronco. Brandon even mentioned that it was Bryce's Bronco."

Betty just rolled her eyes. "Okay, I need to run. I have three more stops before I can go back to the office. Oh, I think you know to never give out your last name in dealing with these parents."

"Yes, I think I remember them saying that in the classes we attended."

"That's right. We don't want a parent looking you up in the phone book and finding the location of your home." Betty ran her hand through her graying hair. "We don't need a non-custodial abduction."

"Oh, I see. Well sure."

"Let's hope you don't run onto Denise or her boyfriend again. Call me if you need anything."

Katie saw her to the door, stood there for a minute, and for the first time in her life she felt vulnerable. She grew up in a small neighborhood where everyone knew their neighbors. She had never known fear. Now with foster children in her home, fear could march up to her doorstep any time. A foster child could disclose their last name to parents. Even scarier, a child might tell his parents where he was staying.

Katie heard the ATV pulling up. Kirk and Brandon soon came through the back door. "What have you two been up to this morning?"

Kirk pushed his hat back a bit, exposing those denim-blue eyes she'd fallen in love with. "We've been inventors today."

"Inventors?"

"We invented an automatic gate opener," Brandon said with an excited tone.

"Well tell me more about this automatic gate opener."

Brandon pointed both his index finger forward. "See, this is how it works. You drive up to the gate and push a button on this little remote thingy. Then the gate opens. But you can't get the gate open if you don't have that."

Katie looked up at Kirk. "So where did we get that little remote thingy?"

"I took a garage door opener that I'd found at a yard sale a few months back, and I did some modifications so it would open and close the main gate up by the highway. I had to weld a couple of pieces of pipe on the gate. Then I used a converter to convert the power from house current to twelve volt. It's now powered by a regular car battery that is hidden about twenty feet away."

"Why would we want that?"

Kirk gave her an "I'll tell you later" look.

Katie ruffled Brandon's hair. "Hey, big guy, you need to go wash up." She saw the green stain on his jeans. "I think you need to throw those clothes in the washer, and then you jump in the shower. How'd you get so dirty?"

"I stumbled and fell down in a cow patty."

"Yuck!"

After Brandon was out of the room Kirk told Katie the reason he had devised the automatic gate was to make access to the ranch a little more secure."

"You think we need to go to those extremes?"

"Honey, I can see where we could be very vulnerable if an angry parent wanted to try something stupid. Your incident in the parking lot the other day got me to thinking. This won't keep 'em out, but at least they'd have to walk in and not drive right up to the house."

"So we're just going to keep the remote in the pickup, just like a garage door opener?"

"That's it. And when I get deliveries for the ranch, they'll call my cell phone, and I'll meet them up at the gate to let 'em in."

"Kirk, actually, I had some thoughts along those lines just this morning when Betty was here. I don't think she trusts Denise and her boyfriend one bit. She reminded me that we were to never disclose our last name when we have a parental visit. But, you know, a child could tell the parent where he was staying. I guess I never thought of those things when we were considering fostering."

"Katie, my thinking is, if Denise would try that in broad daylight in the parking lot of the DFS, who knows what else she might try. We need to be careful."

"Are you in for the day?"

"No, I've gotta go milk. You think Brandon will mind if I go without him?"

"You go ahead. Brandon hasn't had his reading time yet today, so I'll keep him busy with that. Then when you get back, I'll have supper ready."

Kirk bent down and gave her a quick kiss, "Keep him busy if you can. I enjoy his company, but he does slow me down with his never-ending questions."

"Questions coming from a seven-year-old are a good thing. That means he trusts you."

"It also means I don't get much done except answer his questions—some of which I can't answer. He's come up with some doozies. I might be more inclined to give him a better answer if I was his father, but as a foster dad, I hesitate on some of them."

"I think as foster parents, we walk a tightrope. Saying too much could get us in trouble, and saying too little wouldn't satisfy a curious mind."

"See you in about an hour."

CHAPTER 14

Betty called Denise Brewer the day after the incident in the DFS parking lot. She began by telling Denise the importance of being on time for a parental visit. Denise started whining about having a flat on her car. In her fourteen years as a caseworker, Betty had heard hundreds of trumped up explanations for being late. She wasn't going to listen to another rewarmed excuse, so she cut her off and told her it had better not happen again. Then she plowed right into the parking lot incident. "Denise, I told you when we set the appointment that you could not take Brandon during your visit. You need to realize the seriousness of what you tried to do."

Denise cut in with another excuse. "All I was going to do was go get a hungry little boy something to eat—"

"Stop it, Denise! Brandon hadn't even indicated that he was hungry. Even if he had, it would be the foster mother's responsibility, not yours."

"I just don't see anything wrong with wanting to take my son for a Happy Meal."

"Denise, get this through your head; you cannot take Brandon anywhere! If you try that again, you will be looking at kidnapping charges!"

"Okay, so when do I get to see my son again?"

"I don't know. After the stunt you pulled, it may be a good while."

"I should have guessed that, coming from you."

"Look, with an attitude like that, you make it difficult for me to work with you. Now, tell me about Bryce Collier."

"What do you wanna know about him?"

"I told you the only way you will ever have a chance of regaining custody of Brandon is if you get rid of Bryce."

"And I told *you* Bryce doesn't live with me anymore."

"So what were you doing with him at the zoo? And what were you doing driving Bryce's vehicle to your parental visit?"

"You didn't say I couldn't ever see Bryce. You just said he couldn't live with me."

"Well, I'm telling you now! Bryce Collier is not to reside at your residence, and you are not to be with him again. Is that clear enough?"

"You can't enforce that!"

"You're right, I can't enforce it, but I can assure you that you will never get your son back as long as you are seeing Bryce. The injuries he inflicted on your son are criminal. And you, of all people, should be very angry with him instead of dating him again."

Denise started to give another excuse for being with Bryce at the zoo.

"I'm not listening to any more of your lame excuses. You know the rules. Betty disconnected the call and rolled her eyes.

Katie was pleased with Brandon's progress with reading. Their daily routine was pretty well fixed by now—breakfast, then helping Kirk on the ranch, lunch, some math flash cards, and some free time before helping Kirk with the late afternoon milking, supper, reading, prayers and bedtime. Katie found *The Children's Living Bible* at a used book store. The words were too difficult for him, but after she read to him, he enjoyed seeing the pictures while they talked about the story. One story Brandon liked was when Moses struck the rock and water came out. Brandon told her he tried that on a big rock out by the well house, but it didn't work for him.

Their bedtime prayers always meant that Kirk, Katie, and Brandon would kneel at his bedside and take turns praying. Kirk might pray that the Lord would help Brandon grow into a strong, healthy young man that loved the Lord. Katie's prayer often had to do with Brandon learning and loving to read. Brandon's prayer always had to do with his mother. He asked God not to be mad at her. Then he frequently asked God to give her a new boyfriend.

Katie continued to search for books for Brandon. One book in particular that Brandon loved was *Building with Dad* by Carol Nevius. The construction sites and massive equipment fascinated Brandon. The story was about a little boy whose father was working on the construction of his son's new school. The boy was proud of that. The acrylic and colored pencil illustrations were realistic with each page looking like a photograph.

Another one of Brandon's favorites was *Hachiko: The True Story of a Loyal Dog* by Pamela S. Turner. Katie read most of it as Brandon looked on. She would point to the words as she read and let Brandon say the words he knew.

"Brandon, this book is based on a true story about a dog named Hachiko, who waited almost ten years at a Tokyo train station for his master, who never returned. And did you know there is a statue of that dog in Japan? A festival is held every April honoring Hachiko."

"That's so cool! Old Chubby waits up by the gate for me to get off the bus."

Two days later Kirk, Katie, and Brandon were surfing the channels to find something decent to watch when a Hallmark movie about the dog came on. Brandon was so excited that he wanted to read the book again, and he talked about it for days.

Kirk was amazed at how Brandon seemed to be enjoying reading now. "Hon, you're working miracles with that kid's reading ability. I'm so proud of you."

"If I didn't take time to sit down with him and find books that a seven-year-old boy would enjoy, he would always hate reading. You have to make it fun. Brandon enjoyed the book about Hachiko, but when he saw the Hallmark movie it excited him, because he had first read the book."

"But didn't you read most of it to him?"

"It doesn't matter. What mattered is that I sat down with him and pointed to the words as I read. He started saying the words we would come to that he knew, and he did that on his own. I didn't prompt him. I also read slowly so that he could *see and hear* the words he was unfamiliar with."

"You are so good for him."

"And you are the father figure he has never had. So that makes us a good team."

"For sure. Hey, I wanna take him fishing soon. The fish will be biting about now since the water has warmed to about the right temperature."

"What about tomorrow?"

"Yeah, that'll work. Now I just have to figure out where I put my tackle. I think I have a small pole that would be about right for him. We'll catch some minnows and maybe some crawdads in the creek here beside the house."

"Have Brandon help you catch them."

"Oh for sure."

"Kirk, we are so fortunate to be able to live in a place like this. It's so beautiful. I know you must question that when it comes time, in the scorching summer heat, to put up hay for the winter."

"When all the machinery is working right, it isn't bad. What I hate is when the tractor quits on me, or the mower, rake or bailer breaks down—all very old equipment—that's not good when I'm working against the clock to get the hay in before a rain sets in. But you're right, it is beautiful here, and we are fortunate to be able to enjoy all four of God's wonderful seasons."

With the morning milking finished, Kirk and Brandon went back to the house, got a minnow bucket, and retrieved dozens of minnows from the little creek on the north side of the ranch house. Brandon found three crawdads.

Katie had made a couple of sandwiches and filled a thermos of cold milk for them. Kirk tied the rods and reels to the front rack of the ATV, along with a small cooler chest to hold any fish they caught. The minnow bucket was tied to the rear rack. Brandon held on to the bag with the thermos and sandwiches. Chubby followed along beside them to the big pond.

Brandon stared at the glassy clear water, not a ripple from bank to bank. "Where's the boat?"

"There is no boat," Kirk said. "We bank fish today. But, hey, let's keep an eye out for a used john boat for sale. That would be perfect for this big pond."

Chubby made himself a bed in the grass by the ATV while Kirk showed Brandon how to bait his hook and hold the rod to cast out into the pond. After about an hour of nothing biting, He helped Brandon bait his hook with a small crawdad. As soon as the bait hit the water, a fish took it, and the little red and white bobber disappeared under the surface ripples. Kirk reached around Brandon and showed him how to set the hook. Together they reeled in a small mouth bass. Kirk said, "Wow, I didn't know we even had any bass in this pond." After Kirk removed the hook from the bass, Brandon put another crawdad on and did the cast by himself.

"You're getting good at casting—oh, you've got another one. Set that hook!" Brandon jerked back on the rod, setting the hook, and reeled in another small mouth. "Hey, buddy, you did that one all by yourself."

"Can I take the hook out?"

"You'll have to be careful. You know how sharp those hooks are. Trust me; you don't want one of those in your finger."

The hook was barely set just in the front of the fish's mouth. Brandon had no trouble removing it. He was so excited about getting the hook out by himself that he forgot how slippery the fish was, and it escaped out of his hand and back into the water. A crass little word slipped out of his mouth.

"Brandon! Have you ever heard me talk like that?"

Brandon ducked his head and whispered, "No."

Kirk reached his arm around Brandon, "God hears every word that comes out of our mouths. We have to be careful to say the words that would be pleasing to Him."

"What should I say?"

"Anything you want to say, but just leave out the little nasty word."

"I'll just say, *oh Bryce!*" He paused. "But that's a nasty word too."

Kirk laughed. "So I guess you'll have to pick something else."

"So what can I say?"

"How about *oh shoot?*"

Their last crawdad was used to pull in another bass. Apparently the fish weren't hungry for minnows. "Brandon, next time we'll fish for catfish."

"How is that different?"

"Catfish are bottom feeders, so we'll use a little lead weight, like this one, to take the bait down to the bottom of the pond."

"What do they eat?"

"Catfish will eat about anything. I've seen guys use corn, pieces of liver, or even wieners. There are some big ones in this pond—big enough to make a meal for the three of us."

"When do we eat? I'm hungry."

Kirk opened up the sack of sandwiches. He was glad to see that Katie had put in a packet of hand sanitizing wipes. As they sat there on the bank eating their sandwiches Brandon asked Kirk, "Am I going to live with you forever, or will I go live with my mom again?"

"Brandon, that all depends on some things that are out of our control. Your mother has to work out some things in her life before you live with her again."

"I want to live here with you, but I want Mom to live here too."

Kirk hesitated. *How am I supposed to answer that one?* "Brandon, you should pray that God will work it all out for your benefit. He knows what's best for you, and He fixes problems much better than we can. So we may want to leave that one up to The Big Guy Upstairs."

Brandon looked like he was deep in thought; then he said, "Well I don't know how to fix it, so I guess I'll have to let God do the fixing."

"Yep, you're right. Now let's gather up our gear and tie it back on the ATV. You can give Chubby that bread crust if you don't want it."

CHAPTER 15

Sunday lived up to its name with an abundance of sunshine. Brandon had already picked out his clothes for church. It was his time to say grace at the breakfast table. "God, I thank you for our breakfast. Help my mom to work things out so we can be a family. Since Kirk can't be her husband, you will need to find one for her because she hasn't done a very good job of finding one for herself. Oh, and thank you for letting us catch the fish yesterday. Amen."

As they approached the main ranch gate Brandon pushed the remote on the visor of the pickup. The gate opened. He looked at Katie and carefully chose his words. "How do you like our invention? Isn't that just the cat's meow?"

"Where did you hear that?"

"I don't remember, but I think it was on TV. I thought it sounded cool."

Katie said, "You can hear a lot of stuff on TV. That one is okay, but you'll need to be careful what you pick up and say in public."

"I don't say any of that stuff that Bryce used to say. I know it was ugly."

The little country church was about four miles from the ranch gate. Kirk and Katie could see that Brandon had been listening to the sermons. This Sunday, as they were heading back home, Brandon said, "I asked Jesus if He would be my friend."

Kirk said, "Wow! That is great."

"I was pretty sure Jesus wouldn't answer my prayers about my mom if I didn't. I don't understand everything the preacher says, but I'm pretty sure I want Jesus to be my friend."

"Well I know Jesus is very happy to be your friend. This is a very special day for you."

Three weeks went by and Betty hadn't called for another parental visit. Brandon had asked several times when he would get to see his mom again. He loved the farm chores, which kept him busy and not thinking too much about her. He had come to love the reading time in the evening. Katie made several trips to the used book store because Brandon kept asking for more. It was good to see that change in him. She and Kirk talked about how Brandon wasn't stretching the truth anymore, which was also good to see.

There was finally a phone call from Betty. "Katie, I have made an appointment with Brandon's mother for a parental visit tomorrow at four-thirty here at the office. Will that work for you?"

Katie glanced at the calendar on the wall, "Sure, I can be there then."

"Just so you know. I am making sure that I can be there. I've also asked Bob to remain at the office until Denise is gone. I don't want to take a chance on another parking lot fiasco."

When Kirk heard about the planned visit he told Katie he would be going with her this time. Katie shook her head. "There will be two caseworkers there, including Bob, so I think it'll be okay if you need to stay here and do the milking."

"No, I'm going with you. It sounds like it may take two of us men to tether that wildcat. You know, that woman doesn't deserve a son like Brandon."

"Kirk, I've been praying that Denise will see her wrong ways and want to change her life. Brandon needs her."

"Yeah, but he doesn't need her the way she is now."

"Well help me pray for her. God is in the business of changing lives."

"I agree, but a person has to *want* to change."

"Just the same, I'm going to show her some kindness and compassion. I want her to see that she can have a better life."

"Good luck with that."

Kirk pulled into the DFS parking lot at exactly four-thirty. Brandon was anxious to see his mom. Katie looked around the parking lot and said, "I don't see the white Bronco. That could be good or bad."

"How's that?"

Katie whispered to Kirk, "Good if she's ditched the Bronco and its owner or bad if she's not going to show up."

When the elevator opened up to the third floor offices, Brandon's mother was tripping through a thorny outburst of foul language, Denise Brewer style.

Katie looked at Kirk and nodded back toward the elevator. "Why don't you take Brandon down to the vending machines on the first floor and get him a Coke or candy bar.".

Kirk grinned. "You are very wise, Mrs. Childers."

Katie waited at the door. The prickly outburst continued, and she inched into the room where Denise stood facing Betty and Bob.

With her arms crossed in front of her in obvious insolence, Denise was shouting, "My son deserves to be with me. You can't keep on hiding him…"

She turned and saw Katie, "I suppose you're gonna take their side—"

Katie interrupted, "Denise, your conversation up to this point is none of my business. My job is to have your son here at the appointed time for a visit with his mom, and that is what I have done. Brandon and Kirk will be back up in a minute. Kirk took him out of earshot and down to the vending machines."

Denise stared at Katie. "Thanks. I didn't mean to get so loud."

Katie could see Betty's eyes bug out, and her mouth formed the silent word, "Wow!"

"Denise, I have a thought." Betty and Bob waited to see what Katie had up her sleeve. "Here's a suggestion. When you come for a visit with Brandon, it would mean a lot to him if you would bring him some little something—maybe a Matchbox car, or a little book. It doesn't have to be expensive, even a piece of paper that you have made into a card with words of encouragement for Brandon. You know, he talks a lot about you. Do you have a picture of yourself?" Katie reached for Denise's hand, "If you have a picture of just you alone or with Brandon, bring it next time. Brandon would love that."

"That's a good idea," Denise said. "It'll give him a picture or something to hold onto while he's away from me."

Betty stood speechless, not sure that she was hearing the instant transformation in Denise's dialogue. Her lips formed the word, "Amazing!"

The civil conversation between Katie and Denise continued until Brandon zipped through the door, chocolate on both sides of his mouth, and grabbed his mother. But then, a look of fear overtook him. With a barely audible whisper he said, "Did Bryce come with you?"

With her volume turned up loud enough to make sure the others could hear, Denise said, "No, Baby. He is long gone. I told him to get lost and never find his way back."

"Good, 'cause he is mean."

Betty motioned for Kirk and Bob to remain in her office while she ushered Denise, Brandon, and Katie into the conference room. She pulled the door closed behind her and punched the lock on the knob below the frosted glass insert. Then she turned to see the smile on Kirk's face. "Your wife did in thirty seconds what I hadn't been able to do since Denise walked in the door—incredible!"

"Betty, my wife has a gift of kindness and grace that breaks down all barriers. I've learned to shut my mouth when she does that to me, because I know she's gonna win the argument."

"Well she sure knew how to extinguish the fire that was rampant in here."

Kirk glanced toward the frosted glass door. "I'd give anything to hear what's going on. It's pretty quiet in there."

"You're welcome to go in."

"No, I think this should be just the three of them."

At five-twenty, Betty peeked inside the door. "Can you guys wind it up in a few minutes? I have a foster home visit after I lock up here."

Katie stood up and moved toward the open door. "We can continue this conversation at your next visit."

Bob followed Kirk, Katie, and Brandon out to their pickup truck, while Betty made her way to her car. Denise got in her little Pinto wagon.

Katie looked back at the caseworker, turned bouncer. "Thanks, Bob. I'm glad we didn't need you this time."

"Yeah, me too," Bob said.

Kirk watched as Katie buckled herself in. "I'm dying to know what transpired in there."

"Later, honey. Let's go get Brandon a Happy Meal."

That night when they were alone, she snuggled up against Kirk and filled him in. "Denise was on her best behavior. We had a good conversation. She told me she saw something very different about me. I must have frowned because she said, 'No, it's not bad. How is it that you can come into a room and calm everyone down so quickly?' I told her I just wanted her to have a nice pleasant visit with her son."

"We talked quite a bit and toward the end of the visit she said, 'Katie, I can see how you and Kirk are good for Brandon.'"

"Wow! She said that?"

"There's more. Get this. She said, 'Katie, I'm tired of my life; I feel like it is spinning out of control. I want to be more like you.'

"I hesitated, silently praying that I'd choose the right words; then I knew what I had to say, and I spoke with a confidence that I didn't even know I had."

"So what did you say?"

"Denise," I said, "years ago I decided to reject anything that had the appearance of evil. Christ brings a peace to my life; without Him I would be a mess." I paused to let those words sink in.

"She looked deep into my eyes. 'You really believe that, don't you?'

"'Yes, Denise, I really do.' I could see the beginnings of a transformation in attitude come over her right then.

"That's when Brandon told her that he had asked Jesus to be his friend, and that's when Betty opened the door. I knew my message had to be put on hold."

"There'll be a next time."

"I hope so. She was so ready to hear more of what I had to say. She was in such a penitent mood. My heart ached for her."

"Katie, you've planted the seed. Now it needs time to sprout."

"I hope you're right. Denise is such a beautiful girl. Brandon needs his mom."

Kirk put his arm around Katie, got inches from her face and whispered, "But if she wants to throw him away, we'll take him. One way or the other, Brandon will be loved."

CHAPTER 16

Denise's situation continued to dominate Katie's thoughts. She was alone again with Kirk. "Honey, I can't get Brandon's mother off my mind."

"Come on Kate, don't you think we've done our part?"

"No doubt, yes we have. But I'm looking at it from Denise's standpoint. How can the girl get out of the mess she is in? She needs another wage earner in the household just to pay the bills."

"Okay, but the last one she chose cost her more than he was worth."

"True. What she needs is a decent man that will love her and hang onto his job."

"First she has to examine her own life—get her priorities straight. You can't hit a home run if you are wandering around outside the ballpark."

"What's that supposed to mean?"

"Denise has to start running with a better crowd. She's gotta be seen in the right places, and she's gotta pay attention to what's being hurled at her."

"I'm not sure I can convince her of that, but I've got to try."

"Why? So she can get her son back and fall right back into the same old lifestyle? Katie, I think you better think that through. Brandon deserves better than that."

"So you think I should mind my own business?"

Kirk grinned, "That might be in everyone's best interest."

"Kirk Childers! I am overwhelmed by your compassion!"

"Katie you know I love that kid. I don't wanna see him get right back in the same stinking lifestyle he was in. That is exactly what will happen if Denise gets him back, and you know it."

"I'm thinking about how Denise told me she wanted to change her life."

"Honey, she already changed. She learned how to manipulate you and Betty to get what she wanted."

"So you don't believe a person like that can change for the better?"

"Yes, a person like that *can* change for the better, but they have to *want* to. I'm not convinced she wants to. That's all I'm saying."

With school out for the summer, Brandon followed Kirk almost everywhere. Kirk took time to take him fishing again in the big pond. This time they caught two nice channel cats. Brandon had never seen a catfish. When they got back to the house he watched as Kirk cleaned the fish. "Are we gonna cook them?"

"No, that's Miss Katie's job. She has agreed to cook them if we clean them."

"Does she know how bad they stink?"

Kirk grinned, "Yeah, she's cooked them before."

Brandon's demeanor changed. "Kirk, I wish my mom could move out here… 'cause I don't wanna live where she lives. It's no fun. There's nothing to do there. I like it here better."

"Brandon, happiness is a state of mind. We can decide to be happy where we are, or we can be sad and grumpy. Katie and I want you to be happy where ever you are."

"Well I'm happy here, but I want my mom to be here too."

"That's a difficult situation. Maybe you should pray that God will work it out for you."

"I already did, and I guess He didn't like the way I prayed."

"Did you try to *tell* God what you wanted him to do, or did you *ask* Him to work it out for the best?"

"I *told* Him 'cause He wasn't doing anything."

"That's where you made your mistake. We aren't supposed to *tell* God what to do. He knows a lot more than we do, and He knows what is best for us."

Brandon looked down at the floor. "I wish He would tell me so I'd know."

"Give it time, Brandon, you'll know. Now, let's get these fish in the kitchen so Katie can fry them up."

"What do we do with the fish heads and all this yucky stuff?"

"We'll take it down to the hogs; they'll eat anything."

"That is gross!"

"You can stay here and watch Miss Katie fry them up while I go down and serve the hogs their appetizer."

"Okay, but don't get in the pen with them. I don't think they're happy where they are."

Kirk thought about that for a second, tipped his head upward just a tad, and his little one-sided grin appeared. "You're quite a kid."

CHAPTER 17

Kirk steered the big pickup into the Wal-Mart parking lot. "You got the list?"

Brandon pulled it out of his pocket, "Right here."

"Okay, you read each item off to me when we get in the store. Katie said it would all be in the food section this time, so that'll make it easier."

"I might not know some of the words."

"That's okay, just …."

Halfway across the parking lot someone hollered, "Brandon!"

Brandon must have recognized the voice. "It's Bryce!" he said through clinched teeth.

"Just ignore him and keep right by me."

Kirk saw the coward moving toward them. Brandon grabbed Kirk's hand and tried to hide behind him. Bryce kept coming and was now within an arm's length away. He tried to move around behind Kirk, but as he did, Kirk turned and Brandon turned with him.

Bryce shouted into Kirk's ear. "Why don't you tell that little —— there with you to quit hiding."

"Just get on out of here and leave the boy alone," Kirk said.

Bryce's voice escalated and anyone in the parking lot could have heard him. "Hey, you little ——! You're the reason I had to move out of my house."

Brandon was glued to Kirk's back. "It's not your house; it's my mom's," he muttered into Kirk's shirt.

Bryce must have heard him. "Boy, don't you get smart—"

Kirk felt his own right fist tighten into a ball. "Back off!"

Bryce continued to turn to reach Brandon. Kirk grabbed him by the shirt. "I said back off! Leave the boy alone!"

The heated dialogue had drawn a few stares from onlookers. Bryce reached around Kirk and grabbed Brandon's arm. Brandon screamed!

Kirk, still clinching Bryce's shirt, lost all patience with the bully. "Turn him lose NOW before I knock them crooked teeth out of your stinkin' mouth!"

Bryce wouldn't give it up, spewing his liquor laced breath in Kirk's face. "You ain't b-big enough to make me."

With his left hand still holding Brandon, Kirk swung his right fist into Bryce's face. Bryce tried to return it, but Kirk caught his arm in midair. The other arm was heading for Kirk's face.

"Run to the truck," Kirk hollered at Brandon. He grabbed Bryce's other wrist just as it plowed into his cheek bone. Kirk held his grip on both of Bryce's wrists and kneed him with the strength of a two thousand-pound bull.

Bryce doubled over. Kirk turned loose of his wrists and watched as the scrawny misfit hit the pavement. "Get up and get on out of here before I really get angry."

With Bryce still doubled over in a fetal position on the pavement, Kirk turned away, and jogged over to the pickup where he had told Brandon to go. When he didn't see him, he called his name. Brandon peeked out over the bed of the truck. "Come on, buddy; let's go find another grocery store. This one's got snakes in its parking lot."

Brandon climbed on the side of the truck bed, and held out his arms. Kirk's two strong arms reached out and held him while he jumped down. Kirk then opened the driver's door and Brandon crawled over to the passenger side. "I saw you punch him—way to go! I knew you'd win."

Kirk was looking in the mirror and rubbing his cheek. "Brandon, a fight is bound to end with both guys taking hits. It's best to avoid one when you can. But sometimes you just can't."

The Food For Less parking lot proved to be a friendlier place. Brandon was able to read all but two of the items Katie had written on the list. Kirk was impressed. "Hey, buddy, you are reading so much better. I'm proud of you."

"Miss Katie is a good teacher; she makes reading fun."

Several times Kirk caught Brandon looking at his right cheek. It was throbbing and he knew it was probably swelling as well. When they got home, Kirk and Brandon both grabbed grocery bags to carry in. As soon as Kirk opened the door, Katie greeted them and saw his face. "What on earth happened to you? Your face is swelling up."

"I had a little clash with the infamous Bryce in the Wal-Mart parking lot."

"What? You got into a fight with Bryce? How did he know you were there?"

"He didn't. He just saw Brandon tagging along behind me and started smarting off at the mouth—called Brandon a bad name—and was yelling that Brandon caused him to get kicked out of his house. Brandon whispered that it wasn't *his* house and Bryce must have heard him. I tried to get him to back off but he wouldn't."

"That is just plain weird!" She reached up and touched the swelling cheek. "What kind of animal is he?"

"Katie, the guy was drunk. If I'd struck a match to his breath, he would have gone up in flames."

Brandon piped up with excited eyes. "Yeah, and Kirk punched him in the face and kneed him in the—."

Katie didn't let him finish. "Well it looks like someone else got punched in the face too. Kirk, we better get some ice on that."

"We've got more groceries in the truck."

"Brandon can get them. Come on in, and I'll get an ice pack out of the freezer."

"Honey, first let me tell you how proud I am of Brandon. I handed him the grocery list for him to read each item to me so I could find it on the shelf. He read all but two on the list!"

Katie touched Brandon's shoulder. "See, I knew you were reading better. Now, would you go out and get the other bags from the truck while I grab an ice pack?"

When Brandon was out the door Katie turned to Kirk. "I am reporting this to Betty."

"What good would that do?"

"Maybe she could get a restraining order or something."

"Katie, I think I can handle any future rendezvous with the little shrimp. He's about six inches shorter than I am and at least fifty pounds lighter." Kirk felt of his cheek. "The little firecracker wouldn't have gotten this punch in but I had turned to tell Brandon to run back to the truck. As I turned back around, I saw his fist coming at me."

"Just the same, I'm reporting him to Betty."

The next morning, Katie was finishing up the breakfast dishes when the phone rang. She glanced at the clock on the oven—only nine o'clock.

It was Betty. "Katie, I know you and Kirk haven't fostered a full six months, but the Department is in a bind for foster parents. All my foster homes are full. Is there any way you can take a couple of newborn twin girls?"

Katie swallowed before answering. "Betty, I—I don't know. Did you say they are newborn?

"Yes, the girls were born premature and their mother didn't make it through the birth. She died a couple of minutes after the last one was born."

"Where is the father?"

"The hospital records show the father as *unknown*. In fact, the records show that the next-of-kin was marked *n/a*."

"Oh, so they don't even have anyone to notify?"

"That's it. The hospital called us to take the babies after they had spent two months in the neo-natal intensive care ward."

"Betty, that is awful! So they are two months old. What do they weigh now?"

"I think the hospital told me they both weigh about five pounds each."

"What happens next with them? Will they be adopted?"

"If no father or other relative comes forward, they will be up for adoption."

"So we could have them for a long time 'til that happens?"

"As soon as the time is up for someone to come forward, the adoption process will be very quick. Infants are the first to be adopted."

"If you have no other home to place the babies, I guess we should take them. It's just that I wasn't prepared to care for such a tiny little person, much less two at once!"

"Katie, you'll do just fine. Any first time mother has those same uncertainties. You'll do much better than the little teen mothers. When can I bring them out?"

"What time is good for you? I'll be here all day."

Betty told her she would head on over to the hospital to pick them up and then head out to the ranch. Katie remembered to tell her to call when she got to the ranch. "I'll have to drive up and open the gate for you."

Kirk and Brandon came back to the house after the morning chores were done. Katie told Kirk about the babies.

"Are you serious? We're taking two infants? Where are we gonna put them?"

"Kirk, we do have the spare bedroom. I wouldn't have said yes, but Betty seemed desperate. She said she had no other place for them. Their mother died right after they were born, and the hospital records show the father as *unknown*."

"So how long are we gonna have them?"

"Betty said the legal notice will be posted, and after the allotted time, if no father or other relative shows up, they will be placed for adoption. She said infants are always adopted first, so that shouldn't be a long wait."

Kirk rolled his eyes. "Whew! Katie, I don't know about this. What are we getting ourselves into? We don't even have stuff for babies—diapers, cribs, formula."

"Honey, I don't know. We'll work it out some way."

"I don't think I can be much help with this. Brandon and I will just try to stay out of your way. So, good luck!"

"Thanks," Katie said with a hint of aggravation in her voice. "I didn't think I could count on you this time."

"Honey, I'm sorry. I didn't mean it that way. It's just that I know nothing about tiny babies. I don't see how I can be any help to you at all. I don't ever recall even *holding* a baby."

"Let's just hope it's very temporary."

CHAPTER 18

It was after lunch when Betty called from the ranch gate. Katie drove up to let her in and Betty rolled down her window. "When did we get the electronic gate?"

"Oh, Kirk and Brandon installed that a couple of weeks ago. I think Kirk was worried that Denise would find out where we live and try something."

"I can see how it makes the ranch a little more secure. Hopefully it won't be needed. Let's get these little darlings up to your house and snuggled in."

Betty pulled up to the house behind Katie. The babies were belted in their infant seats in the back seat of the Buick. Katie opened the passenger door and was overcome with unexpected tears. "Oh, they are beautiful—and so tiny!" Both girls were sound asleep.

"Let's try to get them in the house without waking them." Katie worked to unbuckle the one while Betty got the other one. After both were in the house, and still asleep, Betty went back to the car and brought in diapers, baby wipes, baby bottles, formula, blankets, and both infant car seats.

Katie continued to stare at the tiny babies. "They look so fragile and *alone* in the world." Her emotions faded just long enough to ask, "What are their names?"

Betty looked a bit puzzled. "They were only known as *Baby Smith A* and *Baby Smith B* in the hospital. I guess the mother didn't live long enough to name them. So it looks like you get to name them, at least for now."

Katie's eyes were locked on the infants. A minute later she was able to break away from the spell she was under. "You may need to run through the formula routine with me before you go."

"Yes, there are several things we need to go over. Let's start with the formula. We should get some ready, because they will be awake soon and hungry."

Katie managed to pull herself away from the little ones and followed Betty into the kitchen. After the bottles of formula were made, the two had a chance to sit down to visit a bit. Betty asked how Brandon was doing.

"He's doing great. His reading has improved dramatically."

About that time Kirk came in, followed by his young shadow. "So I guess you brought us a couple of twins, uh?"

Betty looked up at Kirk and saw his bruised cheek. "What happened to you?"

"I ran onto Bryce in a Wal-Mart parking lot. He started mouthing off to Brandon with several nasty little slurs. I kept telling him to back off, but he wouldn't give it up. I wasn't gonna stand there and listen to his abusive language aimed at Brandon. But when he reached behind me and grabbed Brandon, I'd had enough of the little weasel. So we took a couple of pops at each other, and I left him doubled over in the parking lot. We got in the truck and went to another grocery store."

Betty just shook her head. "Was Denise with him?"

"I didn't see her."

After Betty left, Katie took Kirk's hand and led him toward the bedroom. "Honey, come see these two tiny darlings." She opened the door to the newly defined nursery. "Shhh, they're asleep. Don't wake them."

"Wow! They are identical—and so little!"

"Honey, these could be our babies. Their mother died just after giving birth, and the father is unknown. You may be looking at your own daughters."

"Hold on, Katie. Let's not get ahead of things here. These babies surely have kin folk that would want to take them. What're their names?"

"Betty said they haven't been named yet."

"Oh, come on now. What do their birth certificates say?"

"Betty thinks the birth certificates are being held up until a custodial parent is found."

"So what are we gonna call them for now?"

"Baby A and Baby B, until I come up with a couple of names."

"You? You're gonna name them?"

"Kirk, they have to have names. We can't just continue to call them Baby A and Baby B."

One of them started to cry, and that woke the other one. Kirk turned and dashed out of the room. "Well one thing's for sure; they've got good lungs!"

Brandon was squatted down outside the door. Kirk spotted him and could see there was a problem. "Someone lost his happy face. What's wrong, buddy?"

"Nuthin."

"Well, *Nuthin*'s got you all sad. Why don't you and I go feed Dandy and Lilly."

After feeding the horses, Kirk and Brandon got back on the ATV and rode over the pasture looking for newborn calves. Kirk stopped down by the pond where they had fished, turned around and looked at his partner. "Are you feeling better now?"

Brandon tipped his head down. "Sorta," he whispered.

Kirk wrapped his arm around him. "Would you tell me why you're feeling so sad?"

Brandon's eyes were tearing. "I'm—I'm afraid you'll adopt the babies and not me."

"I didn't know you wanted us to adopt you."

The tears were streaming down his face now. "If my mom doesn't want me, I was hoping you would."

Now a tear was forming in Kirk's eye. "Oh, Brandon… buddy! Katie and I would love to adopt you if your mother can't take you back. I promise, buddy. If there is any way that we can, we will."

Brandon put his arms around Kirk and Kirk leaned his head down on Brandon's helmet. Kirk sat there on the ATV for a minute, holding his little buddy. Then he pulled Brandon's chin up so he could see his eyes. "Feel better now?"

"Yeah."

"You wanna go back to the house to get our fishing gear, then come back here and see what we can catch?"

Brandon shook his head, looked up at Kirk and grinned. "Let's go."

Back at the house, Katie was busy feeding the babies. Kirk and Brandon got busy in the kitchen and designed each other's sandwiches. Kirk drew a smiley face on Brandon's with mayo and Brandon drew a house on Kirk's. "This is our house," Brandon said.

Kirk stood watching Brandon put the finishing touches on the sandwich. *He's gotten attached to me as much as I have to him. This is gonna hurt both of us if Denise gets him back. Dear God, I need wisdom right now. Please give me the right words to say to him.*

Their designer sandwiches and cold milk, along with the fishing tackle was loaded on the four-wheeler racks, and the guys were bouncing down toward the pond. A couple of hours later, they came back to the house with three small mouth bass.

Brandon ran into the house, slammed the door, and hollered, "I caught one and Kirk caught two." That not only got the attention of Katie, it got the attention of both twins and their stereophonic wails burst through the previously quiet house. Kirk apologized and explained to Brandon that they would have to be quiet when they were around the babies.

"I was never *that* loud!" Brandon said. "They hurt my ears."

Kirk grinned. "Maybe that's because there are two of them and only one of you."

The guys took their catch out back and Brandon wanted to clean his fish. Kirk told him to watch as he cleaned one and to do the same thing to his. He did exactly as Kirk had done. They rinsed them off and took them back into the kitchen—tip-toeing all the way.

Two weeks passed and Betty hadn't called. With each passing day, Kirk could see the hope building in Katie. He knew she was counting on no relative coming forward, opening the door for an adoption of the twins.

She had decided on names for them—*Kaitlin* and *Kayla*. Kirk could see what was behind the naming of the babies. With each passing day, he could also see that Katie was becoming more and more attached. He had to admit, her maternal instincts combined with her innate teaching abilities would make for a wonderful mother. But what about Brandon? Three kids would be a huge responsibility. Kirk tipped his head upward. *God, you've got to help me on this one.*

CHAPTER 19

"Kirk, Denise wants another visit with Brandon. Do you think you could take him? I'd have my hands full with the twins."

"No problem. There's only one catch though. We get to stop by Maggie Moo's on the way back."

"Well, go ahead," she said, "enjoy that Oreo and ice cream thing you guys like. Think about me here with the squalling babies the whole time you're eating it."

At four-thirty Kirk and Brandon took the elevator up to the third floor and into Betty's office. One of the other caseworkers, Bob, was waiting for them and told Kirk that Betty had an emergency in one of the foster homes and had asked him to cover for her. Kirk had skimmed through most of the magazines on the table next to him. Bob kept looking at his watch, and Brandon was getting bored. At five minutes till five, Denise burst through the door saying, "I'm sorry I'm late. I had a flat on my car."

Kirk gave her an icy stare, "Denise, don't you think you've over-used that excuse? Surely you could come up with a new one now."

"Are you calling me a liar?"

"Hey, I'm just saying you ought to think of a new excuse. We're all kind of tired of hearing that one."

Denise popped back, "If I'd known you were the one showing up here, I would have found someplace else to go."

"Ouch! What happened to that penitent attitude I was told you had last—"

Bob broke into what was becoming a heated exchange. "Denise, why don't you and Brandon go on in to the conference room now?"

Brandon jumped up and said, "I want Kirk to come in with me."

Denise gave Brandon an icy stare. "I don't want *him* with us if he's just gonna insult me more."

Brandon latched on to Kirk's hand and looked straight at his mother, "He's not insulting you! You're the one that was late! And I'll bet you forgot to bring me a picture too."

"Oh, baby, I'll bring you one to our next visit. I promise you Mamma was in a hurry today."

With Brandon latching onto his hand, Kirk followed Denise into the conference room. Kirk and Brandon sat down while Denise took a chair on the other side of the room by the window. She turned and glared out, without saying a word. This continued for several minutes until Brandon got up and said to Kirk, "Let's go; I think the cat got her tongue."

Kirk grinned and started toward the door with Brandon in tow. Bob met them in the outer office with a quizzical look. "She didn't want to talk," Kirk said, "so there was no reason for us to stay."

Bob shook his head in disgust. "That…" He caught himself before lashing out in front of Brandon.

Kirk looked at Bob with understanding and a *Yeah, I agree* look. Then he and Brandon took the stairs down to the first floor, out to the pickup, and headed to Maggie Moo's. Brandon was silent, even after he got his Oreo cookie treat.

Katie waited to greet them as they approached the door. "How did it go?"

"Don't ask. I'll tell you later."

But Brandon saw no need to wait to give an account of the visit. "I'll tell you how it went. Denise was a jerk!"

Katie looked up at Kirk, and he motioned to her with his head to move on. "I'll explain later," he whispered.

Katie made her way toward the big room, turned and said, "Thanks, guys, for keeping your voices down when you came in. I just now got the twins to sleep."

"Come on Brandon; let's get changed into our work boots and old jeans. We've still got the milking to do."

It was Sunday. Katie made no attempt to go to church with their expanded family. The twins were both fussy and their little country church didn't have a separate nursery to take them to when they cried.

Kirk agreed that she should stay home with them. He and Brandon would go. Brandon knew the routine; he showered, got dressed, and ate all of his scrambled eggs—then asked for more. Kirk forked some off his own plate and gave it to Brandon. "Man, you keep eating like that, and you'll be bigger than me." Brandon's eyes sparkled.

After church, as Kirk came in sight of the ranch gate, he recognized the dark blue Mustang convertible; it was Katie's parents. He pulled up beside them, and rolled his window down. "You two look like teenagers, running around with the top down. How long you been waiting?"

Katie's mother spoke up. "We just got here. I didn't know what to do when I saw the closed gate. I called Katie and she said you'd be coming in a few minutes."

"Sorry you had to wait. I need to buy another remote for the gate… But—wait—that wouldn't do any good. Katie couldn't load both babies on the ATV and come up here. We need another car."

He pushed the remote in the truck and the gate opened for the Mustang to go through. He then followed and pushed the button again to close the gate.

Brandon was eying the Mustang. "I sure like their cool car. Can we get one like it?"

"Yeah sure, when you have enough in your piggy bank to buy one."

Back at the house Brandon went over to Lynn and Carol's little car as they were getting out. "Kirk said we can get one just like it when I've saved enough money to buy one—but that sure sounds like a *never* to me."

Lynn ran his fingers through Brandon's hair. "You know, I think you've grown a couple of inches since we saw you last."

"I'm eating lots of scrambled eggs so I can get bigger than Kirk."

Carol said, "Well let's go see these little twin girls Katie told me about."

The visit lasted a couple of hours, and just as they were leaving, Brandon looked up at Lynn, brazen-faced, and said, "So I guess you will be my grandpa when Kirk adopts me."

Kirk rolled his eyes and said, "Let's not get ahead of things—"

But Lynn interrupted his son-in-law. "If that should ever happen, I would be honored to be your grandpa."

Brandon grabbed a deck of Old Maid and handed it to Lynn. "Come on, Grandpa; see if you can beat me. You shuffle."

One game led to three, and then Brandon wanted to show Lynn some of his books that Katie had just bought for him. He read one and started on another when Lynn interrupted. "Hey Brandon, you're gonna have to hold off on reading this one to me until our next visit. Right now, Carol and I need to start back. It looks like rain, so we may have to put the top up."

Brandon told them that he wanted to ride in the Mustang the next time they came out for a visit. Kirk and Brandon followed the little car back to the ranch gate. On the way back Kirk was getting bombarded with Brandon's questions—all about adoption.

"Brandon, you need to understand that Denise is your mother; she loves you very much. I'm sure she is trying her best to get you back home with her. There are several things she has to work out for that to happen."

"I don't think she's trying at all! She didn't even show up in time for our last visit; then she lied about having a flat."

"Don't be angry with her. You don't understand her situation. Let's give her the benefit of a doubt."

"But she wouldn't even *talk* to me!"

"Brandon, she was angry at me—not you. I shouldn't have said what I did to her."

"No, she doesn't care about me!"

"Hey man, don't say that."

"Well it's true!"

"I think you're wrong about that. Hey, let's go get out of these church clothes and go check on Dandy and Lilly."

"Can I drive the ATV?"

"Sure. After you turn eighteen."

Brandon grinned.

CHAPTER 20

Kirk stood at the door and listened as Brandon finished reading to Katie. "Hey buddy, I'm amazed at how well you are reading now. That's amazing."

"Yeah, Katie is a good teacher, and she's buying me lots of books to read during the summer."

Katie took the book and returned it to the shelf. "Well, now that I've got the twins to care for, our trips to town for more books may be pretty limited."

Brandon ducked his head and said nothing. Kirk had seen him do this before when he was disappointed. "Okay, Miss Katie can stay here and take care of the babies while you and I run to the bookstore. Would you like that?"

Brandon jumped up and headed for the door. "Get your hat, let's go."

The trip to town took about thirty minutes, and not one minute of that was in silence. The first book he saw was *Because of Winn Dixie* by Kate DiCamillo. His eyes gleamed as he told Kirk about the movie he'd seen—although Kirk had seen the movie also. The book was marked for third grade level. Kirk opened it to see if Brandon had any trouble reading. He rambled through the first three pages without even slowing down. So that book went in their basket. The next one was *Judy Moody* by Megan McDonald, another third grade level. Brandon had no trouble finding books he wanted to read. He picked up *Frindle* by Andrew Clements and was telling Kirk about the story.

Kirk fanned through the book and thought it was too hard for Brandon, but he grabbed the book and started reading with no help. "Okay, I guess that's gotta go in our basket, uh?" Kirk held up the bulging basket. "Hey, buddy, I think we've got enough to keep you busy for a long time. Now I wonder how much this is gonna cost me. Too bad our little town doesn't have a public library."

When they got back home Brandon was showing Katie all the books they got. She listened through all of them and silently patted Brandon on the shoulder, but Kirk read right through the silence and knew something was wrong.

"Brandon, take these new books to your room and organize them in the bookcase. I need to talk to Katie for a few minutes."

As soon as Brandon was out of the room, Katie looked into Kirk's eyes. The dam broke and the tears rolled. "Honey, we lost the twins."

"What?"

"Betty came and picked them up about an hour ago." Through the sobs, she managed to relate what had happened. "The girl's aunt came forward and wanted to take them."

"Just like that?"

"Betty said this aunt was already an approved foster parent, so the adoption process was shortened by at least six weeks. Betty didn't want to tell me until it became final. She knew I had hoped we could adopt them and knew it would be hard on me."

Kirk wrapped his arms around his wife and kissed her tear moistened cheek, "Oh, honey, I am sorry. I knew it would be rough on you when this time came."

"Kirk, those babies were still so fragile, and I thought they had no one to even claim them. I knew better than to get so attached—I even told you that. But I couldn't help it. I thought they needed me."

"Honey, they *did need* you, and you gave them what they needed and more. I'm so proud of you for the care you gave them while they were here. I'm sure it wasn't easy caring for them with all of your other responsibilities. Hey, you can bet that aunt will be good to them. You said she was already an approved foster parent, so I'm pretty sure she loves children."

Kirk held her close and kissed her again. "Katie, God had other plans, but that doesn't mean he has no plans for us. We just have to be patient. Come to think of it, I think you have reminded me of that once or twice—or dozens of times."

Brandon came back in, and with a sly little grin he said, "Are y'all through kissing now?"

Kirk grinned. "Why, yes Brandon, I believe you took care of that for us."

Brandon thought about that for a second, and his hidden grin slowly leached through his face. "Cause if you're through I want you to come see my bookcase now. It's all organized. I put the ones I haven't read yet on the top shelf."

As they went past the room where the twins had been, Brandon started to ask, "Where are the—"

Kirk shushed him and led him into his room. "Hey buddy, this bookcase is about full. What can we do when you want more?"

"You can build another one." Then he tried to revert back to his original question. "So what hap…?"

Kirk put his *please be quiet* finger up to his lips. "Let's go check on that new calf that was born this morning. We need to make sure he's been up on his feet and eating."

Before he started the ATV he explained that the babies had been taken to their new home. "They're gonna live with their aunt."

Brandon said, "I guess Miss Katie is sad, uh?"

"Yeah, Brandon, we don't need to remind her of it. Mothers get sort of teary eyed when their babies are taken from them." As soon as he had said that he knew it was a mistake.

"All except *my* mother."

"Come on, buddy. You don't know that. Denise is having it kind of rough. She doesn't have a husband to help her, so she's counting on you to come through with some of your famous *Brandon hugs.*"

He ducked his head and Kirk knew it was coming. Under his breath, and with his lips hardly moving, Brandon said, "She don't want my hugs."

Kirk ignored that. "Come on, man, get your helmet on. Let's go."

CHAPTER 21

Now that Katie had a little more free time, she wanted to check Brandon's math abilities. Over his objections, she had him stay in the house one morning and not go with Kirk. She found the second grade math workbook she had purchased earlier. Her goal was to make sure Brandon was at or near the end of second grade math abilities. Adding or subtracting numbers up to eighteen was no problem for him, as were the basic geometric shapes. She assigned him addition problems which required him to carry to reach the answer. He zipped through them with no help from her. "Brandon, you amaze me! You seem to have conquered your math so far."

"I like math. Miss Bates told me I did good."

"She probably said that you did *well*?"

"Yeah, that's what I said."

"Okay, smart boy, maybe we should work on your English."

Brandon heard the ATV pulling up. "Are we through now? 'Cause Kirk needs my help."

"Sure, you can go with him when he goes back out. I think he must have smelled those brownies I have in the oven." With a wink she continued, "But if he needs you now, you guys can get your brownies later today."

"No, I'm pretty sure we can wait to go back to work."

"I thought so."

For the remainder of the day Brandon was glued to Kirk's side. He told Kirk about the math workbook Katie had used to test him, "Miss Katie told me I did good."

"You did *well*."

"That's what I said. I think you and Katie both have a hearing problem."

"No, we don't have hearing problems; you have a grammar problem. Come on, squirt, grab that hay hook. We need to get a bale of hay for Dandy and Lilly."

"Did you already give them their oats?"

"No, they'll get that this evening—Brandon, you forgot your helmet!" Brandon felt the top of his head for the helmet that wasn't there. "If Miss Betty catches you bare headed and riding the ATV or Dandy, we'll both be in big trouble."

"So what do we do?"

"You stay here at the barn, and I'll run back to the house and get it. Don't go anywhere; stay right here."

When Kirk got back to the hay barn with the helmet, Brandon was nowhere in sight. He ran around to the other side of the barn—but no Brandon. He looked down toward the big pond where they had fished. *There is no way he would have had time to get all the way down to the pond.* But he thought he might be just out of sight on the other side of a little rise in the pasture, so he jumped back on the ATV and headed down toward the pond. Still there was no Brandon. He then circled back up to the horse pasture. Dandy and Lilly heard him drive up, but Brandon was nowhere in sight. He drove back up to the main barn, got off the ATV, and searched the stalls while calling his name. He walked back behind the barn to the pig pen. *Where could the kid have gotten off to?*

Kirk looked up in the direction of the main ranch gate. He had a sinking feeling in his stomach. *Did I leave that gate open?* He jumped back on the ATV and full-throttled it toward the main gate. Suddenly he became aware that he was holding his breath. Only when he came in sight of the closed gate did he release the pent up air in his lungs. *Okay, that's one alarm silenced.* But panic was still building. He squeezed the brake on the handle without using the foot brake, which threw the ATV into a skid, doing a one-eighty in the cloud of red dust, and then he raced back to the hay barn. He drove all the way around the fifty by two hundred foot barn stacked high with baled hay. He cut the engine, called Brandon's name, and listened for the voice that just wasn't there. What began as apprehension had turned into a full blown panic. He pulled out his cell phone and called Katie. "Honey, I can't find Brandon. Is he up at the house with you?"

"No, You came back to get his helmet. Where was he then?"

"I told him to stay put at the hay barn while I rode back to get his helmet. I've looked all over for him. It seems like he has just vanished."

"Do you think he would have gone down to the pond?"

"No, I rode down there. I searched the main barn and then I checked with Dandy and Lilly, thinking he might have gone up to see them. We were about to throw a bale of hay on the ATV rear rack when I saw that he wasn't wearing his helmet."

"What about the milk barn; did you check there?"

"Yeah, honey, I don't know where else to look."

With sudden alarm in her voice Katie said, "Oh Kirk! You don't suppose you would have left the main gate open, do you?"

"That thought did enter my mind, but I covered that too. It was closed."

"If you did forget to close it, could someone drive through and close it on the way out?"

"No, they would of had to use the remote to close it. Hold on! I think I hear him. BRANDON!" Still holding the phone, Kirk darted inside the barn, stared at the stacked bales of hay, and called again, "BRANDON!"

"I'm coming up in the pickup now," Katie said.

Kirk pulled out his flashlight that he always carried in a case on his belt. "Katie, I see a shoe!"

"A shoe! Oh, dear God! Do you think someone grabbed him? Kidnap—"

"No, it looks like he may have tunneled in between the hay bales. I see a spot he might have crawled through."

Just then a muffled voice filtered through the wall of hay. "Kirk, help me." The words were barely recognizable.

Kirk threw his cell phone down in the loose hay on the ground. He climbed up several feet and started to squeeze in between the bales. "Brandon, keep talking to me!"

"Help me!" Several feet of baled hay softened Brandon's voice.

"Keep talking pal. I'm coming toward you."

When he got about six feet in between the stacked bales he saw that they had collapsed from the top, trapping his little buddy. He knew it was going to be impossible to move them from where he was. There was no room to muscle them aside. "Brandon, keep talking."

Katie drove up in the pickup. When she got out and ran into the hay barn, she saw the soles of Kirk's shoes sticking out of a small opening between the bales of hay about ten feet up from the ground. She ran back to the truck and got a flashlight.

She heard a muffled, "Katie, is that you?"

"I'm here, Kirk."

"Crawl up on top of the bales just to my left and try to remove those that you see collapsed."

"Okay. I've got a flashlight here by your feet if you need it."

"Well, I could use it. The batteries just went dead in mine, but I'd have to back all the way out, and I don't want to take a chance on more bales collapsing."

Katie crawled up on top to get to the area above Kirk. She tugged on a bale. It was not budging. She moved on to the next one. The bales were very heavy because they were from fresh cut alfalfa and still contained a lot of moisture, even though it had lain out in the field to dry for a few days before it was baled. She tugged again, but it wouldn't budge.

Kirk yelled, "Brandon, I don't hear you!"

Then he heard the muffled and now failing voice, "I'm here, Kirk."

"Honey, don't try to move the lowest ones—they're probably wedged. Start with the bales on the perimeter of where the collapse is."

Then Kirk faintly heard, "I can't breathe."

"Hang on buddy, we're getting you out."

Katie was frantic, "Kirk, I can't budge these either. I'm just not strong enough."

"Crawl back down and get the hay hook hanging on the wall over there to your left."

Katie started to crawl back down and took a spill, tumbling down to the hay covered ground next to the wall where the hay hook hung. Kirk heard her say, "Well that's one way of getting down." He also thought he heard a cry coming from Brandon—at least he hoped he heard it. He wasn't sure, but now he heard no sound.

"Brandon, keep talking to me. I need to hear your voice."

Nothing—except his own accelerated breathing.

Katie climbed back up the mountain of hay bales. At the top, with her hand wrapped around the handle of the tool, she slammed the hook into a bale that she had already tried to move. With the hook planted deep in the bale, Katie pulled with all her 130 pounds. The bale moved. She changed her position just a bit and pulled again. This time the bale was under her control. She moved it out of the way and stabbed at another. With it out of the way, she was then able to pull the three collapsed bales out of the way. Kirk saw daylight and said, "Way to go, babe!"

"Honey, I see Brandon's hand just to the right of you." She began to work on pulling a couple of bales above his hand and was able to free up a space big enough for Kirk to reach in and grab Brandon's arm.

"Katie, there's an air space cleared now for Brandon. I'm gonna squirm my way back out and come on up and move the other bales above him."

"Thank you. My strength is giving out on me."

Kirk wriggled his way back out and took the hay hook from her. With one quick stab he pulled the first bale from the top and pitched it over to the side, then another, and another. Finally the last bale was pulled from on top of Brandon, but Brandon didn't appear to be breathing. Kirk grabbed his arms and pulled his limp little body up on top of the bales. "BRANDON!" There was no movement. "BRANDON!"

Katie was at Kirk's side now and whispered, "Oh, dear Jesus. Give Brandon your breath."

Kirk moved his limp body again and cupped his mouth over Brandon's. When that didn't seem to be working, he hollered to Katie, "honey, grab my cell phone and call 911."

"How is an ambulance supposed to get through the gate?"

"Tell 'em to bust through it and come on quick."

Kirk kept on trying to revive Brandon with the air from his own mouth. Finally Brandon coughed. His eyes opened; then another cough, and he started breathing on his own. "Hey, buddy, are you okay?"

Brandon shook his head and reached for Kirk. He picked him up and dug his boot heels into the hay, making his way down to the ground. "Honey, maybe you should call back, and tell them everything is okay now."

Katie made the call and took Brandon's hand. "Come on with me back to the house." They both got into the pickup while Kirk was climbing on the ATV to follow. Once they arrived back at the house Kirk dismounted, ran over and grabbed Brandon as he was starting to get out of the pickup. He threw his arms around him with one hand covering the back of Brandon's head. Tears were sliding down his cheek. He held his little buddy in a tight grip. "Hey pal, you scared me half to death. Don't ever go into that hay barn without me."

Brandon laid his head on Kirk's shoulder. "I won't. I promise."

CHAPTER 22

Later in that same week the owner of the ranch came up to visit his nephew. When he arrived at the main gate and found it closed he called Kirk's cell phone. Kirk grabbed the remote from the truck, rode the ATV up to the gate, and punched the button to open it. After his uncle drove through, he rolled down the window and asked about the automatic gate.

"It's something I rigged up from an old garage door opener. Since we're keeping foster children we wanted a little more security."

"Security?"

"Yeah, we've got one mother that might try to snatch her son. It would be pretty easy for her to find us if she found out our last name. The only problem with my automatic gate is one of us has to drive up and let a visitor in. I've told my feed distributor and a few of the contractors to call me when they get to the gate, and I'll come and let them in."

"Kirk, I like the idea of having the ranch a little more secure. I've heard there have been some thefts in the area. They're taking farm implements right out in broad daylight—hay balers, discs, rakes—one rancher even had a tractor stolen."

"Yeah, that was the farm next to us on the east. They got hit last week, so I thought this gate might be a deterrent for that too."

"You were pretty resourceful, but I've got a better idea. I'll call around and get the best price on automatic gates. They will come out and put in a brand new gate configured to work with a combination key pad. That way you can give the combo to the people that need it, and you guys won't have to drive up here to let someone in."

"Man, I like that idea, but what do those things costs?"

"I'll search around and find the best price, but whatever it is, it will be worth it just for the theft protection alone. With the ranch as big as it is, I worry about some hooligans coming in here and loading up cows and calves. It'll also keep out unwanted guests."

"Fantastic!" Kirk said. "That will be much better than my little homespun invention."

"Hey, don't cut yourself short; that was pretty ingenious—and from an old garage door opener! I must say, I would have never thought of that."

"Hey, follow me on up to the house. I want you to meet my little buddy."

After they both had pulled up to the ranch house, Kirk's uncle asked, "How many new calves you got now?"

"As of yesterday we're up to a hundred and eighty-three."

"I'm guessing they weren't all easy births, uh?"

"I lucked out so far–only had to pull two."

"You do it yourself or call the vet?"

"No, I wasn't able to get them myself, so I had to call our vet. Between the two of us we saved the calves and the young mothers." He opened the back door for his uncle. "Come on in and meet my helper."

Brandon heard Kirk, and he came barreling out of his room. "Hey Kirk!"

"Hey buddy; I want you to meet my Uncle Carl." Without hesitation, Brandon stuck out his right hand toward Carl.

"Uncle Carl, this is Brandon. Brandon's my main helper now around the ranch."

"Well it looks like you've got yourself a mighty good little helper. Does he help with some of the chores?"

"Man, this little guy is stuck to me like glue. He helps me milk and separate the cream—even washes up the separator equipment. So far we haven't had to feed the cattle much."

"Yeah, that grass is looking good," Carl said.

Brandon piped up, "Kirk says I can drive the ATV." Then a sly little grin spread over his face.

"Yeah, I said when you turn eighteen."

"Kirk, where's that pretty little wife of yours?"

Katie came around the corner with a potholder mitt still on her hand. "Here I am. I was just pulling some hot cinnamon rolls out of the oven. You'll have to come in and try one."

"I thought I recognized that delightful aroma. So I guess I timed my visit about right."

"I was just getting ready to put on a pot of coffee."

"Oh, that sounds great. Hot cinnamon rolls and fresh coffee—Wilma's gonna wish she'd come too."

Kirk told Katie about his Uncle Carl's idea about the ranch gate. She turned back around from the coffee pot. "Oh that would be fabulous! There have been several times that would have been so much easier. Brandon's caseworker has to call me when she gets to the gate, and I just hope Kirk hasn't taken the truck with the remote in it."

Katie, I'll make some calls when I get back, and we'll get you a gate with a combo pad just as soon as possible."

After the cinnamon rolls and coffee, Kirk took his uncle in the pickup. They drove around the ranch, over the pastures, around stands of post oak-blackjack trees, looking for newborn calves. The air smelled like rain. The calves were running and kicking up their heels with tails flying above their backs—beautiful Black Angus calves enjoying the fresh ozone filled air, knowing their dinner stood close by. Carl Childers looked at his nephew. "Kirk, this is as good as it gets."

"You are so right. I wouldn't trade this for all the real estate in New York City. I'm glad you bought the ranch and even more glad that you asked me to come and manage it. I love it! Katie and I still talk about how fortunate we are to live like this."

"Is she going to teach next year?"

"I don't think so. After last semester's leave of absence she decided she could be more help here at home, and now that we are fostering, that seems to be the answer for her love of children."

"I admire you two for taking in these kids. It's got to be a huge commitment on Katie's part—and yours too. I know I couldn't do it."

"I guess it is, but it's the kind of commitment both of us were looking for. I'll tell you, that Brandon is quite a kid. He has been a real joy to me. Katie has worked with him since the end of May. She believes he is now a full grade level ahead of what he was then. His second grade teacher had planned to retain him—wanted to hold him back to second grade—but we think he may be ready to move on to third."

"Kirk, I'm proud of you both. I'm also proud of the way the ranch looks. I see someone's been spending some time with a paint brush and white paint. Those white fences look impressive all along the highway and on each side of the lane coming into the ranch."

"Brandon's been helping me on those. He's a good little worker; he never complains."

"Let's head back to the house; I've got something for Brandon."

On the way back, Kirk spotted a heifer that was having problems giving birth. "Carl, I need to see if I can help this little mother-to-be. Both men got out of the truck, put on gloves, and assisted the heifer to a successful birth.

Carl removed his gloves and threw them back in the truck. "We may have just saved that calf and the mother too. That's a good eight hundred—maybe a thousand dollars—saved. Of course, you know I'm always looking at the money end of things. But it also makes me feel good that we were in the right place, at the right time, to help that beautiful creature."

"And they really *are* beautiful creatures. I love Angus. As far as I'm concerned nothing comes close to a good thick Angus steak. They're the best tasting beef there is."

"Okay, get me back to the house. I've got something for Brandon, and then I'm gonna have to head back home."

Brandon heard Kirk's pickup and came running out to meet them. Carl pulled out a ten dollar bill and gave it to Brandon. Brandon acted surprised and asked what the money was for. "Hey, I hear you have been helping Kirk here on the ranch. Are you the one that painted those white fences up by the road?"

"Yes sir."

"Well you deserve that ten dollar bill. The fence looks great."

That special *Brandon sparkle* lit up his eyes. "Thank you. I'm saving up to buy a Mustang convertible."

"Well, Brandon, that's great, but maybe you ought to get a driver's license first."

"I'm almost eight now. When can I get a driver's license?"

"Gotta be sixteen, son."

"Oh."

Carl opened the door to his pickup. "Kirk, everything is looking good on the ranch. Tell Katie bye for me. I'm gonna get on the road."

As Kirk and Brandon were going back in the house, Kirk saw Old Chubby lying next to his dog house. "Brandon, you've been feeding Chubby, haven't you?"

"I feed him every day, but he's not eating. He just lays there."

"You mean he just *lies* there."

"Kirk, that's silly. How can he lie; dogs don't talk?"

"Brandon, I think you know what I mean. The correct word is *lies*. Chickens *lay* eggs, but dogs *lie* down."

Kirk reached down and petted Chubby. He could feel his rib bones under all that mass of wavy black hair. Chubby didn't move. "Brandon, Old Chubby may not make it. He's almost fifteen. That is old for a dog. Just make sure he has plenty of water next to him.

"Shouldn't we take him to the vet?"

"If he was a younger dog, but since he is as old as he is, it may just be his time to move on to doggie heaven."

"He hasn't been following us on the ATV either. I don't want him to die, but if he does, can we get another dog?"

"We'll see when the time comes."

CHAPTER 23

It was toward the end of the summer vacation. Katie was having second thoughts about retaining Brandon. She felt that he was now ready for third grade. If he was retained, he would become very bored. She figured Miss Bates would be working in her second grade room, so she decided to pay her a visit. The main door to the school was locked, but Miss Bates saw Katie and walked around to let her in.

"Hi, Katie. I see you survived the summer. Do you still have Brandon?"

"Yes, that's what I wanted to talk to you about."

"Come on in. My room is still a mess. I should have been up here last week working. Of course the janitor removed all of the desks and chairs to wax the floors, so I've just got all of them back in place. I haven't even started on lesson plans yet. So how is Brandon doing?"

"Well, Miss Bates…"

"Oh, please, honey, call me Donna. I'll hear that *Miss Bates* enough once school starts."

"Donna, I have worked throughout the summer break with Brandon. His reading has improved dramatically. I'm buying him books marked for third graders and he is having no problem reading them. He's whizzing through them without even slowing down. Kirk went with him to the bookstore in the city and came back with a couple of fourth grade level books along with about six third grade ones. I was just sure he wouldn't be able to read the fourth grade level, but he did pretty well with them. There were a few words he had to have some help with, but I was amazed. I bought that second grade math workbook you recommended and some math flash cards. Donna, he is quite proficient in math. I'm thinking if he repeats second grade, he will become bored. I wish you could see him reading now. You know, that was the main worry you and I had for him going into third grade."

"Katie, that is good news. You must have devoted a lot of your time to him if he has made that kind of progress."

"Yes, but I think a big factor in his progress is the stable environment he's been in. The ranch is good for him. He is stuck like Duct Tape to Kirk. Kirk says he is a big help to him with the ranch chores."

"I can see how that might help him. When a child is upset at home his grades will always show it. It sounds like you both are just what he needed."

"We've had to pull him out of a couple of scary situations on the ranch. One time Kirk had to pull him out of the pig pen with the old sow attacking him; another time he tunneled in between the bales in the hay barn. Some bales collapsed on him and he was stuck. It took both of us to get him out. When we did, he wasn't breathing. Kirk gave him mouth-to-mouth resuscitation and revived him. Just last week he climbed up the big Sycamore by our house and was afraid to come back down. Kirk got a ladder and coaxed him down to the top of the ladder. He is quite a boy."

"Why don't I get an appointment with our principal for the three of us? We'll discuss Brandon's achievements and see if we can't pass him on to Mrs. Dalton's third grade. It sounds like he's ready to me. Bring a few of the third grade books he's reading. It's better to promote him now than after school starts. That would be almost impossible."

"Thanks Donna. I'll wait to hear from you in the next day or so."

When Katie drove back to the ranch, a crew of men was already starting to work on the new gate. She drove on to the house, and when she got near Chubby's dog house by the back door, he wasn't there. She called but he didn't come. Later that afternoon Kirk whispered to her that he had taken the dog to the vet earlier that morning and had him put to sleep. When Katie protested, Kirk told her the vet had told him the dog was eat up with cancer and would only suffer more if he wasn't euthanized

"Honey, what are we going to tell Brandon?"

"I've already prepared him for what might have to happen; I think he'll understand. I promised him I'd try to get him another dog if Chubby didn't make it."

"What if we get him a dog and then he has to go back to Denise? I don't know if she would allow him to have a dog or not."

"I'm not gonna worry about the *what-ifs*. I'm gonna give that kid all the love and attention I can now, even if that means getting him a dog that he has to give up later. As long as Brandon is with us, I'm treating him like he is my own son. And my own son *would* have a dog!"

"Kirk, you're framing yourself in to be hurt when he's taken from us."

"That's just another *what-if*, and I'm ignoring them."

"Okay, but you know we had this discussion back when we were considering fostering, and we both agreed to go in to this adventure with the knowledge that a child wouldn't stay with us long. We would have to give him or her up."

"Hey, you used the word *adventure*. I have volunteered to help form what we are calling the Boy's Adventure Club at church. These are boys, aged six to twelve to start with. We'll teach them many of the things they would learn in Boy Scouts, but with more of a Christian influence."

"What's wrong with just going with the Boy Scouts instead?"

"Katie, there are no Boy Scouts out here. Remember, we live out in the boonies. Jack Newton and I will be heading it up. We'll take them on camping trips, maybe some horseback riding, if we can round up enough saddle horses, some fishing trips, and a trip to the planetarium. Jack's gonna teach the boys archery—I've never even held a bow, so I guess I can learn right along with the boys. He's thinking about seeing if he can get us into some archery competitions.

"I think that's a great idea. How many boys are you talking about in our little country church?"

"I've counted about six or seven boys that age, but we hope other boys will want to join, even if they don't go to our church."

"So when is this going to start?"

"Pastor is going to announce this next Sunday. I've agreed to call the ones that we know of. I'll visit with their parents about it. I told Jack that our first outing can be a fishing trip here on the ranch. He liked that idea, and he's working on some other trips. We'll meet at the church and have most of our teaching sessions there—like good citizenship, first aid, camping essentials, etc."

"Why couldn't you two just start your own Boy Scout troop?"

"I don't know what all that would involve, but I guess I could find out."

"Well you'd have that familiar name, a handbook, and you might even be able to talk one of the Scout masters in the city to come out and get you started."

"You may have something there. I'll see what Jack thinks about that."

"I would think that would be easier than blindly starting out on your own. At least you'd have a handbook to go by and some tutoring from a Scout master."

"Yeah, I see your point. We'll see."

CHAPTER 24

Kirk searched the internet to see how to go about forming a Boy Scout troop. What he found was not encouraging for a rural area such as theirs. First, you have to find an organization to support the unit. Their church would be okay, but no one in the church had an affiliation with the Scouts, which was one of their requirements. Plus the organization had to have enough eligible boys and interest to start up. After reading the seven requirements to start a troop, it seemed to Kirk that forming a Boy Scout troop would have to be put on hold and see how many boys they could recruit for their own Boy's Adventure Club.

He relayed what he had learned on the internet to Katie. "Honey, it looks like we'll need to start with our own little club. Then, when we have enough interested boys, we can think about converting that into a Boy Scout troop."

"Whatever you decide, the boys are going to love it. I know Brandon will—if he's here long enough."

"You think there is a chance DFS will return him to Denise?"

"Yes, I do. A birth mother is always going to have the trump card when all things are equal—and even when they are not so equal."

"But anyone can see Brandon is much better off here on the ranch with us than stuck in that drug infested neighborhood with a mother that thinks more of her current alcoholic boyfriend than her own son.

We've seen how he has progressed since he's been here with us. Don't they take that into consideration when deciding his fate?"

"Like I said, Kirk, the mother is always going to have the trump card. As long as she abides by the rules and does what the caseworker asks, the child will be returned to her."

"That is just so unfair! Brandon will revert back to his old miserable lifestyle. His future will be very bleak. He probably won't go to college—may not even graduate from high school. He won't have a chance at a good life. It's just not right!"

"Honey, all we can do is what we are doing now. We point him in the right direction—get him caught up on his education level, introduce him to the spiritual side of life, and show him what a loving family looks like. We're doing all of those things. Then we pray that what we've done is enough to carry him to a happy and prosperous adulthood."

"Fat chance of that if Denise gest him back!"

"Kirk, what we both are doing now will have a lasting impact on Brandon. Trust me; he will *never* forget his time with you. Our efforts will not be wasted. We *will* have made a difference in his life."

"Okay, call me selfish. I want to be the one to see that difference ten years from now."

"He'll know how to find us."

Kirk shook his head in disappointment. "Well, Katie, I can't think about this anymore right now. I'll be up at the barn if you need me."

"See if Brandon wants to go with you. Oh, by the way, did you see the guys working on the new gate?"

"No, I haven't been up there. I'll ride up and see how it looks."

"Don't forget Brandon."

❧

Just after the guys left the house, Betty called and had scheduled an appointment for a parent visit for Brandon. Katie kept her on the phone for a few minutes while trying to detect Betty's feelings toward Denise's possibilities for regaining custody of Brandon.

Betty opened up a bit. "Katie, if I had my way about it, Denise would never get her son back. She hasn't shown that she is willing to accept her responsibilities as a mother. However, I have to abide by a set of strict guidelines set out by the Department, and if she meets those guidelines, then I have no choice but to restore custody to her. This next visit will show me where this is headed. I have driven by her house several times and haven't seen Bryce's old Bronco. If this next visit goes okay, I will schedule another in-home visit to see what that environment looks like now."

Katie hesitated a little bit and then said, "Betty, if Denise ever has her parental rights terminated you do know that we would want to adopt Brandon."

"I thought you might be willing, but please don't get your hopes up. This could go either way, and right now, if Denise follows the rules and her house is in order, I will have no choice but to restore her parental rights."

Kirk and I talked about this very situation prior to applying to foster, but he and Brandon have become such inseparable buds, it will be hard for Kirk to accept."

"I'm sure it will be equally hard on Brandon. I know Kirk has become a true father to Brandon."

"So I assume the scheduled time will be the same as usual?"

"Yes, we'll see you about four-thirty tomorrow."

After Betty had said goodbye, Katie held the phone to her heart and prayed. *Oh, God, help Kirk and me to accept the outcome of this to be your Divine will and know that it will be in Brandon's best interest.*

Katie was still standing there, holding the phone to her heart with a finger holding down the disconnect pegs in the phone cradle, when another call rang through. She let go of the pegs. "Childers Ranch; this is Katie."

"Hi Katie, this is Bob Murphy with DFS. You remember me?"

"Of course, Bob. You came to my rescue out in that parking lot, and you've been there for our last two parent visits."

"Yeah, how's Brandon?"

"Bob, he could not be better. He loves it here on the ranch, and his reading skills have shot up a full grade level or more. He is one happy little boy."

"Katie, what I've called about is another little boy just younger than Brandon. I believe he is about five or six. I'm looking for a home for him. As you know, the Department is again short on foster homes. Betty Sawyer told me that you might have a spare bedroom."

"Sure, we do. But can you give me a little background on this child?"

"I can't tell you much because of the privacy laws and the fact that *we* know almost nothing about him, but I *can* tell you his name is Timmy, and he comes to us with quite a bit of baggage."

"Baggage?"

"Yeah, Timmy ran away from home and was seen by a concerned person in the area. He was emaciated and a bit delirious. I have yet to meet with his parents or guardian. Timmy wasn't talking. We're still working on that. He is a very disturbed little boy and will need professional counseling. I was hoping Brandon might be good company for him. Betty sings praises for you and Kirk—says you are the best foster parents she has."

"So you know nothing more about Timmy, anything that would be helpful for us to know?"

"I'm afraid that's it. We don't know what his home situation is yet. He is *refusing* to clue us in on where he lives or anything about his parents. He either doesn't know or is refusing to tell us his last name. So you see what we are up against? Police are working on it too, and

Timmy will be on the six o'clock news this evening, with the hopes that a parent will contact us. The bruises on his arms tell us he has been abused, but we don't know by whom. He has clammed up, and we are getting no useful information out of him."

"Bob, that is awful!"

"Would you and Kirk be willing to take him in until we can locate parents and determine who has abused him?"

"I know you can tell I am hesitant, but I don't know how we could say no. We do have a parent meeting for Brandon tomorrow at four-thirty. I just hung up from visiting with Betty about it. Would we be allowed to bring Timmy along?"

"Oh sure; no problem there."

"When did you want to bring him to us?"

"I can head your way right now, if that's okay."

"Okay, I'll see you in a bit."

Katie was a bit stunned. She had still been thinking about her conversation with Betty, and now this—a runaway little boy with multiple problems. She called Kirk's cell and said, "You guys need to come back to the house soon because Bob is bringing a little boy to us."

The sound of the ATV broke Katie's trance, and she met them at the door.

Kirk stepped in the door. "So what's his name?"

"All Bob knows is his name is Timmy. He is a runaway and they have no clue where his parents are, or who they are. Bob said there will be a bit about him on the six o'clock news with the hopes that a parent or relative will come forward."

Brandon looked excited. "I will read some of my books to him."

"This little guy may not be ready for that. Bob said he is emaciated and appears to be a bit delirious."

"What's emaciated?" Brandon said.

"He hasn't been eating. He may be skinny and pitiful looking."

"Well we can fix that easy enough," Kirk said.

"Kirk, I forgot to tell Bob he would have to call me to come let him in the main gate."

"All he'll need is the combination. They have already installed the gate and left. He will need to punch in seven-four-two."

"That's pretty easy to remember."

Brandon said, "Yeah, the *seven* is for me—my age, then *four* you *two*. Seven for two."

Katie stared at him; then said, "I don't get it."

Brandon said, "You should try to listen to me. I said it is *seven for two*, meaning me, *I'm seven*, for Kirk and you."

Katie still stood there with an awkward stare. Kirk looked at her and said, "He's saying *a seven year old boy for me and you*, 7-4-2."

"Okay, that is quite a stretch, but I think I will remember it now."

Brandon tugged at Kirk's arm, "Come on. I want to show you one of my newest books. It's one that you bought me last week at the bookstore, but you didn't see the surprise in it."

Brandon kept Kirk occupied for the next half hour with the fourth grade level book. He had read most of it but needed help with some of the harder words. The *surprise* was a combination to unlock the last page of the book. Two numbers in the right sequence were required to open the last page.

Kirk looked at the way that last page was locked up. "That's a pretty cool idea, but how do you know the combination?"

"You have to buy the next book. It's on the first page of that book."

"So the only way to open it is to tear that thick page up or buy the next book so you can have the right combination. I'd say that was some pretty sneaky marketing on the publisher's part."

Bob called from the main gate and Katie gave him the combination. A few minutes later he was at the front door. "That's a nice gate you got up there."

Katie told him it had just been installed. "You may be the first to try it out."

"Brandon piped up, "No, I already tried it, and it opened right up."

Bob was holding on to a very shy and scared little boy. He looked as if he hadn't eaten in a week. She knelt down in front of him, tried to take his hand, but he pulled back. "Timmy, this is Brandon. He can be your buddy while you are here. And this is my husband, Kirk. I am Katie Childers. What is your name?"

"Timmy Cox."

Katie looked up at Bob. He was standing there in disbelief, with his mouth forming the word *Wow!*

"Timmy, would you like to come in and have a cookie? These cookies are Kirk and Brandon's favorite."

Timmy looked up at Kirk. His eyes widened and he started to pull back. A slight whimper was made, and an unexpected wet spot appeared in his pants. When he realized what he had done, he started to cry.

Kirk knelt down by Katie and started to take Timmy's hand, saying, "It's okay, Timmy. Don't worry about tha…."

Timmy pulled away and ran screaming back toward Bob's car. Kirk stood speechless, with a bewildered look on his face.

Bob said, "He did the same thing to me at first. I would be willing to bet that some man has abused him. I guess you saw the bruises on his arms." Timmy was standing next to Bob's car hiding his face. Bob went over, consoled him and coaxed him into going back inside.

Kirk looked at Katie, shook his head, and whispered, "Honey, I don't know that we are equipped to handle this one."

"Kirk, I can't believe you! We are as equipped as anyone. This little boy needs us—he needs you!"

Kirk stuck his hands in his pockets and tipped his head upward a bit. "I hope you're right."

She knelt down in front of Timmy again. "Timmy, come on in. I'll get you some dry pants to put on." Kirk retreated into the kitchen so he wouldn't scare the boy any more.

Timmy went with Katie to the spare bedroom where she had stored some of the second hand clothes Betty had brought out. She started to pull his wet pants down—Timmy screamed and pulled away. Katie whispered to him, "Timmy, I'll turn my back and you can change into these nice dry pants. Tell me when you're ready for me to turn back around."

She heard a very faint, "'k." When she turned around she saw he had the pants on backwards, but she wasn't about to correct that.

She then asked if he was ready for his cookie. The only acknowledgement she got was a quick blink and his face dipped downward.

Okay, I'll take that as a yes.

He followed her back to the kitchen. She pulled out a chair opposite Kirk at the small breakfast table. Timmy promptly pulled back. Kirk told Katie he would finish his cookie at the other end of the big room.

Bob followed him to the big leather couch in front of the fireplace. He looked over at Kirk. "This may take a lot of counseling to get him out of his shell."

"Yeah, I may need some of that counseling myself to know how to deal with this. Did he treat you the same way as you were driving out here?"

"Yeah, I'm afraid he did. He never said one word the whole way here. He kept his face glued to the side window— never looked at me."

"What do you think has happened with him?"

"I'm pretty sure some male has hurt him—physically and maybe sexually. It may take a long time for you to win his trust."

"Yeah, if ever."

Katie came over and joined the two men. "Bob, I'm going to need some help tomorrow with Brandon's parent visit. We have to bring Timmy with us and it looks like Kirk won't be able to sit with him at the office. Do you think Betty might be available to sit with him while we are in with Denise?"

"I'll ask her, and if she can't, I'll get one of the girls from the office to sit with him. At this point I think Kirk and I would both be out of the question. He's too afraid of males."

"How long do you suspect that he was alone out there with no shelter or food before he was spotted?"

"That's a good question. He looked like he had slept in his clothes, but that doesn't tell us anything; most of these kids sleep in their clothes at home. Most of them wouldn't know what pajamas are. Some have never slept in a bed; it's always on the floor, or maybe an old dirty and stained mattress thrown on the floor, with no sheets."

Katie was shaking her head. "Oh, those poor kids! I guess we could expect that in a third world country; but right here in the United States, the most prosperous nation!"

The silence was broken by Timmy and Brandon talking to each other. Brandon had asked him if he wanted some milk to go with his cookie. Timmy said he did. But then he said, "I like your house."

Brandon told him about Dandy and Lilly and catching fish in the big pond. Brandon got up and poured both of them milk. "So, where do you go to school?"

Timmy said, "I don't go to school."

"Why not?"

"My mom said I wasn't allowed to."

"What's your mom's name?"

Bob, Katie, and Kirk stopped all conversation and had their ears open to the conversation on the other end of the big room. "Get this," Katie whispered.

Timmy turned up his glass of milk and drank most of it before setting it down. Then he said, "Her name is Tanya Cox. She works all day, so I have to stay home."

"So why'd you run away?"

"I don't like my dad. He's mean to me. When mom's not home he does ugly things to me. I hope I don't have to see him ever again. Maybe you could ask Mr. Bob if I could stay here with you."

"I know you can. That's why Bob brought you out here."

"Is your dad mean to you?"

"Oh, Kirk? He's not my dad, but he's not mean. In fact, he would be about the best dad ever. I'm hoping someday he can adopt me."

"So he won't hurt me?"

"No, why should he?"

Silently, the three adults let the boys ramble on for several minutes. With the innocence of a child, Brandon asked Timmy *how* his dad hurt him. Timmy described in sordid detail what his dad had done.

Bob started to protest. He didn't think Brandon should hear what Timmy was saying. Kirk held his hand out, palm down, as if to say it's okay. Let him talk.

Timmy continued telling Brandon what his dad did to him, withholding nothing. "That is disgusting!" Brandon said. "He really did that?" Timmy started to cry again. "I'm sorry. I know that won't happen to you here. Kirk's not like that. You're safe here."

Bob got up to leave. "Timmy, I'm going to go now. You will be safe here just like Brandon is."

Kirk and Katie followed him out the door. Bob turned toward them. "I just learned more right there than I thought possible. You might see what else he tells Brandon. If he discloses anything else of importance, write it down. It looks like Brandon is going to be our main source of information."

"Wish us luck," Kirk said.

"I'll see you tomorrow back at the office."

CHAPTER 25

Timmy continued to shy away from Kirk. When Kirk came near him, the boy would quickly move away, usually toward Brandon. He allowed Katie to come close to him but would never open up to her. Brandon was the only one that could get Timmy talking. Brandon liked his new friend, but when it came time for the ranch chores, he kept his routine and went with Kirk, leaving Timmy alone in his room.

Katie peeked in and saw Timmy sitting on Brandon's bed with his head down and his hands lying idle in his lap. There were toys all around him, but he was ignoring them. Seeing the little frail boy sitting there, Katie went back to the kitchen and made him half of a peanut butter and jelly sandwich. When she took it back in to him, he never looked at her and remained silent. She laid the sandwich on a napkin on the bed beside him. "Timmy, this will tide you over 'til supper." He didn't move, and she left the room. Later, she peeked back around the door. The sandwich was gone, but he was still sitting in the same spot on the bed.

Brandon knew how to use the cream separator now. He considered that his job. He also washed and dried the equipment for the next use.

Kirk walked in to the separator room, and found his buddy deep in thought.

"I've been thinking about Timmy," Brandon said. "I don't think he wants his mom to find him. That's why he didn't want to tell Bob his last name or where he lived."

"So what has he told you that made you think he didn't want his mom to find him?"

"He said his mom was always drunk. There was never any food in his house; he was always hungry. His dad wasn't his real dad, and he only lived there part of the time." Brandon kept drying the already dry equipment. "Timmy told me he got hungry and found a house that had a dog in the back yard, so he went back there and ate the dog food right out of that dog's bowl! Kirk, you just gotta help him. He really is a nice boy."

"Brandon, I'll do all I can. He is very afraid of men. It may take a long time for him to trust me. I can't be much help to him 'til he does."

Brandon laid the towel down and looked up at Kirk as if a new day had dawned. "Now, I have a question. When are you gonna get me that dog that you promised?"

"Wow! You don't beat around the bush. I hadn't thought much more about it. How about tomorrow? We'll go to the pound in town and you can pick out one."

"Good, because this dog is gonna have to like Timmy too."

When they got back to the house, they washed up for supper. Brandon got Timmy to follow him to the table. Katie had made pork chops, mashed potatoes, and green beans. Timmy picked up his pork chop and started to bite into it. Katie placed her hand next to his plate. "Timmy, we always say grace before we begin our meal. If you'll put your pork chop down, Brandon will say the prayer for us."

Timmy laid it down, and Brandon said his quick little prayer. When Timmy saw Brandon start to eat, he did the same. He devoured the pork chop and moved on to the mashed potatoes. No fork, just with his hands. Brandon stared at his friend in horror. Kirk and Katie both saw what Timmy was doing but waited for Brandon to say something to him. After breaking his stare, Brandon pointed to Timmy's fork. "Timmy, you need to go wash your hand, then come back and use your fork to pick up the mashed potatoes."

"Brandon, maybe you should help him wash up and then show him *how* to use his fork," Kirk said.

Timmy was embarrassed and started to cry. Brandon took his hand and led him over to the sink to wash up. "It's okay. You don't need to be embarrassed. I was embarrassed when I came here because I didn't know how to read good, and Katie taught me—"

Katie interrupted, "Brandon, I think we still need to work on your English skills. The word should have been *well*. Brandon grimaced.

Back at the table, Timmy watched Brandon use his fork and made a crude attempt at copying him. He ate everything on his plate and asked Brandon for more.

Kirk and Brandon were back at the barn the next morning. He reminded Kirk that he had promised to take him to the pound to get a new dog. "Timmy has to come along. The dog has to like Timmy too."

So after the morning chores were done, the boys climbed into the back seat of the truck, and Kirk started to back out. He saw that Timmy was looking at his seat belt as if he didn't know what to do with it, so he asked Brandon to help him buckle up.

When they walked into the isle between the kennels, pandemonium broke out. The dogs were barking with an ultrasonic intensity. Dogs of all sizes and breeds were pouncing at their gates. Timmy held his hands over his ears. Brandon scouted out the various dogs. He came to a beautiful black and white Border collie mix with a white blaze running up his muzzle and between his eyes. The dog was lying in his kennel with his paws reaching over his head as if he was trying to drown out the noise. When Brandon stooped down and held out his hand, the dog rose and licked it through the wire gate. The animal shelter attendant asked Brandon if he would like to pet the dog. Brandon's eyes lit up like two beacons.

As soon as the gate was opened, the dog leaped into Brandon's arms. "It looks like this is love at first sight," Kirk said. Timmy reached over and ran his fingertips down the dog's back. A smile came across his face, the first since his arrival at the ranch.

"How about it, guys? Is this the one?"

Brandon and Timmy gave no indication that they even heard him. They were both charmed by this dog's affection. Kirk looked toward the attendant. "I think that means this is the one." Kirk told Brandon he and Timmy could remain there with the dog while he took care of the paperwork.

In the front office, Kirk paid the sixty dollars for the neuter fee and shots. "How did this beautiful animal come to find his way here?" The attendant didn't know but agreed that particular dog was, in his opinion, the pick of the pack.

The boys sat in the back seat with the dog between them. Kirk glanced at them in his rearview mirror. "What can we name him?"

Brandon thought for a minute and then his eyes gleamed. "Let's name him Noah."

Kirk was puzzled. "Why would you wanna name him that?"

"Because he was stuck in there with all of them noisy animals, just like Noah was."

Kirk smiled. "Is that okay with you, Timmy?" Timmy turned to Brandon, looked for confirmation and nodded his head.

"Then boys, this is Noah!"

After a stop by a pet store to buy a collar, leash, and dog food, Kirk pulled up to the ranch gate. With his index finger to his temple, he pretended to be trying to remember the combination. Brandon gawked at him. "Kirk, it's *seven-four-two*. I think you've got a memory problem."

Kirk eased forward a bit and rolled Brandon's left window down. "Punch 'er in, bud."

∽

It was time to head toward the city for Brandon's parent visit. Brandon questioned Katie. "Can I stay here, and just let you go?"

"No, Brandon, you may not stay here. She is not my parent; she's yours." Before that last word got out of her mouth, she regretted saying it because she knew what the response might be.

He looked down toward the floor. "She don't wanna be my parent."

"Brandon! You don't know that. Denise loves you."

He looked at Katie with a bit of contempt in his eyes. "She don't love me. If she did, she'd not forget to bring me a picture of her."

"Brandon, don't say she doesn't love you. You don't know what all she is dealing with."

"She doesn't care about me. She only cares about herself."

"Honey, I wouldn't be so quick to accuse her."

"Well, I don't wanna go!"

"Brandon, you have to go. You and Timmy can play with Noah after we get back."

"Can we take Noah?"

"No, Brandon, I don't think Noah would be welcome there. You need to hurry and change clothes. Wear some clean jeans and that new shirt we bought you."

Brandon stomped off to his bedroom, making sure Katie knew he wasn't happy about it. Timmy followed close behind him.

We learn Timmys father was a drunk & that he was always hungry. Brandon got a dog & named him Noah.

CHAPTER 26

Kirk pulled into the parking lot of the DFS offices at four-twenty. Since they were a few minutes early, he took the boys downstairs to the vending machines while Katie waited in the hallway for the elevator to return with the green up arrow.

On the way down, Kirk noticed Timmy in the far corner, pressing up next to Brandon, and hiding his face in Brandon's back.

When the elevator door opened, Brandon ran to the Coke machine and requested a cherry Coke. Timmy indicated he wanted one too. "Can we take these up with us?"

Kirk knew his little teacher wife would have corrected his grammar, but he let it drop. "I don't see why not. Let's go."

Up on the third floor, Kirk found Katie in the outer office thumbing through an out-of-date *Mother Earth* magazine. "No Denise yet?"

"No, Bob and Betty aren't going to be here either. Jennifer has agreed to stay here with Timmy while Brandon is in with his mother."

Katie forgot she hadn't introduced Jennifer. "Jennifer is the receptionist here. She and I had an extended visit last time when we were waiting for Denise to get here."

Kirk noticed Brandon kept looking at the clock on the wall. At ten 'til five, Denise stormed through the door saying, "I'm sorry I'm late. The traffic is really bad out there." Katie got up to go into the conference room and Denise snarled at Kirk, "Do you like that excuse any better?"

As Brandon got up to follow them in, it appeared that Timmy was permanently attached to him. Jennifer came over, took his hand, and said, "Timmy, you're going to stay out here with me."

Timmy jerked his hand free and clung to Brandon. "You should just let him come on in with me," Brandon said.

Katie told Jennifer that she saw nothing wrong with allowing Timmy to stay with Brandon. Jennifer grinned and said, "I guess that leaves me baby-sitting Kirk."

Katie winked. "Make sure he behaves."

Inside the conference room, Timmy insisted on sharing the same chair with Brandon. Katie sat next to them, and Denise took her favorite chair across the room next to the window. She had yet to greet Brandon.

Katie was thinking how sad that was when Brandon jumped up from his chair, looked straight at Denise and said, "I guess you forgot how to say *hello!*"

She didn't even reply to her son, just continued to stare out the window.

Katie attempted to jump-start the conversation by telling Denise about the new dog they had just adopted. Denise ignored her and interrupted, asking, "Who's that kid?"

Katie started to answer, but Brandon was quicker. "This is my friend, Timmy."

Denise pointed at the scared little boy. "What's he doin' here?"

Katie jumped in and explained that Timmy was a foster child that had come to stay with them recently.

"Why is he latching onto my son like that?"

Katie was appalled at Denise's behavior, but didn't want to start any verbal attacks. "Timmy is a scared little boy, and Brandon has befriended him." Just then Timmy dumped his cherry Coke over, and it spilled on Brandon's jeans and on to the floor.

Denise went ballistic. "Now look what he's done!"

Timmy started to cry.

Katie rescued the can, hurried over to the door and asked Jennifer to get her a couple of paper towels. Denise sat in her chair, picking at her nail polish. The room was silent, except for Timmy's whimpering.

Brandon pulled himself away from Timmy and walked over to Denise. "I guess you forgot to bring me a picture—again."

Denise started with a lame excuse, but Brandon cut her off. "I think this meeting is over!"

"Brandon!" Katie was embarrassed for him. "That was rude. Your mother drove all the way over here to see you."

Timmy was clinging to Brandon again and sniveling. Denise glared at Katie. "You should get that retard off my child."

Katie had enough and was now full of venom. "Denise, don't *ever* call a child that! Don't you know your words can damage a child permanently?"

Denise said in a loud voice, "That child is already damaged!"

"All right, I've had enough! Brandon, I think you were right; this meeting is in fact over!" She got up to leave, walked over to Denise, and pitched the wet paper towels in her face. "Girl, you are the one that's damaged!"

She took the boys by their hands and started to walk back through the door into Betty's office. Denise crowded in ahead of them, cursing as she went, and disappeared through the outer door.

Kirk sat immobile, holding his empty Coke can and grinned. "I see you had a positive influence on her again today."

"Yes, you might say we got off on the wrong foot, and never recovered. Anyway, let's get out of here so Jennifer can close up and go home."

❧

They got back to the ranch just in time to catch the six o'clock news.

This just in: This little boy was found wandering the streets this morning on Southeast Twenty-ninth. He will only say that his name is Timmy. It appears that he has been without food or shelter for several days. Timmy is in the protective custody of the Department of Family Services for now. If anyone has any information about Timmy, please call the Del City Police or this station.

Katie commented, "I can't believe they put his picture on there. Shouldn't that be private?"

"What?" Kirk said, "how could anyone recognize him if there was no picture?"

"Okay, you're right. I just hate to see his picture made public like that."

"Where are the boys now?"

"I sent them out to play with Noah. I thought Timmy shouldn't be in here when this came on. Hey, let's go join them. I haven't got to see this new dog. By the way, why did Brandon want to name him *Noah*?

"Honey, we were wandering through the aisle between the kennels, and all of the dogs were barking their fool heads off, except for this beautiful little black and white Border collie toward the end. He was lying there, scratching his ears with his paws—probably had fleas. Brandon took it that he was trying to cover them and muffle all the noise in the kennel. He proclaimed that his name should be *Noah*, because that is what he thought Noah was doing on the ark with all of those noisy animals bothering him."

"That's pretty clever. That kid has quite an imagination. Maybe he'll write a best seller someday."

Noah was inside the yard fence, lying in the shade of the silver leaf maple on the west of the house. The boys weren't there. Kirk called Brandon, but got no answer. "What's the little bugger gotten into now?"

"I don't know, but he is a boy, you know."

Kirk grinned at her. "Yeah, and I hear that's sometimes a problem."

After checking around the other side of the house, they both jumped on the ATV and headed toward the barn. "Kirk, do you think they could have gone all the way down to the barn in that short time?" Katie's question was drowned out by the engine noise of the ATV. Kirk steered down the slope toward the chicken house. As they got closer, they could see the boys. The big old rooster was attacking Timmy. Brandon was kicking at the big bird, then the inevitable happened—he fell back on his bottom and the rooster came after him. Lying on his back in the chicken yard, Brandon kicked the rooster with all his might. Feathers flew, and the rooster went down. A few feet away, Timmy was crying and slinging his hands, trying to free them from the awful stuff he'd landed in.

Kirk jumped off the ATV, yanked open the gate to the chicken yard, and ran in to rescue the boys. They were both a mess, head to toe! "Okay, guys. You're gonna have to walk back to the house. I just washed this ATV. It's nice and clean; I wanna keep it that way."

Katie was trying to keep from laughing. "Kirk, how did you know they were down here in the chicken yard?"

"It was just a hunch. I knew Brandon hadn't gathered the eggs yet, so I figured he thought he'd take Timmy with him and teach him to gather eggs."

"I doubt that Timmy will ever go near that chicken house again."

Back at the house, the boys got a quick rinse with the garden hose before going in for their baths. Timmy was not only still crying; he was trembling.

"Kirk, do you think you could help him with his bath tonight?"

"Honey, he would freak out. I think he can bathe himself. If he needs help, he'll ask Brandon."

The following morning Betty Sawyer was on the phone. "Katie, Jennifer told me a little bit about the parent visit yesterday. I guess it wasn't a very pleasant scene."

"No, it was a total melt-down. Denise never greeted Brandon—never even said one word to him the whole time. She looked at Timmy and growled, 'Why is this kid clinging to my son?' I explained, but she could say nothing good and never said anything to Brandon. She sat over in the corner picking at her nails and looking out the window. Finally, Brandon quizzed her about the picture she had been promising him. She started to make an excuse and Brandon traipsed over to her. Got in her face and said, 'I think this meeting is over!' Brandon came back over to his chair and Timmy latched onto him. Denise yelled out, 'Get that retard off my child.' That's when I had had enough. I wasn't going to continue to allow her to talk like that about Timmy."

"I guess Jennifer didn't hear all of that. If she did, she didn't relay it to me. You know, Katie, I've about had it with that crabby little saucebox. I wish I could have been there. Miss Denise will be getting an earful from me!"

Katie asked Betty if she had heard Bob say if a parent had been located for Timmy.

"No, I've heard nothing. I saw that piece on the news. I understand he's one sad and disturbed little boy."

"If he stays with us, I think Bob's gonna have to arrange some counseling for him. It's clear to me that we can't fix Timmy's problems on our own."

"For sure. I'll have Bob call you."

Brandon wanted to go to the barn and help with the milking chores. Timmy whined and tried to get him to stay at the house with him. Brandon told him to just stay there in his room and play with his toys. "I'm going to the barn to help Kirk."

As soon as they were out the door, Bob called. Katie started to ask him about getting counseling for Timmy. Bob interrupted her and said Timmy's grandmother had contacted them, and Timmy would be going to stay with her until she could locate her daughter.

"Bob, that is somewhat of a relief, Katie said. "I don't think we can be of any help to this little boy."

"You're probably right. I'm only about five miles from the ranch now. Will it be okay if I come by and pick up Timmy now?"

"Sure, you remember the combination to the gate?"

"No, I'm sorry I don't."

"Seven-four-two."

"Gotcha."

Katie called Kirk to warn him that Timmy might be gone when he and Brandon got back to the house.

"You mean Brandon will be free from Tag-a-Long Timmy?"

"Kirk! Brandon will hear you."

"Actually, he won't. He's got the milker on Old Gertie and it provides enough noise to make you wanna cover your ears, like Noah did."

"Okay, well I thought I should give you a heads-up. See you guys in a little bit."

When Bob came for Timmy, Katie had a fight on her hands. Timmy made it clear that he had no intentions of going. All the coaxing did no good. Timmy ran out the back door before Katie or Bob could catch him. When they caught sight of him, he was already out the yard gate and running down the road toward the barn where he knew Brandon would be. Katie started toward the ATV. "Bob, I'm gonna catch up with him. You can stay here, or you can jump on with me."

Bob looked at her straddling the four-wheeler—looked down at his dress pants—hesitated, and climbed on behind her. She turned the key. It acted like it was going to start and then died. She tried again. This time she'd flooded the engine. "Oh great!"

"Why don't we just walk; it's not that far."

"I had hoped to catch up with him before he got to the barn." Katie didn't give up. She waited a minute, then punched the start button, and it finally started. She took off so fast, she was afraid Bob might be headed for the dirt. She turned to look, and he was white-knuckling the left grab bar to the side with one hand, while holding onto his hairpiece with the other. It was then she remembered neither of them had on a helmet.

Katie was still accelerating just before she reached the barn; then she braked a little too hard, sliding sideways a bit and kicking up a cloud of dust. She jumped off, leaving Bob holding one grab bar and his hairpiece, coughing with the Oklahoma red dust cloud hanging around him in the calm air.

She ran inside and—just as she thought—Timmy latched onto Brandon as he was seated on the three-leg stool beside the cow. This startled Brandon, and he tried to keep his balance while holding onto the milker. The milking machine noise scared Timmy. He pushed hard against Brandon. They both went down. The milker suctions were knocked loose from Old Gertie, and she was freaking out. Kirk had turned loose of the cow he was milking and ran over, just as Old Gertie kicked. Brandon screamed! She'd kicked him in the head. Timmy was bawling his eyes out. Old Gertie had somehow managed to free her head from the stanchion and was tromping around trying to leave the scene.

Kirk grabbed Brandon up from under the big cow, bringing the attached Timmy with him part way, 'til he fell to the floor. Katie grabbed Timmy and ran outside with him. Kirk followed with Brandon in his arms. Katie handed Timmy to Bob, and that started the screaming and kicking all over again. She ran back to Kirk. "Is Brandon okay?"

Kirk pulled Brandon's hair back and saw the blood oozing from his temple area. "Hey buddy, are you okay?"

Brandon was trying not to cry, but tears were sneaking out anyway. "I'm okay, but my head sure hurts."

"Come on buddy, let's get you to the house and get that taken care of."

"Why did you take the truck?" Katie said. "You always ride the ATV to the barn."

"Honey, I flooded it. So I just jumped in the pickup."

"Oh, so it wasn't me that flooded it."

"No, not this time. You take Bob and the boys in the truck; I'll follow you on the ATV."

Inside the pickup, Timmy had latched onto Brandon again. This time Brandon pushed him off. "Leave me alone."

Timmy's crying accelerated. By the time they reached the ranch house, his screams were deafening. Bob wasted no time in getting out of the truck. He then pulled Timmy out, kicking and still screaming.

Katie took Brandon in the house. Kirk flew off the ATV, ran inside, and went to Brandon. "Hey buddy, I'm so sorry. Are you gonna be okay?"

Katie washed the wound, and put him to bed. She then made a quick ice pack, improvising with a frozen bag of peas, and placed it on the side of his head with a small towel between.

Brandon rose up and whispered in Kirk's ear. "Yeah, I might be better now that Tag-a-Long Timmy will be leaving."

"Brandon, he didn't mean to cause all of that. He doesn't understand cows like you and I do."

"Yeah, he's a city boy."

"Hey, don't be too rough on him. You were a city boy not too long ago."

Katie blurted out, "Kirk! We have forgotten about Bob and Timmy out there." She ran out the back door and couldn't see either of them, but she could still hear the screaming. It was coming from the front of the house. As she turned the corner, she saw Bob trying to get Timmy inside his SUV. Timmy was fighting him. He was kicking; then he turned to biting. Katie ran over, thinking she might help calm him down. It did no good. He bit Bob's ear. A four-letter word slipped out of Bob's mouth. Finally he got Timmy in the back seat. Sweat was rolling down his forehead. He gave Katie an exasperated look. "Now, I don't have a clue how I'm gonna get the little tiger strapped into that car seat."

"Don't even try to put him in a car seat. I think he's about big enough to just use a seat belt."

"Yeah, good idea." He managed to wrap the belt around Timmy's now urine soaked lap and buckle it. Before he could get around to the driver's side, Timmy had unbuckled and was coming out the back passenger door.

Katie grabbed him and firmly set him back inside. She placed her hands on either side of his face and in a calm voice said, "Timmy, we're not going to play this game with you anymore. You will cooperate with Bob!" The screaming stopped. "Bob is taking you to your grandmother. She's worried about you. It will be just a short drive to her house. You will be safe with her."

His face flooded with tears, and he was still whimpering. "Okay. Bye." He ducked his head and wiped at his eyes.

Bob turned around, looked at Katie, blinked, and started to say, "How...?"

"Have a good trip, Bob," Katie said. "Good luck."

Another parent visit:
Denise is late again does
not aknowlege Brandon.
Timmy brought to his
grandmas house

CHAPTER 27

By alternating the timing for use of the make-shift ice pack, Brandon's swelling in his temple was minimal. Katie started toward the kitchen to make another ice-pack. She turned back to Kirk. "Whatever you do, don't let him go to sleep. It's dangerous to allow sleep right after any head injury. Try to keep him talking. Oh, and don't ever give him an aspirin."

"Yeah, I know—Tylenol."

Brandon looked up at Kirk. "So, is Timmy gone now?"

"Yep, he's being taken to his grandmother. She called in to the TV station after seeing that piece on the six o'clock news."

"Well, I'm glad! I was getting tired of him hanging on to me all the time. He's a big crybaby."

"Yeah, he is, but maybe he'll be better after he gets to his grand-mother's house."

With school about to start up again, Katie devoted a lot of her time going over math problems with Brandon and checking his reading comprehension. She even allowed Noah to come inside with them so she could see if he could remain on task with the distraction of the dog. Happy to be inside the house, his four-legged friend pawed at Brandon's jeans, trying to get his attention. Noah was persistent, so she got him a Milk Bone to keep him busy. The treat disappeared quickly, and Noah returned to pawing at Brandon. She knew study time was over for the day.

Katie walked out of his room, called, and talked with the third grade teacher, Mrs. Dalton. She explained Brandon's previous home situation and his problems back in second grade.

"Katie, Miss Bates has already visited with me about his progress over the summer. I'll let you know if I see him falling behind."

As soon as she hung up, the phone rang. She heard Betty's familiar voice and burst out, "Betty, if Denise is asking to see Brandon, I can't take another catastrophic visit with that woman! I'd probably wind up slapping the bejeebers out of her!"

"Katie," Betty laughed. "I don't blame you. I'd like to do the same, but that's not why I called. I have a foster parenting couple that would like to get away for the Labor Day weekend. They will be celebrating their twenty-fifth wedding anniversary and would like to spend the weekend in Texas, down on Padre Island. They have been fostering two pre-teen girls for about a year now."

Katie held the phone out from her ear and ran her fingers through her hair. Then she brought the handset back to her ear and listened as Betty continued non-stop.

"You know about our respite program, where another foster parent agrees to take the child for a short period of time, while the other foster parents take a break. So I was wondering if you and Kirk might be able to take the girls, just for four days."

"Oh Betty, we have just said goodbye to a very demanding little boy that Bob sent to us. I almost feel like we are the ones that need a break. Brandon will be starting school Tuesday, and even he needs an opportunity to have some down time after little Tag-A-Long-Timmy caused numerous problems here on the ranch. Can't you call on someone else this time?"

"Sure, Katie, I can do that. I know Timmy was a handful. I was glad to see his grandmother come forward."

The dreaded Denise visit was never mentioned, and Katie felt good about saying *no* to the respite plan this time.

Labor Day weekend at the Childers Ranch was relaxing for a change. Brandon had taken over milking Old Gertie again, while Kirk milked the others two cows. The two were able to squeeze in one more fishing trip to the big pond. They also saddled up Dandy and Lilly for a long ride over the ranch's huge spread Saturday afternoon. The eighteen hundred acres was comprised of a variety of terrain for horseback riding. The area around the barns gave way to a gentle slope down to the back pond. The big bluestem grass in this area reached four feet high. White puffy clouds skimmed above. The silence was broken only by the sound of the horses treading through the tall grass. Kirk looked over at his little buddy riding Dandy. Brandon's hat was tilted back a bit, exposing a face full of contentment and sheer joy. The two spoke few words, but the tacit communication they shared was priceless.

Farther east, the big bluestem grass gave way to timber. The guys followed the trails through the timber, spotting a few wild turkeys and a beautiful doe with her twin fawns. They stopped and watched the mother and her babies from a distance. Brandon looked at Kirk and asked, "How do twins get to be two and not just one?"

Kirk repositioned his hat and made an attempt at a safe answer. "Brandon, sometimes God will cause a fertilized egg to split in two. Other times there are two fertilized eggs to start with."

"Eggs! I thought chickens laid eggs, not people and deer."

"Oh man, maybe we ought to leave that part for a science lesson later. You can learn all about that when you study that in school. For now, let's just say that it is sometimes possible for a female to have twins or even triplets, or more."

"Well, I don't want my wife to have twins; they're too noisy!"

"I don't think you need to worry about that just yet. You aren't even married."

A little farther into the timber they saw a big tom turkey with his huge tail spread in his typical male fashion. Kirk held up his index finger to his mouth to signal Brandon that they needed to be quiet and just watch. The big tom turned and looked in their direction, a beautiful sight! Just then a gunshot broke the silence. The tom dropped his tail feathers and fled into the brush.

Kirk sounded off. "I can't believe someone is shooting! It's not hunting season, for deer *or* turkeys." Then another shot rang out. This time the sound was way too close to them. Kirk's anger flared. He cupped his hands around his mouth and yelled into the trees, "HEY! Wha'd'ya think you're doin'!"

There was silence. Brandon searched Kirk's eyes. "You think they heard you?"

"Yeah, they heard. Come on, let's get outta here." Once they had cleared the timbered area, Kirk clicked his tongue and gave Lilly a loose rein. She flattened her neck and switched to a lope. He looked back, and Brandon was following suit.

They rode upland toward the eastern edge of the timber, near the dirt road that ran alongside the fenced ranch. A white Ford pickup was parked beside the road. Kirk rode up to the barbed wire fence, handed Brandon Lilly's reins, and dismounted. He climbed over the fence, and when he found no one in the pickup, he pulled out one of the ranch business cards and a pen from his shirt pocket and wrote, *In case you didn't bother to look, this is private property. Childers Ranch allows no hunting on any area of the ranch. You should also know this is not official hunting season. A game warden often drives by here. You got a problem with this, call me.* He signed it, *Kirk Childers.* He climbed back over the fence, and from the usual left side, mounted Lilly. Brandon handed him the reins.

"You wrote them a note; what'd you say?"

"Told them they were trespassing, and it wasn't even hunting season. I told them if they had a problem with that, they should see me."

"Way to go, Big Kirk!"

That brought a grin to Kirk's face. "Hey, buddy, you wanna ride west, over to the other side of the ranch? There's an old falling down cabin and a well I wanna show you."

Two hours later they headed back to the barn. Inside the tack shed, Brandon went to work. He had learned how to loosen the cinch on Dandy, but the saddle was too heavy for him to manage. Kirk grabbed it with both hands, pulled it off Dandy, and stored it back on the saddle rack horse. Brandon grabbed a rag and saddle soap to clean the saddles like he'd seen Kirk do. After a good rub-down, the horses were led back out to their pasture. Brandon wasn't quite tall enough to reach Dandy's bridle, but Kirk was amazed at how much he could do around the ranch. While Kirk was removing the bridles, Brandon ran over to the horse trough to check their water. After they put the bridles back in the tack room Brandon said, "I think Dandy deserves some carrots. He carried me a long way today."

"Hey, grab your helmet and we'll go to the house and get him some." Kirk jumped on the ATV. Brandon crawled on behind him, but this time Brandon didn't use the grab bars. He wrapped his arms around Kirk's waist and laid his head into Kirk's back. Kirk smiled. *Now, that is what being a 'dad' is all about—I love it!* And once more, the words of his uncle Carl came to him. *It just doesn't get any better than this!*

Katie says no to a
Betty when two girls
need a place to stay.
Kirk feels like a father

CHAPTER 28

After the first day of school, Brandon came home excited about his new third grade teacher. "I think Mrs. Dalton likes me."

"And just why do you think she likes you?" Katie said.

"She had me read a story to the class, and then she said that I was a good reader. We did math problems on the blackboard. I was the first one through—and I got 'em right."

"Well, it sounds as if our studying over the summer did a lot of good. Let's keep it up and make you the head of the class."

"Oh, I already am!"

"You're also a bit arrogant. Now go in your room, and read the book I laid out for you on your bed. After that, you can go help Kirk with the milking if you want. When you guys come back, you can tell us about the book. Kirk hasn't read it, so you'll need to tell the story to him in detail. He's already down at the barn, so you'll just have to walk. Noah's going to stay here so I can give him his flea and tick treatment."

Later, at the dinner table, Brandon began telling the story he read earlier. He was excited about that, but not so excited about eating his meal. "Brandon, maybe you should wait to finish telling the story to Kirk after we've eaten."

The phone rang. It was Lynn Reynolds. "Katie, do you and Kirk have anything planned for this evening?"

"No, why, Dad?"

"If it's okay, we'd like to come out to the ranch. I have something for Brandon."

"Sure. You remember the combo to the front gate?"

"Seven-four-two?"

"You got it. We'll see you soon then."

Kirk asked who had called. "It was Dad. He said he had something for—"

Brandon picked up on that. "Is he bringing *me* something?"

"Why don't you finish your plate of food? You'll find out when they get here."

After they had finished their meal, Kirk and Brandon moved over to the big leather couch. Kirk turned the TV to Channel Four News.

Charges for DWI, and possibly manslaughter, are being filed against a Dell City woman after broadsiding a minivan, killing the passenger. Denise Brewer was traveling east on Norton Road when she failed to stop at the intersection. Ms. Brewer was taken to Baptist Hospital for minor injuries. The name of the victim is being withheld until the next of kin have been notified.

Kirk was stunned. He looked at over at Brandon to see if he had been paying attention. He was thumbing through the book that he had started telling the story at the table and gave no indication that he'd heard the reporter. Katie looked across the room at Kirk and mouthed the word, "Denise?"

Kirk acknowledged her. He knew it was terrible that someone had lost their life, but a somewhat sinister thought entered his mind. *Will this be enough to terminate her parental rights?*

Brandon looked up at Kirk. "Can I have your attention?"

"Yes, you *may* have my attention. So then what happened to the little boy in the story?"

Brandon went into great detail, giving Kirk a chronological order of the entire story. He laid the book on the end table and looked up at Kirk. "What is a DWI?"

Kirk was astounded! The boy had given no indication that he'd been listening to the news report. "It means *driving while intoxicated.*" Brandon pulled the book back onto his lap and looked down. "She didn't use to drink that stuff. Now look what she's done!"

Kirk couldn't find adequate words. Katie was behind the eight-year-old now and came to Kirk's rescue. "Brandon, you will need to pray for your mother. She needs God to give her wisdom and comfort."

"My mother doesn't care about me; why should I pray for her?"

"Because she is still your mother. God loves us, even when we aren't so lovable ourselves."

"I wish she wasn't my mother. She embarrasses me!"

Katie sat down beside him and wrapped her arm around him. "Sometimes we just have to pray anyway. God has a way of working things out when we don't know the solution."

Brandon's attention had jumped back to the book, quizzing Kirk about one scene toward the back of the book. Kirk was relieved to hear a car pull up out front. He got up and started toward the door. Brandon looked at Katie and whispered, "I could tell he didn't know the answer to that. I don't think he listened very well."

Katie grinned. "Sometimes he doesn't listen to me either, but that's okay; I think we'll keep him."

Lynn and Carol Reynolds were inside now. Lynn was heading toward Brandon. "Hey Brandon, I brought you a present."

Brandon jumped up and hugged Lynn first, and then he took the gift. "Can I open it now?"

"Well, it looks like you're quite capable of that, so go ahead."

Brandon ripped off the wrapping paper and opened the box to find a little midnight blue die-cast Mustang convertible in 1:18 scale. The doors, hood, and trunk lid all could be opened. The wheels looked like shiny spoke wheels in miniature. "This is just like your Mustang—and you bought this for me?"

"Didn't you tell me the last time we visited that you wanted a Mustang like mine?"

"Yeah, I guess I did."

Katie looked at Brandon and said, "What do you say, Brandon?"

"Thanks, *Grandpa!*"

Katie started to correct him, but Lynn cut in, "Brandon, you can call me *grandpa* any time you want!"

Brandon pursed his lips and grinned.

When her parents were ready to leave, Brandon walked out to their car with Katie's dad. Carol and Katie had been saying their goodbyes inside the big room when Carol stopped and put her finger to her lips, motioning for silence. "Listen," Carol said.

They both stood there, eavesdropping on a familiar tune. Brandon was whistling the *Andy Griffith Show* theme song, as he walked hand-in-hand with Mr. Reynolds.

The next morning Betty Sawyer called and asked Katie if she had seen the news about Denise. "Yes, we saw it. Brandon was in the room, but we didn't think he was paying attention. Later he asked what a DWI was."

"Was he upset?"

"No, he said Denise embarrassed him, and he wished she wasn't his mother."

"Well, sometimes I wish she wasn't my case either. She was very close to being able to regain custody of Brandon, but now she's making it difficult for me to grant that. I'm going to try to call and arrange an appointment to come to her house and discuss her case."

"Betty, were you able to find respite care for the two girls you called me about?"

"No it wasn't necessary after all. I thought you might have seen that piece on the news also. The girls have vanished. They were last seen at a quick stop on Eastern Avenue. The store has them on their security camera, but no one has seen them since."

"Oh, Betty! Now I feel bad that I said no to the respite care."

"Katie, the girls would have run anyway, whether it would have been from your house or their foster home. They were troubled girls; it would have happened anyway. Don't blame yourself."

"Yes, but I may have been able to help them sort out their troubles and show them that I cared."

"Oh, not so much in the short time you would have had them. Hey, I've gotta catch this other line."

Katie said goodbye and hung up the phone but still wondered if she could have helped prevent the girls from running—and where were the girls now? Were they safe? She relayed this all to Kirk when he came back in.

"Honey, we can't rescue *every* troubled child. Maybe the most we can do is rescue one child at a time—and we're doing that now with Brandon."

"That brings up a question I've meant to ask. How is the Boy's Adventure Club coming along? I haven't heard you comment on that lately."

"We couldn't get anyone else interested. I don't understand these fathers that don't make time to be with their sons. So I guess it will just be me and Jack with our two boys on an informal basis—no official club.

"That's too bad. Hard to believe no other dad was interested, but I'm sure you guys will enjoy the time with the two boys. I think they get along just fine."

The girls Katie
Refused ran away &
Brandon calls Kirks
dad 'grandpa' after
recieving a gift from him

CHAPTER 29

For three days Betty had tried to call Denise Brewer. Her supervisor at the motel told her that she hadn't shown up for work in over a week and hadn't called in. The home phone she had on file had been disconnected, so she decided to drive by Denise's trailer. There was no car and the house appeared vacant. Those tacked on *rails* on the steps had been removed and tossed over to the side with nails sticking up, waiting for any child to step on them. Betty could see through two of the windows. She saw the sparse furniture still inside, but everything else gave the appearance of abandonment. She drove by the house two more times in the next couple of weeks. The grass and weeds hadn't been mowed, and three windows were bejeweled with multiple BB gun holes and cracks.

After six more weeks with no sign of Denise, Betty started the process of having her parental rights terminated based on abandonment. As she was preparing the paperwork a call came in—from Denise.

"I thought I should let you know that I have moved."

"Yes, Denise, I've driven by your trailer and called your employer. I haven't seen or heard from you in almost two months. Your supervisor at the motel tells me you've not shown up for work in well over a week. Where are you?"

"I'm living with a friend here in Midwest City." She gave Betty the address and her new phone number.

"Denise, I was just now preparing the paperwork to have your parental rights terminated due to your abandonment. You can't just drop off the face of the earth for—"

"You can't do that!"

"Yes, I'm afraid I can."

"Look, I lost my job—"

"Was that before or after your DWI?"

"It had nothing to do with that. I lost my job and couldn't pay my lot rent. My lights and water were cut off. A friend of mine was good enough to let me stay with him 'till I get back on my feet."

"What is your *friend's* name?"

"His name is Tom Smith, and he is the sweetest guy. He's letting me stay here rent free."

"Denise, you have shown no interest in Brandon during your last three visits. I have to assume you just don't care anymore."

"Well, your *assuming* that doesn't make it so."

"I have another line holding, but if you're interested in your son, call me in about a month."

"A month!"

"That's what I said. Goodbye."

The following day Betty decided to drive by the address Denise had given her. The houses in the neighborhood were small bungalows; all painted the same tan color—rentals, no doubt. There was no car at the address Denise had given her. A big red Doberman pinscher was chained to a post about ten feet from the front door. Since the chain appeared to be more than ten feet long, Betty decided it was time to leave. The house sat on a corner lot. She turned there to circle back around to the four-lane road she had come in on. On that street a neighbor's driveway adjoined the back yard of the house with the Doberman—and there it was, a white Bronco.

⁂

Another two weeks passed and Betty accepted another call from Denise. "Okay, what is our next step?"

"I assume I'm speaking to Denise Brewer."

"Yeah, Betty, couldn't you tell from my voice?"

"Yes, but an introduction would have been nice. I talk to a lot of people, Denise."

"Okay, so what happens next with Brandon?"

"That depends on you. I drove by the address you gave me. Are you still living there?"

"Yes, I'm still here."

"What was the name of the friend you said had invited you to stay with until you could get back on your feet again?"

"My friend, his name is Bobby Smith. Why?"

"I thought you told me his name was *Tom* Smith?

There was a slight pause, then "Yeah, it's Bobby Tom."

"Bobby Tom?" Betty couldn't help herself, "You've got to be kidding. His name is Bobby Tom Jones?" She deliberately changed the last name to try to catch Denise in still another lie.

"Yeah, isn't that a crazy name? What was his mother thinking?"

"Yes, and it appears his mother couldn't remember her own last name either. So is it Smith, or is it Jones?"

She'd been caught. Now Denise was faking a coughing spell and then said, "I think I caught this crud at work."

"Is that right? Are you still at the motel?"

"Yes, it's not the best job, but I need the money."

"Denise, I thought you told me you lost that job."

Another pause, "Oh, they called me back in the next day."

"Come on, Denise, can you be honest with me just for the duration of this phone call?"

"Why? Are you calling me a liar?"

"Not yet, but that was going to be my next word. When I called the motel last month, they told me you hadn't showed up for over a week.

Now you're saying they called you back in the next day! Maybe you should prepare in advance for the lies you plan to tell—you know, keep the inconsistencies to a minimum that way.

Betty's ear was blasted with the whack of the receiver being slammed down.

Two days later, another drive-by revealed the same white Bronco parked behind the Bobby Tom Jones/Smith house on the adjoining property, which she could now see, was vacant.

Back at the Childers Ranch, Katie maintained her vigil of having Brandon read, both aloud and silently. She and Kirk both closely monitored his homework, and when his first third-grade report card came, they were both shocked—nothing less than an *A* in every subject! There was a note from Mrs. Dalton that read: *Mrs. Childers, it looks like you were right not to retain Brandon. He is doing very well now in third grade.* Katie knew this called for a celebration. Kirk suggested taking Brandon to Frontier City Saturday.

"Honey, what if we run into the same situation we did at the zoo?"

"Katie, what chance is there that she would be there too? Frontier City is mostly for kids. She doesn't have kids."

"She didn't have kids at the zoo either. Are they not mostly for kids and families?"

"Yeah, I see your point. But we can't be controlled by fear. We've got two sets of eyes to watch."

"That's just the problem. While we're keeping our eyes on Brandon, we don't see Denise and whatever boyfriend she happens to be with at the time."

"No, but Brandon will."

"Honey, I don't wanna take that chance. Can't we go to an amusement park in Tulsa or somewhere besides Oklahoma City?"

"Quit worrying. It'll be okay."

Saturday's blue skies and temps in the low seventies made for a beautiful fall day. Kirk was driving around the crowded parking lot, looking for an empty space when Brandon shouted, "Let's go home!"

"What?"

"That was Bryce's Bronco back there."

"No way, Brandon!"

"Back up, you'll see."

Kirk only had to back up a few feet and there it was. "How do you know it belongs to Bryce?" Katie asked.

"See that bumper sticker? It says *Get off my* ———."

"Yes, Brandon, we can read too. Why do you think it belongs to Bryce? There are probably a lot of white Broncos around town."

"Because I was there when he stuck that on his bumper. Can we just please go back home?"

"Yes, buddy," Kirk said, "we can do that. I was hoping we could all celebrate your good report card."

"You can. Just take me fishing on the big pond."

"You got it, bud." He looked at Katie and grinned, "Bryce just saved me about seventy bucks."

After two months of being a no-show, Denise calls Betty & lies about where she had been. Brandon gets all A's on his report card. They see the white Bronco

CHAPTER 30

Betty Sawyer's supervisor at The Department of Family Services was pushing her for a resolution in Brandon's case. Time was running out, and she had stalled about as long as she could get by with. She had stated her opinion that Denise Brewer was not a fit mother, but her opinion was not sufficient. She had to prove it, within the guidelines set out by the Department. Each time Denise fell within those guidelines she would make a small correction that put her back in the ballgame for having her son returned to her. Betty relayed in her reports how Brandon was thriving in his current foster home. She had also mentioned that his foster parents were more than willing to adopt him as soon as Denise's parental rights were terminated. That wasn't good enough. Rules had to be followed, and Denise always managed to slide just to the right of those rules, just long enough to start the process all over again.

Betty decided to call the supervisor of the motel where Denise had worked. Just as she suspected, she hadn't been employed there since she had walked away several weeks ago and never returned. Denise's cell phone was now disconnected. In a discussion with her secretary, Betty said she was tempted to take a *wait-and-see* attitude. If Denise was interested, she would call. If she didn't call, Betty could start the paperwork again for abandonment. Her plan fell apart when her supervisor pushed her for a drive-by in an attempt to reach the truant mother.

When Betty pulled up to the house where Denise had said she was staying, she was again greeted, in a very unfriendly manner, by the front door sentry. With a low guttural roar the Doberman pinscher displayed his threatening fangs and started toward Betty in an aggressive lurch that forced his visitor to retreat past the length of the extended chain he was tethered to. The big dog's growl was loud enough to have brought any occupant of the house to the door, but the door remained closed, and there was no movement in the closed plastic mini-blinds covering the small vertical windows on either side of the door. Betty went to the house next door to inquire about their neighbor, but no one was home there either. She returned to her car and drove around the corner where the white Ford Bronco had been parked in the neighboring driveway the last time she was there. It wasn't there this time.

The following week Betty again repeated her trip, to be met only by the same threatening Doberman. This time she found the neighbor home and was greeted by a filthy bulldog of a man outfitted only in his once white briefs. Stumbling for words, she pointed next door and asked, "Uh... Can you tell me anything about your neighbor? I'm looking for Benise Drewer—uh, Denise Brewer."

"Lady, I don't know you, and I don't know a Benise, Denise, or whatever you think her name is. I think you're soused! You oughta call a cab."

"How about a guy by the name of Bryce Collier?"

Her only answer was a slamming of the door in her face. She returned to her car and drove around the corner—again, no Bronco.

After a third unsuccessful trip back to the unwelcoming neighborhood the following week, Betty once again started the paperwork for abandonment. Part of the process for termination of parental rights involved a personal visit with the child, whose future was in question.

Given Denise's history of coming in just under the wire before termination of her rights could be completed, Betty saw this required visit as an attempt to prepare Brandon—and the Childers—for Brandon's possible return to his mother. A trip to the Childers Ranch was always a nice get-away. The beautiful rural setting, coupled with people that she now considered friends, was a welcome change from her unpleasant duties of removing a child from a home or hostile encounters with a parent—or a Doberman.

After a call to Katie for a reminder of the gate code, Betty steered her Buick down the little ranch lane, cordoned off on each side by the chalky white fences. Curious, the two horses pranced up to the fence. Betty stopped the car. A third horse was following—a beautiful little paint, with a rope halter. Betty got out and strolled over to the fence. The new little horse hesitated, then gradually made its way over where the other two were greeting their visitor. Dandy's head was reaching over the fence and bobbing up and down in a sociable salutation. Lilly was nuzzling the top rail of the fence, also with anticipation of attention from her visitor. She was rewarded with a pat on the nose from Betty. The little paint held back a bit displaying her wariness of the unexpected guest. Betty's intended brief stopover turned into several minutes as she soaked in the beauty before her. The picture-perfect moment of serenity was broken by the sound of a loud engine approaching. A hundred yards down the lane Betty spotted Katie, perched on the approaching ATV.

Katie pulled up to Betty, stopped and stood up on the running boards of the four-wheeler. "Hey, girl, I was afraid you were having trouble with the gate."

"No, I was just lost in the beauty of this picture. She pointed to the little paint horse. "Isn't this a new one?"

"Yes, Kirk bought her for Brandon at an auction last week. Dandy is a bit too tall for him, but she is short enough that he can mount her without any assistance. He even found a Teskey Pony Saddle at an auction—fits Brandon perfectly."

"What's her name?"

"Brandon named her Puzzle. He said the way she is spotted and marked up, she looks like a jigsaw puzzle."

"Well, I can see that. Some of her spots are even shaped like interlocking pieces of a puzzle. So is Brandon up at the house?"

"Yes, let's go catch him before he leaves. If we don't, we might have to chase him all the way to the barn. Follow me."

Brandon was in his room with one of his favorite books, which he had to show Betty and tell her the story. He summarized the story up to the last few pages, but he insisted on reading the ending. Betty was amazed. "Brandon, you are reading quite well now! I am impressed."

"Miss Katie taught me that reading can be fun. We go to the used bookstore, she helps me pick out the books, and Kirk buys them. See all of these? I've read all but one, and I'm gonna start it after school tomorrow."

"Brandon, actually I came here to visit with you and ask you some very personal questions."

"Shoot!"

"What?"

"That means go ahead—get to it."

Betty grinned. "Okay then, let's start with some questions about your mom."

"You mean Denise?"

"Yes, that's right. Can you tell me a little bit about her?"

"Yeah, she don't know how to pick her boyfriends."

"You may be right about that. One in particular that I know wasn't good for her—or you."

"Yeah. We went to Frontier City and I spotted Bryce's old Bronco, so we left because I didn't want to see him."

"How did you know it was *his* Bronco?"

"Because of the bumper sticker."

"The bumper sticker? What did it say?"

"I don't think Miss Katie wants me to say it, but I'll tell you. It said, *Get off my* ———."

"So you figured that was Bryce's?"

"Yeah, I was there when he stuck it on."

"This was when you were living with your mother?

"Yeah."

"Brandon, tell me about your mother. If you could live with her again, what changes would you want her to make."

"I don't wanna live with her ever! She doesn't love me."

"Well, when I brought you out here to live with Kirk and Katie, you didn't feel that way. You wanted to go back home where your mom was."

It was obvious Brandon was thinking about his answer. He ducked his head, paused, and then said, "She used to love me, but then she loved Bryce more."

"If Bryce was no longer her boyfriend would that help?"

"No, she is selfish! She won't even talk to me at your office."

"But Brandon, she is still your mother."

Brandon seemed to read right through Betty's questioning. "Look. I don't wanna go live with her again. I wanna live here with Kirk and Katie—and that's final!"

"Wow! That's pretty strong talk for a boy your age."

"It's not just talk. It's what I want! Doesn't that matter?"

"Brandon, honey, we will take your wishes into consideration, but if your mother wants you to come live with her, we won't have much choice, will we?"

"Yes, I do have a choice—I'll run away!"

Betty could see she was only upsetting him more and managed to bring the conversation to a close in a way that made him smile. "You really love it here, don't you?"

"Yes, and I forgot to show you what Grandpa brought me."

"Grandpa?"

He took the little die-cast Mustang off the shelf and said, "Well, it's not official; he's not my grandpa yet, but he will be someday."

"That was nice of him, Brandon. I like Mustangs too."

"I could ask Grandpa to buy you one too. But, Miss Betty, I need to go help Kirk at the barn with the milking."

"You help him milk the cows?"

"You wanna come watch?"

"I'd love to some other time, but now I need to visit with Katie before I leave."

When Brandon was out the door, Betty went into the kitchen where Katie was starting supper. She briefed her on their somewhat troubling conversation.

Katie looked into the eyes of the caseworker whom she knew held Brandon's destiny. Her words came slowly at first. "If... Brandon is... returned to Denise, we will never see him again!" Tears were forming.

Picking up the cadence, she continued. "Denise doesn't deserve that kid... No... Denise doesn't deserve *any* kid! Brandon is a gift from God!" Wiping the twin tears that were trickling down her cheeks, she blurted out, "Kirk will be devastated!"

"Katie, you knew it could happen. That's the heartache borne by all good foster parents."

The tears were rolling now. "Does this mean you are taking him from us now?"

"No, but what I'm trying to do is to prepare you guys as to what may happen if I'm unable to prove Denise to be an unfit mother. What I'm counting on is abandonment charges. If she doesn't contact me soon, that could happen. I've already started the paperwork—again—for that scenario."

With a tear induced gleam of hope in her eyes she asked, "You think that may be a possibility?"

"It's possible, but you know how unpredictable Denise can be."

The beginning whiff of burned potatoes launched Katie back into her world. She rushed over to the stove, grabbed a towel, slid the pan from the burner and grinned. "I was going to ask if you'd like to stay for supper, but now I think I may know what your answer to that would be."

"Katie, burned potatoes wouldn't keep me from the supper you're making here, but the truth is I need to get home to my own kitchen. My husband is getting tired of eating out almost every night."

Katie reached out for Betty's hand, "Uh… about Denise—just don't answer any phone calls from her."

As Betty was leaving, she turned and whispered, "Maybe she's moved to Timbuktu."

The minute Brandon came into the barn, Kirk knew something was wrong. Without a word Brandon pulled down the milking machine, sat down beside Old Gertie on his little three-leg milking stool, did the necessary udder cleansing, hooked up the machine to the Jersey, and watched the milk stream through the plastic tubing, accompanied by the noise of the suction from the machine.

"Hey guy, you're not talkin' much."

Either Brandon didn't hear over the noise of the machines, or he ignored him. When it was finished, he disconnected the equipment, carried it through the door into the wash room, cleaned and put it back in its place. He then went back, opened the stanchion, and led Old Gertie out to the cow lot.

Kirk finished milking the other two cows but didn't see Brandon waiting for him as was usual. Brandon always helped Kirk clean and put away the other equipment, but he was nowhere in sight. Figuring he was waiting for him on the ATV, he started out to it, but Brandon wasn't there—he knew something was wrong! He jumped on the four-wheeler, peeled out in the gravel by the barn, and sped toward the ranch house. On the back porch, he kicked off his boots and went straight to Brandon's room. The door was closed, so he gave a quick tap with his knuckle. He heard a faint response from Brandon. He opened the door and saw Brandon lying, stomach down, on the bed. "Hey, buddy, what's wrong?"

There was a little sniffle. "Nuthin.'"

Kirk sat down on the bed beside him, put his arm around him and remained silent for a minute. "Come on, buddy, tell me what's on your mind."

His face was turned to the other side, half buried in the pillow. There was another sniffle and then, "I wanted you to be my dad!"

Kirk could tell the tears were rolling now, and he didn't know how to respond to him. He eased up onto the bed beside him and just lay there with his head next to Brandon's. "I don't know what to say to you, buddy, but I am here now for you."

Brandon turned his face upward and Kirk kissed his cheek. "I love you, Brandon."

With tears still rolling he said, "I know." He swiped at his eyes. "I love you too."

Kirk reached over and grabbed a tissue from the night stand and handed it to his little buddy. "Just rest here for a few minutes; then come into the kitchen. I think I smell supper."

He left the room and was met by Katie, leaning up against the wall. "You hear?" he whispered.

Katie wiped her eye and swallowed hard. "Yes, I heard."

After motioning for her to go to the kitchen with him, he wrapped his arms around his wife." What do I need to know about this?" Then he pulled away a bit, puckered his lips, and his eyes were like burning embers. "Did Denise get her stinkin' custody?"

"Not yet. But Betty was here and talked to Brandon about what he thought of the possibility of living with his mother now."

"And…?"

"As you can see, it has upset him badly."

"Well, why did she do that?"

"I think she was trying to prepare him for that possibility."

"So what did he say to that?"

"He said he'd run away."

"Well, now I just wanna take him and run away!"

"Kirk! We're the adults. We have to be strong for him."

Kirk picked up the mail that was stacked on the kitchen table next to his plate and hurled it onto the floor, not realizing Noah was lying there under the table. The dog yelped and shot out of the room.

Brandon met the little dog in the hallway; then he dashed into the kitchen. "What happened to Noah?

"It's okay, Katie said. He just got spooked when Kirk dropped the mail on the floor next to him. Come on, let's sit down and eat what's left of the supper I managed to incinerate."

"You burned the potatoes, didn't you? I smelled them."

"You've got a pretty good sniffer. Sit down. I'll pour you some milk."

"Where'd Kirk go?"

"He'll be back in a minute." She grinned. "He must have gotten a whiff of those burned potatoes too."

Kirk slunk back inside, sat down at the table, picked up his fork, stabbed at his pork chop, and stopped. He looked at Katie with a still angry twist in his mouth and attempted a forged apology for losing his temper. "I am just so…" He coughed. "I am just irritated with the stinking system that would even think of returning Brandon to a totally unfit and uncaring mother." He stabbed wildly at the pork chop a second time.

Katie could see the bulging veins in his neck. "Kirk, you are still riled up!"

He was already packing out toward the front door again. "Honey, I need a minute to regroup."

Brandon noticed and asked, "Where's he going now?"

"Just letting off a little steam, Brandon—adults have to do that now and then."

"I don't blame him. I'm mad too!"

Then it was Katie's turn to lose it. She dropped her fork on the table. "Okay, you guys go ahead and finish your sacrificial supper. I'm going to go to my bathroom and soak in a very long and hot bubble bath."

Brandon watched her and saw her exasperation. "I'll clean the kitchen and do the dishes for you."

Katie grabbed him, held her arms around him tight, and kissed his forehead. She walked out of the kitchen and down the hallway. *This is truly a very special child!* She then walked into the master bedroom. *God, I sure hope you've got a good plan!*

We don't!

CHAPTER 31

All it took was one phone call from Denise, and Betty was forced to again trash the abandonment papers she had initiated. At five minutes 'til five, the following Monday afternoon, Betty received the dreaded phone call.

"So Betty, when do I get to see my son again?"

"Well, Denise, I didn't realize you had any desire to see him. I've tried to reach you by phone. I've called the motel where you said you had been called back to work, only to find out that you lied about…."

"Look—that's beside the point. I asked when do I get to see my son again."

"Well, Denise, let's start over. I need to ask you some necessary questions first. You have not kept me posted with a current address where you can be found—"

"I thought you said this would be *questions*. That sounds more like accusations to me!"

"If you'll stop interrupting, I will get to the questions." Then a loud crack and the phone went dead.

One minute later, Betty picked up again. "Okay, go ahead and ask your questions."

"Denise, your attitude is making it difficult to have a discussion with you."

"I dropped the phone—okay!"

"Start out by telling me where you are living now." She scribbled out the new address, an apartment in a smaller town on the city's south side. "Who do you share that apartment with?" She wrote down a name. "Is that a fake name too?"

"I don't have to put up with this! I'm getting a lawyer!" Another crack and the phone again went dead.

Three days later, Betty received a call from Garrison Downing with one of the city's largest and most prestigious law firms. An appointment was set up for a visit between the two. Garrison Downing pranced into Betty's office, a hot-out-of-law-school, ambitious youngster in an Armani suit, spit-shined shoes and sporting a Rolex watch. A highly motivated newbie to the profession; it was obvious that Garrison Downing had descended from a family of privilege, and he had the world at his fingertips. The meeting went as Betty had expected, and it was agreed that Mr. Downing would make the arrangements between Betty and Denise for the next parental visit.

The following Thursday, Kirk and Katie escorted Brandon back to the DFS office. At the exact agreed upon time, Denise stomped in, followed by Garrison Downing carrying his alligator skin brief case. Kirk looked at Katie and whispered, "How'd she afford that dude?"

Brandon was uncooperative in every way. Denise tried to hug him, but he pulled away. Probably prompted by her attorney, Denise had brought a picture for her son—a well-tanned Denise in a string bikini standing at the wheel of a ski boat. He stared at it a second then dropped it on the floor beside his chair. Katie glanced at it and rolled her eyes.

Denise babbled on about herself, never asking Brandon anything about himself. No questions about school, his grades, or his friends, but instead, she dispensed a plethora of promises of what would happen when he came back to live with her—video games, water slides, pizza every night, and even his own go-cart. Brandon continued to look down at his balled fists and said nothing. When Denise ran out of promises, the meeting came to an abrupt halt. Garrison held the door for Denise to exit and then told Betty he would be in touch.

Kirk had seen Katie pick up the photo from the floor beside Brandon while they were in the conference room. The three of them walked back out to the pickup. Brandon was buckling himself in the back seat, and Kirk stopped and looked at Katie before turning the key. "Well…" he said.

She pulled the picture out of her purse, changed her mind and put it back in. Brandon saw what she did and said, "I don't want that thing; you can throw it away." Katie tried to look over at Kirk without turning her head. A little grin was sneaking from his face.

Kirk helped Brandon heave the new saddle over Puzzle's back. Brandon cinched her up, put one foot in the stirrup, and threw his other leg over the beautiful little paint. "She's just the right size now, but I hope she'll keep growing as I do."

Dandy and Puzzle carried the two guys to the very back side of the sprawling ranch on the east. The lush pasture gave way to a wooded area of post oak-blackjack trees and then to some sycamores lining the banks of a small creek etched into the red earth. They followed the cow trail through the trees before coming to a clearing. A doe with her twins, probably the same one they'd seen earlier, caught scent of them and fled back into the trees.

Brandon saw it first. An ill positioned crate of well weathered boards, about four feet by four feet, was perched about ten feet up in a Sycamore. It was partially covered by a tattered and faded camouflage-printed tarp. The ruins of what was at one time a deer stand for some hunter hovered dangerously above them. "Kirk, let's climb up and see what's up there."

"You wanna take a chance on that thing taking a tumble to the ground just as we get inside? It looks pretty unstable to me."

"Come on, let's check it out."

"You stay down and I'll go take a look first." Kirk started up the ill spaced two by four board steps nailed to the tree by some unknown hunter. He climbed just high enough to see inside. Empty beer cans littered the floor, along with an unopened can of Beanie Weenies and an abundance of bird droppings.

"Hey, I wanna see! Brandon said."

Kirk stepped back down and held him up to the bottom rung of the improvised ladder. "Okay, buddy, I'm gonna be right behind you. When you get to the top, don't go in, just look. I don't want that rotten old shanty to collapse on you."

To an eight-year-old boy, it was a castle in the sky. "I wanna go in—please!"

"Not a chance, guy. That thing is filthy, as well as rotten. The next good windstorm will send it down to the ground. Come on down now." Kirk slid his thumbs inside Brandon's waistband and gently persuaded his little buddy to back down. After mounting up again, they backtracked, making their way to the ranch house, where they were greeted by Noah, slapping his tail from side to side, with his head raised to the sky and breaking into a half chortle, Border collie style.

Denise unlocked the door to her second-floor apartment, shuffled in, and kicked off her shoes. The latest in her string of boyfriends, stretched out on the couch. Holding a cold one in his hand, motioned for her to come over and sit with him. "What's wrong, babe? Didn't your visit with your son go well?"

"My son has been turned into a snob by that hillbilly couple he's living with. They've got him where he won't even talk to me! I've got to get him away from them before he is permanently ruined!"

"What are you doing?"

"I'm callin' Garrison. I want Brandon outta that house now!"

CHAPTER 32

Kirk Childers walked into the big room and saw Katie sitting at the breakfast table clutching a cup of coffee. Her eyes were focused on a cardinal in the cedar tree outside the window. She made no attempt to acknowledge his presence. He reached down and touched the side of her coffee cup. Cold. He put his callused hand over the top of the cup. Still no warmth. "Kate, how long have you been sitting here? You're coffee's cold, and that bird's got your full attention."

"Oh, Kirk, I'm sorry." Katie turned and hugged him around the waist, plunging her face into his tee shirt. "You know, writing this story was just getting to me. Just imagining what some kids have to endure makes me want to kick some—"

"Kate, you don't have to put yourself through all of that. Just write about the good parts. Leave out all that other junk."

Katie pulled her head up and looked into his eyes. "But that wouldn't be real."

"Well, I heard you say you were writing fiction. Or something about fictionalizing reality, or some nonsense stuff I never understood. So you could just leave out the bad stuff and concentrate on the good."

"Kirk, I can't tell only part of the story. We can't pick and choose what life throws at us. We just accept the whole thing—the good along with the bad."

"True, but if writing about it makes you despondent, write only the good parts." He took her coffee mug and started toward the coffee pot. "What you need is a fresh cup of coffee to pull yourself out of your mulligrubs."

"Thanks, sweetie." Katie ran her fingers through her russet-brown hair and looked out the window again. "Kirk, do you think we've done the right thing—I mean, taking these kids? Sometimes I don't see that we've made a difference."

"Are you kidding!" He set the steaming mug down in front of her. "You just need another cup of coffee! Of course we've made a difference."

"I guess. But sometimes we don't hav‌ to see any changes in them."

Kirk pulled out a chair, turned it aro‌ and rested his arms on the back. "Honey, ‌ ing in Matthew. I think it was in chapter ei‌ welcomes one such child in my name wel‌ hand over Katie's. "Don't you see? We do ‌ kids, and He will do the rest. I'm not gon‌ I've gotta do is welcome a kid and show h‌ both good at that."

"Well it takes a little more than kindness, but I get your point. I just feel so sorry for these kids for what they are up against. Sometimes I wish I didn't know any of the abominable details when the caseworker brings a child to us."

"Katie, I've read some of that story you're working on. It even got to me a bit. Maybe you should take a break from writing for a while."

But she didn't.

CHAPTER 33

Betty Sawyer's day was a typical Monday at the Department. Five separate calls from concerned friends, family, or neighbors about separate cases of what they had seen as child abuse or abandonment. Two of the cases were assigned to Betty. One was at the far southern end of the county and Betty knew she'd better get an early start for the required home visit before the lunch hour traffic hit.

When she pulled up to the address she'd been given, the house appeared abandoned—no window coverings, weeds and grass that hadn't seen a mower in weeks. An empty hummingbird feeder hung from the eave of the porch. But the house was not abandoned. She could see children through the window. She was greeted at the door by the oldest, probably seven. There was no food in the house, only a few pieces of furniture, and no beds. Betty packed all four into her Buick and headed back to her office. She knew that placing all four siblings in one foster home was going to be difficult, if not impossible.

Her next case was even more difficult. There were accusations of sexual abuse and the eleven-year-old girl, who should have been in school, was not talking. A belligerent boyfriend was defended by the mother of the girl, even though two other family members had called in with sordid details of the abuse.

After a call from one of her foster parents pleading for respite care, Betty picked up another line and heard the voice of Garrison Downing. "Ms. Sawyer, my client is requesting that her son, Brandon, be removed from the foster home he is in."

"Mr. Downing, Brandon is quite happy and is thriving in the home that he's been in for almost a year now. I see no basis for removal of the child at this point."

"Well, Ms. Martin is claiming that the foster parents have brainwashed her son and have created a chasm of animosity separating him from her."

"No, Mr. Downing, you are wrong. Denise has done that herself! She fails to show up for parent visits or is very late to them when she does decide to show up. She has sat in the conference room across from her son, never speaking one word to him. He had asked her to bring a picture of her to him. As you know, it took you—her attorney—to get her to bring one to him. And then, she brings a picture that is totally inappropriate for an eight-year-old boy."

"I didn't see the picture she—"

"Well you should have!"

"As her attorney, I feel that it would best serve the interest of all if the boy was moved to a different foster ho—"

Betty interrupted again, "Mr. Downing, as her attorney, you know don't squat about what is best for this child. You haven't watched him progress from the scared little boy with deep cuts in his legs and groin from her boyfriend's belt—"

"That is not—"

"No! You listen to me! You can't just waltz in here with your fancy briefcase and understand what has happened in the life of this child. The home he is now in is the best thing that ever happened to Brandon Hall, and if you have any conscience at all in that perfectly groomed head of yours, you will back off!"

"I can see I'm getting nowhere with you."

"And you won't as long as you are fighting *against* this beautiful child! Goodbye, Mr. Downing."

The rest of her day wasn't any better. A child in one of her better foster homes had been expelled from school because of his inappropriate sexual activity in the boys' room. The foster parents were at their wit's end. "Betty, we don't know how to handle this. This was not the first incident, and we have talked to him about it before. Please remove this child from our home!" The only option for Betty was to send the child to a boy's home, but she knew that wasn't a perfect solution either.

Each of the day's crises was compounded by the magnitude of required paperwork. Every phone call had to be documented. There were forms for this and forms for that. Every time she got in or out of her car, her mileage had to be documented. Most weeks were filled with court appointments that disrupted critical home visits. Sometimes it seemed the main focus of a social worker—the child—was greyed-out by mountains of paperwork and over-confident lawyers that knew nothing about raising a child in the way he should go. In her fourteen years at her job, Betty Sawyer had learned to juggle the heavy workload better than most, but it was the next bombshell that caught her off-guard.

Betty gets a lot more cases. Mr. Bowney calls to convinse her why Denise should get the child back. She yells.

CHAPTER 34

It was a Friday afternoon following a busy week of removals, placements, required home visits, court appearances, and angry parents threatening her. Betty's supervisor appeared and handed her a summons. Garrison Downing, acting on behalf of Denise Brewer, was suing the Department. Ms. Brewer was asking that the court remove Betty Sawyer from Brandon's case and that the boy be moved to a different foster home. Furthermore, it alleged incompetence on the part of Ms. Sawyer and demanded that she be removed from her job with the Department. For good measure, the young upstart lawyer had thrown in "The degrading remarks of Ms. Sawyer to the attorney should constitute an apology on behalf of Ms. Sawyer."

Betty threw the document down on her desk with the force of an F-5 tornado. She looked at her supervisor and said, "I've had it; this job is not worth it! I'm going home to my husband and prepare him a home-cooked meal for a change.

It was a phone call at home Saturday afternoon from Betty's supervisor that convinced her to take some vacation time. "Take a cruise. Go rent a secluded mountain cabin. Take your grandkids to Disneyworld. Just get away, and don't even think about this chaotic mess here."

Betty thought about it. A cruise would be nice, but she decided instead to make a call. "Katie, this is Betty Sawyer."

"Betty, this is Saturday! Don't you ever take a day off?"

"That's just it, Katie. I do need a break from this job. I remember one time Kirk invited me to come out to the ranch sometime, and you and I could go horseback riding. Is his offer still good?"

"Well of course it is. When do you wanna come out?"

"How about Monday morning?"

"Sure, I'll be here. Just come on out anytime that's good for you. Better yet, why don't you come out early, and I'll have a good old fashioned farm breakfast ready before we mount up."

"You know, that sounds wonderful. But I have to tell you, I haven't ridden a horse since I was a kid."

"That's no problem. Lilly's a sweetheart of a horse—gentle as they come."

At nine o'clock, Monday morning, Betty called from the main gate. "Katie, I'm sorry, I don't remember the gate code."

"Seven-Four-Two."

A few minutes later, she opened the door. "Betty, you're just in time. I was just pulling the biscuits out of the oven. Come on in. Hey, I see you're dressed for the occasion. I meant to tell you—jeans, and boots if you had them." She looked down at Betty's boots. "Hon, those boots look like they've never seen a stirrup, or even a mud puddle before. Are they new?"

"I've had these back in my closet for years; I just never had any reason to bring them out."

The two sat down to homemade biscuits, sausage gravy, scrambled eggs, thick slabs of home-smoked bacon, and bold coffee with a vanilla creamer. Betty looked down at her plate of farm fresh food and said, "This sure beats my usual morning dry bagel and sometimes cold coffee from the vending machine downstairs."

"Well, we'll need a good hearty breakfast to sustain us for the route I've got planned. I hope you're up to a pretty good little jaunt. There's eighteen hundred acres here on this ranch, which means we can ride 'til we are exhausted or start to get sore, and never tire of God's own special décor in this incredible chapel under the sky."

"Yes, He's quite an artist. I can't wait."

After they had finished their breakfast, Betty started to help with the cleanup. "Let's just leave these dishes right where they are so we can get on out there."

"Where are the boys?" Betty asked as they started out the door.

"Kirk took Brandon for his dental check up in the city. I called Mrs. Dalton and told her he wouldn't make it back to school today. So we've got the entire ranch to ourselves."

Betty followed Katie toward the ATV. "Why don't we just walk; it's not that far."

Katie was climbing on the four-wheeler. "This will be faster. We'll probably get enough walking in today anyway."

When they reached the pasture where the horses were grazing in the distance, Katie put her two fingers in her mouth and blasted out an ear-splitting whistle, bringing the three horses at a trot toward her.

"Where did you learn to whistle like that?"

"Oh, I've been doing that since I was a kid. I think my daddy taught me. It comes in handy at times." Katie pulled out a few carrots from her hip pocket, and the horses followed her to the stable. Once inside, she asked Betty to shut the gate. Then after she'd placed a thick blanket on Dandy's back, she grabbed a saddle off the rack and slung it over him effortlessly.

"Wow! You seem to have done that a few times."

"Yeah, next comes the bridle. Can you reach that for me over there on the tack wall?" When she had Dandy ready to ride, she saddled up Lilly for Betty. "I always ride up to their water trough to give them a chance to get a good drink before taking off. Do you think you'll need help mounting up?"

"I'm not sure; it's been awhile." Betty struggled but managed to get her left foot in the stirrup. "Now, if I can just vault my big rear over her."

"Here, I can give you a shove."

After watering the horses, they headed west toward the gentle slopes with the big bluestem grass waving in the morning breeze. The weather was perfect for riding, with a seventy-something temperature and low humidity. The blue sky extended into infinity, with no interrupting clouds. Noah was bouncing along in front of them and spooked a covey of quail. Betty pulled back on Lilly's reins and sat in amazement as the birds flew overhead, lighting again some fifty yards away. "Wow! That was beautiful!"

Another quarter of a mile and they were crossing a shallow creek trickling over smooth rocks, some with a blanket of velvety moss covering them. Betty caught sight of something to her left scampering into the brush next to the creek. "Did you see that?"

"I did. You know what it was, don't you?"

"Well, I know it wasn't a squirrel!" She laughed. "Maybe a weasel?"

Katie grinned. "It was a mink."

"A mink!" She turned toward Katie. "You are kidding!"

"No, I'm not. We've seen a few of them down here around this little creek. Kirk says it is an American mink, as opposed to a European mink—those usually have a white patch on their upper lip. The American minks don't.

A trail led off to the right. Fifteen minutes later they came in sight of the abandoned log cabin. A little closer Katie could see some movement just inside the door. She let the reins drop a bit but whispered, "Whoa, Dandy."

"What do you see, Katie?"

"I'm not sure, but I think there is someone inside. Come on, Dandy, let's go check it out."

"Do you think it's safe to go closer?"

"Betty, you can stay here. I'm gonna see who's doing what in that old cabin." A soft touch to Dandy's flanks was all it took, and the beautiful Morgan was bolting forward in a sprint toward the cabin. Ten yards from the cabin door, Katie spotted one of the intruders and hollered, "Hey! What're you doin' in there?"

A teenage boy peeked out and looked at Katie. "Just checkin' it out."

"Who else is in there with you?" Two other youngsters appeared, both with cigarettes hanging from their mouths. "Why are you boys not in school?"

Two were quiet, but the first one smarted back at Katie, "What's it to you, lady?"

"Young man, this is private property. Dozens of signs are posted on the perimeter of the ranch. What's more, this is Monday. You guys are supposed to be in school. And you two hanging back there, spit out them nasty cigarettes!"

"Who's gonna make us?"

Katie reached behind her as if there was a gun concealed there. "I am!"

The younger one dropped his cigarette and whispered to his buddy, "Dude, she's got a gun!"

"You boys get a run on, because I'm chasing you off this ranch." Noah was right there, barking his fool head off at them. The boys turned and headed toward the west fence. Katie nudged Dandy's flanks again and was soon on their tails, hollering, "I'd better not ever catch you hooligans back on this ranch. You go back to school where you belong!" She chased them to the fence, where they stepped on the bottom rail and vaulted over. "Next time, I'm calling the cops on you!"

Betty was laughing when Katie returned back to her. "Katie Childers, you've got guts!" I would never have the nerve to do that."

"Well, they don't need to be snoopin' 'round here and tarring up their lungs. They need to be back in school!"

"Amen, sister!"

Katie grinned, "Come on; I wanna show you the big pond where Kirk and Brandon fish."

By two o'clock Katie asked if Betty thought she'd had enough. Betty bugged her eyes in an I-thought-you'd-never-ask look and said, "Yes, but I'm not sure I can even get off this pony. If I do, I'm afraid you're gonna see one Bow-legged Betty barely hobbling back to the house."

"I think I saw Kirk come home. I'll call and see if he'll bring the truck back to the barn so we don't have to walk back to the house."

By the time they reached the stable, Kirk met them, offering to take their horses and put the tack back in place. "You girls just take the truck back to the house. I'll be up in a little bit. Brandon's in his room, still complaining about a numb lip—doc had to fill a cavity."

Inside the main room of the house Betty's eyes roamed the cathedral ceiling with the wagon wheel chandelier, then over to the massive rock fireplace. "Katie, I could get used to this gorgeous house and this lifestyle. I feel like I'm standing in a huge lodge in some national park, away from all the traffic and sirens of the big city. You are so fortunate!"

Just then Brandon showed his face. "Hi, Miss Betty, I didn't know you were here."

"Well, hi Brandon! Yes, Miss Katie and I have been horseback riding."

"Who'd you ride?"

"I had the pleasure of riding that beautiful Lilly. She's a sweetie!"

"Do you think I talk funny?"

"What?"

"I got a tooth filled and my lip is still crazy numb. I'm trying not to bite it."

Betty sat down on the big leather sofa, facing the massive river rock fireplace, her eyes wandering over the cavernous room, then back to Brandon. "Come, sit down here by me and tell me all about that dentist visit."

Brandon chattered about every detail, as if Betty had never been in a dentist chair herself. He started telling her about the pretty dental assistant and how she had asked him what kind of music he liked. "She put these little ear thingies in my ears, and I listened to music the whole time the dentist had his hands in my mouth." He rattled on some more. "There was this little sink right by my chair. I had to spit after he finished with that drill, but I missed, and it landed on the arm of my chair."

Betty's attention never faltered. "Brandon, that's interesting. Who knows, maybe you'll grow up to be a dentist someday."

"No, Miss Betty, I will own a big ranch like this one."

"You think?"

"Yeah, I wanna work cattle just like Kirk does."

Katie heard the back door open and close. "Okay, Kirk's here. I've got some sandwiches already made up in the fridge. Brandon, you grab that bag of potato chips and I'll get us some drinks."

Betty limped into the kitchen and had already plopped down in the nearest chair. "Katie, I didn't mean to stay for lunch, but I'm not bashful. A sandwich sounds great."

After lunch she said, "I need to be going back now. I hope I didn't overstay my welcome."

Katie smiled at her. "In no way did you overstay your welcome. I have enjoyed our girl's day out."

Betty gave her a quick goodbye hug and said, "This has been a real treat for me; one I'll never forget!"

"Yeah, we'll have to do this again sometime."

"Well, Annie Oakley, as long as we don't run into those hooligans again!"

"Awh, they were just goofy kids, but I'll bet they don't try coming back on the ranch again. I'll have to remember that fake gun move next time. That worked out well."

CHAPTER 35

The following Monday, Betty was back in her office. Her supervisor was a bit surprised to see her back so soon. "I thought you'd take at least two weeks. You even have more vacation time built up than that."

"I thought I'd better get back and see if I still have a job?"

She assured her that she did and told her not to worry. "We'll fight that little egotistic lawyer. I have a feeling this is his very first case."

As she knew it would be, Betty was barraged with a mountain of paperwork, required home visits, parent/child visits, and a new case staring her in the face—with a name that jumped out at her. She stared at the note taken by her secretary. *A Bryce Collier is accused of beating a five-year-old boy while his mother, Joyce Richards, stood by and did nothing to stop the abuse. From her patio, a neighbor saw it all take place in the back yard next door and called into DFS.* The neighbor had left a number to be called back.

After a brief conversation with the neighbor, Betty knew she had to go out and question the mother that allowed her son to be beaten. She wasn't looking forward to a confrontation with Bryce, if he was in fact the infamous Bryce Collier, and if he was there at that house. There was no phone number given for Joyce Richards. "Do you suppose this is the same Bryce Collier?" she asked her secretary.

Arriving at the address she was given, Betty met with Joyce Richards. Joyce even looked similar to Denise. She appeared a bit malnourished and had curly shoulder length, blazing red hair. As the woman described her boyfriend, Betty knew it was the same Bryce Collier. The little boy's injuries were even the same as those suffered by Brandon—deep cuts by a belt to the back, legs and groin area. Betty asked how that happened. The woman aimed a cloud of smoke directly into Betty's face. "The kid was smartin' back at Bryce, okay?" Betty felt goose bumps dance up and down her arms.

"Joyce, do you mind if we turn that TV off? It is very annoying, and we have serious matters to discuss."

"Look, you just need to lay off Bryce. He was trying to discipline Jason."

As she was defending her boyfriend, Betty interrupted and told her the history of Bryce Collier, as she knew it. Joyce already knew about his other girlfriend and brazenly declared, "Bryce flips back and forth between me and Denise. I'm okay with that, because Bryce treats me good. If it wasn't for him, we wouldn't eat."

Betty was stunned. "You mean you would sit by and watch him beat your son and be okay with that...because he treats *you* good?" She knelt down beside Jason and asked if he would mind pulling his pants down at the waist just a bit so she could see where he was hurting.

Joyce blurted out, "Look! Jason deserved what he got! He had been smart-mouthing me and Bryce all day. Bryce didn't realize he was injuring Jason 'til later."

"Oh! So you both knew and didn't even try to get medical treatment for your son?" The woman blew another nicotine cloud toward Betty. Betty waived the smoke from her face. "Joyce, has Bryce ever hit you?"

"Well, I guess a time or two, but he has always apologized and told me it wouldn't happen again. Bryce is a good man. He didn't mean to hurt Jason."

"Uh huh, right! Well, Joyce, I'm afraid I'm going to have to take Jason back with me. He will be in the custody and care of the Department of Family Services until this situation can be corrected."

"You're not taking my son. You have no right!"

"Oh but I do! You stood by and watched your son as he was beaten and did nothing to protect him. Furthermore, you didn't even get treatment for those deep slashes!"

The fire bomb in Joyce Richards exploded, "Lady, you are not taking my son!"

"Joyce, I can call for backup from the Oklahoma City Police if it is necessary. Either you allow me to take him now, or you can face charges from the police."

At the mention of the police, the raging fire suddenly turned to glowing embers. Betty handed Joyce her business card and explained the process of the Department and how they make every effort in an attempt to reunite parent and child. "But Joyce, I have to tell you straight up, your only hope of getting your son back is to get rid of your boyfriend. This is the second child that Bryce Collier has beaten, and you must get him out of your life if you have any hope of regaining custody of Jason."

Jason was silent and clinging to his mother. Joyce snuffed out the butt end of her cigarette and reached for another from the pack next to her. "So I have no choice with this?"

"At this point, no you do not. Now, if you will gather up Jason's clothes and any toys you would like for him to take with him, we will be on our way."

On the way back to the office, Betty questioned Jason about his injuries and got the response she had often heard from children before. "It was my fault."

"No, Jason, you didn't deserve to be beaten like that. You may have been smart-mouthing your mother and Bryce and not obeying them, but you did not deserve to be cut up by a belt."

Back at the office, Betty flipped through the old Rolodex which she still preferred over the newer ways of maintaining contacts electronically. She picked up the foster home listing on her desk that was updated weekly and saw there were no new homes added to the list. She picked up the phone and dialed a number she now had etched in her brain.

For several months Katie had been thinking about writing a children's book. Brandon kept asking for more and more books. Each time she searched for new topics, the plight of foster children kept popping up in her mind. So far, she hadn't found any books that dealt with that topic. Kirk had encouraged her to just sit down and write, but it seemed she never found time. There were farm chores, gardening, preparing meals for her hungry men, and occasionally substitute teaching in the lower grades at the little school in Luther.

It was Monday morning, after the breakfast dishes were cleared, and she was alone in the big ranch house. She sat down at an old Remington typewriter that she'd had since college days, typing out a tentative title for her book, *Where is My Mom?* She sat there asking herself, *now, what do I do?* She had some ideas racing through her head, but that was the trouble—most of them just raced right on through. The only writing class she'd ever taken was part of one of her elementary education classes at OSU, and it was about as basic as it could get. She knew even a children's book had to have a beginning, middle, and end, and most of them tried to teach values to children while providing a fun experience. Just as an idea came into her head for a great beginning, the phone rang.

"Katie, this is Betty. I need a big favor. I have another little boy that needs a home. Incredibly, this little guy has suffered the same kind of wounds as Brandon did—and from the same wimp of a man!"

"What! Are you saying it was Bryce?"

"Yes, I'm afraid that's what I'm saying. It seems Bryce has been keeping two girlfriends, Denise, and now there's a Joyce.

"Is this kid Joyce's son? Bryce is just a boyfriend?"

"It appears that way. I had to remove him from his mother's home after a neighbor called in and described the beating the little guy had taken from her boyfriend out in the back yard."

"So does this Joyce know about Denise?"

"Oh yeah, she knows! Get this; she is even okay with that arrangement. Says he is good to her, buys her groceries."

"And she defended him?"

"Katie, I will never understand these women that won't stand up to a man and protect their child from such abuse. It is disgusting!"

"The man is an animal! He should be put away!"

"So how about it? Do you think you could take little Jason?"

"Well, we might be able to take the child; I'm just not sure about dealing with Bryce again."

"I can have Jason out to the ranch in about an hour. Will you be home?"

Katie hesitated for a second. "Yeah, we'll be here. Seven-Four-Two."

"Yes, I remember. I'll see you about eleven."

Katie put the dustcover back on the old Remington. That inspiration for a great beginning of a children's book had evaporated.

1R

CHAPTER 36

Katie called Kirk and told him that Betty was bringing a little five-year-old boy, and that they would be here around eleven. Kirk rode up to the house on the ATV, just in front of Betty's Buick. He stopped at the house in front of her. "Sorry about the cloud of dust I was leaving behind me. It's been dry here for a long time. You get any rain lately in the city?"

"No, we haven't. My flowers are looking pretty sad. I don't seem to find the time to water them as I should." She opened her door, and Kirk opened the passenger door.

"Who do we have here?"

Kirk, this is Jason. I've told him about the big ranch where he would be staying for a while."

"Did he get to see the horses as you came in?"

"Yes, he said he'd never seen a horse, except on TV."

"Well come on in so he can meet Mamma Katie."

Jason was quiet but didn't seem as timid as Timmy had been. He was looking all around. When he spotted Noah, his eyes lit up, and he asked if it was okay for him to pet the dog.

"Sure, it's okay. In fact, he can follow us in the house. You can play with him while Miss Betty talks to us."

Betty relayed all the details she knew (and was allowed to tell) about his mother, Joyce. Katie hadn't had the chance to tell Kirk that Jason was whipped by Bryce, just as Brandon was, so when that came up in the conversation, Kirk's eyes narrowed, his shoulders straightened, his lips tightened, and he glared at Betty. "You mean that—I started to call him a Bozo, but there is nothing funny about that man—you mean he has done the same thing to this boy?"

"I'm afraid so," Betty said.

"Why is he still walking free? Shouldn't he be locked up for what he's done?"

"You know Denise won't press charges, and it appears to me that this mother won't either."

"Can't DFS press charges?"

"Kirk, I suspect that just may happen. It's costing taxpayers' money. Jason will be assigned a guardian ad litem, so I look for him to file charges on behalf of the child."

Katie asked if Jason had started kindergarten. Betty said she didn't know. "Let's just ask him."

Noah and Jason were chasing each other around the big room. Betty touched his shoulder as he came by. "Jason, do you go to school?"

Jason stopped, stared at Betty as though he thought he was in trouble. "I went one time, and my mom moved, so I never did get to go back."

Katie jumped at her chance, "Well, Jason, you're gonna get to go to school now while you're here at the ranch." She turned to Kirk, "By the way, where is Brandon?"

"He's finishing the cleanup of the milk station. He should be here any minute. I asked if he wanted to postpone finishing up and ride up here with me, but he said he'd go ahead, finish and just walk home."

"Why don't you take Jason up to meet Brandon while Betty and I visit? That way Brandon will have a ride home."

"Good idea. I'll take the pickup. We don't have an extra helmet."

"Let him wear mine; it might fit."

"I don't think so; we'd better take the truck." Kirk nodded toward the side of the house where the pickup was parked. "Brandon's keeps asking me if he can drive. I think I'll see how he does."

"You've got to be kidding! He's not old enough."

"Awh, Kate, it's just here on the farm. He's already driven the old tractor. A farm boy oughta know how to drive a truck, don't you think?"

"You just make sure you've got your foot ready to hit the brake." She glared at him. "But I want no part of this. I still say he's way too young."

Katie searched Betty's eyes for her take on it. Betty let a tiny grin escape her lips and shook her head. "Boys will be boys," she whispered. "But, for the record, I didn't hear any of that conversation."

As they were leaving, Betty went back to her Buick and brought in a small plastic shopping bag of Jason's clothes that Joyce had sent—two pairs of underwear and one shirt. "Katie, do you think any of those things I brought out months ago will fit Jason?"

"Maybe. If not, I've held on to most of the things Brandon has outgrown. They should fit him."

The two talked for just a few minutes, but Betty told Katie that she wanted to be gone when the guys returned. "I hate to say this, but I would rather not have to say goodbye to Jason. I've seen my share of child abuse cases over the years, but for two children from different homes to be beaten to a pulp like this by the *same man*, it is really getting to me. This old grandma just wants to go kick his.... Okay, see, I do need to go. Call if you need anything."

Jason's injuries were almost identical to those Brandon had received. This time Katie went ahead and took him into the clinic to see Dr. Chandler to start with. A couple of stitches were needed and prescription strength antibiotic ointment was given.

Jason seemed to be in awe of everything at the ranch. He'd asked to ride a horse, but Kirk told him that would have to wait 'til his injuries healed. He sat quietly in the barn door and watched Brandon as he did his milking chores. He loved the outdoors. Sometimes Katie would see him standing out in the front yard, staring at the big trees or sitting beside the little creek that trickled over rocks along the north side of the house. One evening the little improvised Childers family sat out on the back patio. Jason sat gazing at the night sky and told them he had never seen stars before. "We don't have stars where I live."

"Oh they're there alright," Katie said, "you just can't see them because of the city lights."

Brandon took to his big brother role and reveled in sharing his vast knowledge of ranch life with Jason. The boys were good for each other.

Katie knew reading might be a problem for the boy, as it had been for Brandon. After quizzing him a bit, she learned that he had yet to learn his alphabet. He couldn't even count to ten. He had trouble naming all of the basic colors. Katie's job of tutoring was starting all over. The books they had bought were still filling that bookcase Kirk had built, as well as the two window sills in the foot thick walls of Brandon's room. Brandon's favorites held their own special place under his bed within his easy reach. Katie started with picture books for Jason. She brought out her packs of flash cards for numbers, colors, and the alphabet. Then she remembered Kirk had bought an electronic flash card game, knowing that would be more appealing to a child than the old fashioned paper flash cards. When she enrolled Jason in kindergarten, she explained that he was a foster child and had been deprived of any early pre-school education. The teacher knew Katie from the praises of other elementary teachers that Katie had subbed for. She said she was confident Jason would do just fine with the good at-home parental help Katie would provide.

Brandon took up some of the tutoring responsibilities of Jason after Katie explained to him that the picture books were about all that he could handle for now. The picture books would help him develop a love for books that would migrate into a pleasant experience of actually reading the stories later.

CHAPTER 37

The apartment manager walked into number Two-Oh-Five to find it in shambles. Several pieces of furniture had been abandoned there. A huge bleach spot in the center of the living room carpet had become the main focus of the room. There were dirty dishes piled in the sink and surrounding counter top, and the fridge reeked with spoiled food. It appeared the trash had never been taken out. It was spilling out of the trash can. Some had even been pushed over to the corner on the floor where a roach made his way out of the debris to the edge of the cabinet. Dirty clothes covered the floor in the bedroom.

After receiving the eviction notice, Denise had abandoned everything and moved in with Jackson. She had met this man at the bus station downtown, where she was about to board a bus back to New Jersey. She had hoped to look up one of her friends that she'd met when she lived there with her first husband, and just hoped that she'd be willing to take her in until she could find a job. Denise wasn't sure if *Jackson* was a first name or a last name, but everyone just called him Jackson.

She got up the nerve to tell Jackson about Brandon. Even though he had four children by his ex-wife, Jackson suddenly became interested in Denise's story of Brandon. His ex-wife had gained full custody of their children and moved to California, leaving him virtually no way of having contact with his kids.

Jackson had managed to get the house, along with the mortgage, in his divorce. It was a thirty-year-old three bedroom ranch with an attached two-car garage, typical of homes in the older part of Oklahoma City. Denise was happy. She had a roof over her head, food in the house, and a set of wheels. Jackson was good to her, and Bryce was out of her life. But Jackson didn't last long. Within a week of moving in, Denise realized this man was not who he pretended to be. A more recent wife appeared on the scene and Denise took Jackson's old car and moved out—or rather, into the car.

On the other side of town, after moving in with Joyce, Bryce Collier had given up on Denise Brewer. He admitted to Joyce that Denise was one wildcat he just couldn't tame. Joyce knew she now had her ticket to a full time food pantry. She knew Bryce wasn't her idea of a man to spend the rest of her life with, but she kept telling herself that he loved her, especially now that Denise was out of the picture. But now she found herself faced with quite a dilemma—keep Bryce Collier and lose her son, or lose Bryce and get her son back. For Joyce Richards, the choice was simple. She needed a man in her life.

Yes, they fought. And yes, Bryce often lost his temper and went into a rampage, throwing things, including her. The huge hole decorating the living room wall, and outlining Joyce's image, was evidence of his rage. Once he even beat Jason's dog with a two by six, leaving the dog to die in its own pool of blood. But, hey, the dog just wouldn't stop barking.

The violence escalated, and three times she had called nine-one-one, only to retract and immediately call them back to dismiss her allegations as a mistake.

Joyce knew it wasn't every little girl's dream for the perfect family, but still it was a good arrangement. Bryce needed a place to stay, and Joyce needed a man. But mostly she needed the meal ticket that came with the man.

CHAPTER 38

It was a warm Saturday afternoon, following a brief shower—enough to track in mud. Kirk kicked his shoes off at the door and called for Brandon and Jason. "Hey guys, you wanna ride down to the pond and get in some fishing?"

Brandon shot out of his room and wasted no time answering. "Yeah, let's go!"

He turned back and saw Jason still sitting on the edge of the bed, looking down at his feet. "What's wrong, Jason? Haven't you ever been fishin'?"

"I don't know how."

"Come on; I'll teach you. It's easy. Piece o' cake—nuthin' to it."

Kirk and Brandon had made a worm bed by salvaging an old rusted out water trough. They had dug out an area in the ground to drop the bottom twelve inches of the tank into. Then Kirk added horse manure, some of Katie's potting soil, and Brandon cut up cardboard into small pieces, soaked them and then wrung them out. This was added to the bed and a pocket of food scraps had been added on one end of the tank to partially decay and provide food for the five pounds of red wiggler worms Kirk bought at a feed store in town.

"Hey guys, pull the tarp back, and let's see if those worms are happy with their new home."

Kirk took one of Katie's little garden tools and scratched down into the surface of the organic bedding material. Brandon squealed as several of the fat squigglers surfaced.

"Okay, guys, reach in there and grab some and drop 'em in this coffee can," Kirk said. "Be sure to get a little of the soil with it to keep 'em moist so they won't die before we get 'em on our hooks.

Brandon knelt down by the tub and buried both hands into the soil, filtering several worms through his fingers. Jason just stood there, staring into the bed of fat jellied worms. Brandon noticed and said, "Come on Jason; they won't bite."

When they had the can half full, Kirk told the boys that was enough. "Let's grab our fishing gear and jump in the truck."

Brandon popped up, "Can we ride in the pickup bed?"

Kirk looked at Brandon, winked, and said, "Sure, but one of us has gotta drive." Brandon gave Kirk a playful shove on his shoulder and Kirk returned the nudge, saying, "I guess that would leave me, uh?"

Brandon was first to crawl over the tailgate. He then reached his hand over for Jason.

"You guys have to sit your butts flat down in the pickup bed." With his side window down, Kirk headed toward the pond.

The boys were chattering like the flock of cedar waxwings in the tree last winter by the back door. A big Angus bull was pawing the ground fifty feet away. Jason stood up. Brandon scolded him, "Get back down on your bottom and hold onto the side! If Kirk hits a bump, you'll bounce out of this truck like that super ball we were playing with this morning." Jason grinned and obeyed his big brother.

As soon as Kirk pulled up beside the pond, Brandon jumped up, grabbed the rods and reels with one hand and the coffee can full of worms with the other. Then he told Jason to crawl out and he'd hand him the worms.

Kirk watched as Brandon showed Jason how to bait his hook. Then he handed the rod and reel to him, stood behind him, and grabbed

Jason's right arm to bring the rod back for the cast. The first time the hook landed only a few feet from the shore. "Watch me," Brandon said. He took the rod, reached back, and gave it a quick swing toward the water. This time the lead weight and hook, followed by the red and white bobber, sailed out a good twenty feet before dropping into the pond.

He handed the rod to Jason and set about baiting his own hook. But before he finished, he noticed Jason's bobber go under. "Pull back! Set the hook."

Jason stood there staring like a deer caught in headlights. Finally he said, "I don't know how."

Brandon dropped his rod, ran and grabbed Jason's. "We may have lost him." Brandon did a quick yank backward on the rod; then started reeling. "Nope, he's on there!" He handed the rod back to Jason and told him to continue to reel him in. "He's all yours; bring him on in."

Brandon went back to baiting his own hook.

Kirk looked up just in time to see a big mouth bass leap out of the water; it then took a powerful dive back into the pond. The red and white bobber disappeared. Jason was holding tight onto the rod with his finger hooked around the finger hold like Brandon had taught him. Suddenly the boy's body propelled forward with incredible torque. Jason belly flopped into the mossy water.

Brandon looked up, saw the splash, and dropped his hook and worm. "Dang!" he blurted; then he jumped to his feet, but Kirk was already on the move.

Kirk had jumped over the can of worms, ran over, and was squatting down, grabbing Jason's legs. He then turned loose, stepped into the water, reached his arms around the boy's chest, and pulled him up out of the pond.

Jason coughed, sputtered, and started to cry.

"Are you okay, pal?"

A big glob of green moss was hanging from Jason's hair. Brandon laughed. "Get your camera, Kirk. I want Katie to see this." Kirk pulled out his cell phone and snapped a picture while Brandon waded into the water and recovered the rod and reel. The bass had escaped.

Still dripping wet and the initial fear factor gone, Jason laughed and wanted to try again. This time he baited his own hook, took up the rod and reel, reared back with it as he was asking Brandon, "Like this?"

Before Brandon could answer, Jason's line was being thrust over the water. About two minutes later, his bobber disappeared under the surface again. Jason spread one leg back behind the other to brace himself this time, set the hook, and started reeling in his catch.

As the fish came closer to shore, Kirk yelled, "Hey, man, you got yourself a nice big bass there! Bring him on in." Kirk then reached down and readied himself for grabbing the line when the bass reached the shore.

Jason was grinning from ear to ear.

Kirk patted him on the back. "You just caught us some supper, pal!"

Another hour produced two more bass, smaller than Jason's. Brandon had caught both. By now the sun was beaming down and Kirk asked if the boys were ready to head back. "If we stay out here much longer, my head's gonna be blistered."

"There you go, forgetting to wear your hat again." Brandon grinned. "Come on, Jason, Kirk's just mad 'cause he didn't catch anything."

Back at the milk equipment room, Jason got another lesson. He learned how to clean fish. The fish were each split open, and the heads and tails removed, along with the guts. They dropped them in an old rusty, never used, milk pail. Then Kirk showed Jason how to fillet the fish. When they were finished, the stainless steel sink and surrounding countertop was washed down, sanitized, dried, and ready for Brandon to use to clean up the separator equipment at the next use.

Brandon shook Kirk's hand. "Major fish surgery accomplished!"

Kirk held on to that young innocent hand. "Yeah, or autopsy," he said.

Kirk stood back for a minute, thinking about the little boy he had come to know and love. *Brandon has come so far from where he was when he came to us. We've seen a total transformation in this kid. He's smart, he's happy, he's fun to be around, and he's no longer bashful. Now if I can just brand Jason with a similar outcome.*

Katie fried potatoes and made a slaw to go with the bass. At the supper table, Kirk pulled out his cell phone, retrieved the picture, held it up to her, "This is what it took for us to have fish for supper tonight."

Katie held the phone in her hand, stared at the picture of Jason, draped in moss. She shook with laughter and finally pushed herself away from the table. Still holding the phone with the picture displayed, a tear escaped from her eye—a happy tear.

Kirk took the phone from her and scrolled to the next picture with Jason proudly holding up his first ever bass. "Jason caught this one himself and reeled it in all by himself—no help from us!"

"Oh, Jason! That's a nice one," Katie said.

Brandon grabbed his fork and held it up in a *let-me-speak-now* gesture. "Okay, now take a picture of us *eating* that bass."

That night, Katie snuggled up to the man she had become so proud of. "Kirk, you are so good with the boys. They are both so fortunate to have you with them at this time in their lives."

He whispered, "Okay, I'm honored that you feel that way, but look what you've done with Brandon. He's gone from a total non-reader to an avid reader. I can't seem to buy him enough books to satisfy his appetite. And look at what his grades have done. He's good at math as well as reading. You deserve big kudos for that."

"Thanks, but you are the father both of these boys never had. Maybe I can teach them how to read, but you can teach them how to become men!"

"I'm privileged to be placed in that position. There's more to this life than milking cows, mending fences, and paying the bills. God has given me an assignment that I am glad to accept with these boys."

"Kirk, every boy should have a father like you!"

CHAPTER 39

Betty made two more trips to Joyce's home. She was determined there would not be a parent-child visit until she was assured that Bryce Collier was no longer in Joyce's life. Joyce was still protective of the beast, even though she said that he had moved on. Betty knew it was a lie the minute she saw the fast lube uniform shirt lying on the floor beside the bed. The pocket was monogrammed "Bryce." She stared at Joyce, waiting for the woman to look her in the eyes. "Joyce, this is all up to you. Your son will stay where he is until you send Bryce packing! Then he's got to stay gone and out of your life!"

Joyce's response was almost like a defense lawyer, minus any words more than the usual four or five letters long. "You are trying to make Bryce into a criminal. He's a good man and deserves a fair chance."

"No, Joyce, he doesn't deserve a fair chance, not when it comes to beating small boys. And yes, that is criminal! But you know; I may not have to worry about that too much longer. I expect he'll be spending a long time in a six by eight cell for what he's done to these little guys."

"I'm telling you, Mrs. Sawyer, Bryce was only—"

"And I'm telling you I have to leave now. You know how to contact me if anything changes."

Katie had wondered how long it would take. Jason was starting to miss his mother. The new had worn off of ranch life for him. He no longer played with Noah; he'd lost all interest in any of the picture books; and now he'd lost his appetite. The fresh-out-of-the-oven homemade cinnamon roll sat cold and untouched. "Jason, I know something is wrong. Do you want to talk about it?"

With his head ducked, he whispered, "No."

"Come on; it'll do you good to tell me what you are feeling."

"I miss my Mamma." A tear dripped down onto his shirt.

"Oh, honey, I know you do. Can you tell me a little bit about your Mamma?"

The tear had now produced a sniffle. "I just miss her. I'm sorry I was bad and had to be taken away from her."

"Jason, honey, you were not bad. It was not your fault…"

"Yes it was! I was smartin' back at Bryce."

"Jason, you weren't separated from your mother because you had smarted back to anyone. You were brought here to get you away from him. Those deep cuts and lashes on your back and legs are *his* fault. He was wrong to beat you like that."

"Will I ever get to see my Mamma again?"

"Jason, she will have to make Bryce move out before you can go back home. He would just beat you again, and we don't want that to ever happen again."

"If he don't move out, can my Mamma come and live here?"

"If he doesn't move out, she will have to find a new place to live, but she wouldn't be allowed to live here. Look, I don't think you should have to worry about it. Your Mamma will work it out."

Jason wiped his eyes on his shirt sleeve. "Couldn't I just tell that lady again that I'm sorry and I won't sass back to Mamma again?"

"Jason, please understand, this was not your fault. You did nothing wrong. Most all little boys sass their moms at times. This wasn't your fault!"

Kirk came in and saw the tears. He reached down and grabbed up Jason in his arms, and squeezed him tight. "Hey pal, let's go for a ride on the four-wheeler, just you and me. I wanna show you a brand new calf that was just born a few minutes ago." Kirk borrowed Brandon's helmet for Jason to wear, strapped it on him, and then headed for the ATV. "Hold on tight."

The cow and her new calf were just east of the barn. Kirk pulled up, stopped, and held his hand out for Jason to climb down. He took a few steps forward when Kirk put his arm on the boy's shoulder. "Maybe we shouldn't go any closer. She won't want us to come any nearer to her baby."

"Why's she licking him?"

"That's what Mamma cows do; it's their way of saying 'I love you...'" He immediately regretted those words.

Jason ducked his head. Barely audible, he whispered, "I love my Mamma. I wish she was here."

Kirk took his hat off and wiped his forehead. "Why don't you talk to God about that? You know, pray about it—He can fix anything."

"I don't know how."

"Hey pal, it's easy. Just talk to Him like he was standing here in front of you." Kirk started, paused, and then—much to his surprise—Jason did just that. He started talking to God, asking Him to take him back to his Mamma.

The cow struggled, but she managed to get up on her feet. Kirk knew this was good. He had worried when she had just laid there. That would mean problems. His attention refocused on Jason. "That was a good prayer. See, you can talk to Jesus, just like you would talk to anyone else. He wants to be your friend."

"Will Jesus talk to my Mamma?"

"She'll have to be quiet and listen, but yes, He will talk to her."

"If Jesus talks to Mamma, I hope He'll tell her I'm sorry I sassed her, and I won't do it again."

"Jason, she already knows that."

"But He should tell her anyway."

"He'll do that. He will."

A loud round of thunder roared over the horizon. Jason's eyes were wide when he looked up at Kirk. "Wow! That was loud. I hope she heard Him."

Kirk laughed and ruffed up Jason's blond hair. "Come on kid, I think that might have been telling us to get home."

As they were pulling up to the house, the rain started. There was no warning with sporadic raindrops. It was an instant downpour. Kirk opened the back door and pushed Jason inside. He looked down at the flagstone floor, already pooled with water from both of them standing there.

Katie heard them come in and peeped around the corner to see. "You guys look like drowned rats! Hang on; let me get you a couple of towels."

The rest of the afternoon was spent at the big dining room table around a game of Monopoly. Brandon had no consideration for the rest of them and managed to buy up Boardwalk and Park Place, along with Pennsylvania Avenue and the railroads. Jason had to have a bit of help when it was his turn. Kirk counted the money for him, and Katie tried to clue him in on what he should do when he landed on a spot. But Jason's attention drifted, and Kirk knew his mind was several miles away.

When it was time to go do the milking, Brandon invited him to come along. Jason shook his head and trudged toward his room. Kirk and Brandon climbed in the pickup and headed toward the milk barn. The thunder continued, and Kirk wondered if Jason thought that God was still talking to his Mamma.

❦

While they were gone, Betty called to see how Jason was doing. "Well, Betty, it seems like the honeymoon is over. He is missing his Mamma. I can't get him to eat much, and he seems a bit lethargic."

"I was afraid of that. Are those cuts healing up okay?"

"Yes, they're looking good. We've kept them plastered with that antibiotic ointment Dr. Chandler prescribed. The stitches will be coming out soon. Kirk took him down to see one of the newborn calves, thinking that might get his mind off his mom."

"Katie, I wish I had two dozen foster parents like you and Kirk. Maybe then I could sleep at night. I worry about some of these kids. Sometimes I get the feeling that I may be placing the child in a home that's not much better than the one he was removed from. No sleeping pill will erase that from my mind."

"Has anyone ever thought about a privately sponsored or a faith-based organization to recruit good foster parents? I have to admit, the foster parenting classes that Kirk and I attended were cold and never stressed the importance of *loving* these kids. It was just all about what we could and could not do to keep ourselves and the Department out of lawsuits. We need parents that consider foster parenting to be their mission. What we don't need is a person that sees foster parenting as a paycheck, as pitifully low as it is. Loving a hurting child is far more important than looking forward to that little end-of-the-month stipend they receive for each child."

"Katie, I think that is a great idea. Of course that organization would have to be sanctioned by the Department, and there would have to be mandatory training."

"Sure. But I think a faith-based organization responsible for recruiting foster parent homes would come up with better quality homes. Those people would be doing it as their way to give back, not to receive."

"I like that!"

CHAPTER 40

Betty's supervisor paraded in and slapped a legal document on her desk. She glanced only at the top page. "What's this?"

"A present from Denise Brewer."

"This doesn't sound good. Should I start gathering up my personal items and turn in my key?"

"No, I don't think that's going to be necessary now."

As Betty skimmed through the three page document, she was relieved to learn that Denise's lawyer had dropped the case. The reasons given were that she no longer showed interest and had failed to meet her obligations with respect to financial arrangements with the law firm. "In other words," Betty said, "Garrison Downing never got paid. That figures!" She handed the document back to her supervisor. "Amazing! It took three pages to say they had dropped the case!"

Kirk finished his chores for the day, kicked off his boots by the back door, and made his way into the big room. "Where are the boys? Brandon never came down to the milk barn like he usually does."

"He and Jason are in his room." Katie placed a package of ground beef in the microwave to thaw. "He's been so wrapped up in reading to Jason; I think he forgot about the milking."

"That's okay. I don't mind doing it myself, but I just enjoy having him around." Kirk headed for his big La-Z-Boy recliner. "What book is he reading to Jason?"

"When I checked in last, it was *Arthur's Honey Bear.*"

Kirk reclined the big chair and flipped on the evening news. As he sat there listening to the local reporter, he suddenly popped the recliner back up. "Oh my, God—No!"

"Kirk, what's wrong?"

"Didn't you hear that?"

"No, this microwave is too noisy."

"Honey, we need to have Brandon take Jason outside for a few minutes."

"Why?"

Kirk was already headed toward Brandon's room. After he had convinced Brandon to take Jason outside and play with Noah for a while, he came back in to the kitchen, hugged Katie, and relayed the details as best he could from the news report. "I just heard on the news that a Joyce Richards was found dead in her southwest Oklahoma City home. She had bruises on her neck and it appeared she had been strangled. Her boyfriend is being held for questioning in her death."

"Kirk, that does sound like Jason's mother. Wasn't her name *Joyce?*"

"Yeah, I'm sure that's what you told me, and I remember you saying that she lived over in the southwest part of the city."

"Honey, if this is Jason's mother, we cannot tell him. He is still very much attached and misses her. We're going to have to get some professional counseling for him."

"Well, Katie, *Joyce Richards* is a fairly common name. Let's hope it's not his mother. But you know, maybe we should try to keep the boys away from the TV anytime local news is on. I wouldn't want the kid to find out that way. That little boy is way too fragile to be subjected to a sudden upheaval like that. He's already pretty unstable; this might push him over the edge."

❧

The next morning, while the boys were still sleeping, Katie turned on the early edition of the local news.

A southwest Oklahoma City woman was found dead in her home yesterday. Joyce Richards appeared to have been strangled, and her boyfriend is being held for questioning in the incident. Neighbors have told KOKY that they had witnessed several incidents of violence lately from the backyard of Miss Richards' home, one in which a small boy had been severely beaten by the boyfriend. The neighbor said she had reported that incident to the Department of Family Services and believed the little boy had been removed from the home. DHS has refused to comment at this time.

Katie picked up the phone and dialed Betty Sawyer.

"Betty, please tell me that was not our little Jason's mother I just heard about on KOKY."

"Katie, I'm afraid it is. I was just getting ready to call you."

"Betty!" There was a pause. "I know…you told me that Bryce was the boyfriend that whipped Jason. Do you suppose it might have been him that kill—"

"I'm not allowed to comment on that."

"Okay—I understand. Now, what are we going to do about telling Jason?"

"How would you feel about telling him yourself?"

"Oh, Betty, I don't know. What's this going to do to that kid? He's already unstable from being removed from his mom. This is going to do the little fellow in!"

"I assume he's not heard the news on TV."

"That's right. We've kept the boys away from the TV for that reason."

"Katie, we need to get some professional help involved with this. As soon as we hang up, I'll make an appointment for him with a counselor. It might be better if both you and Kirk were there with him. He's going to need some good warm hugs that you two are so good at. It might be best for Brandon to not go with you to the psychologist's office. If you need me to, I could probably arrange some respite care. Brandon's not old enough to be left alone."

"First let me see if my parents would be free to sit with him while we're away. You know, they went through the classes and got approved as foster parents just so they could step in for us if needed. Brandon loves them. Dad brought him a little die-cast replica of their Mustang. Maybe they'll be able to come out to the ranch then, or we can take him into them. Besides, I may need some support from my own mother to help me get through this. What an awful thing to have to tell a child!"

"Okay, well, let me know if I need to arrange any respite care."

Katie talked to Kirk about her conversation with Betty. "I'm pretty sure it is Bryce that they are questioning in Joyce's death."

"You're right. I figured it was the bully!"

"The reporter on KOKY said this morning that it's the station's policy to not disclose a name until the person has been charged with the crime."

"Wow! This is getting even worse. Brandon is now involved."

"Honey, what's he gonna think?"

"If I know Brandon, he'll convict him on the spot."

"Kirk, we both have a big job ahead of us. These boys are going to need us more than ever."

"You're right, but it may also work to their benefit that they have each other."

Katie called her mother and explained their situation. Carol Reynolds told her they would just reschedule anything that might be on their calendar on the day she needed them.

"So would you want us to bring Brandon in to you?"

"No, you'll have your hands full. Besides, we love coming out to the ranch, and Brandon is a jewel of a kid. We both enjoy him. Who knows, Lynn may have a couple more of those little cars to bring out for Brandon and Jason. His collection in the downstairs den is getting out of hand—looks like a mall parking lot there in that huge display case of his."

"Thanks, Mom."

"No problem; just let us know when."

Katie uncovered the old Remington and sat down to put some of her thoughts on paper. Her idea of writing children's books was fine, but somehow she was now being drawn away from make-believe characters to real life situations that kids find themselves in the middle of. *I have to find a way to incorporate some loveable little imaginary characters into these unvarnished circumstances kids face in today's world.*

Her thoughts were again interrupted by the phone ringing. "Katie, I've got an appointment set for you and Kirk to bring Jason to the Brimm Institute on Northwest Sixty-Third tomorrow morning at eleven. Will that work for you?"

"Sure, I'll just need to make sure Mom and Dad are okay with that time. She said they would come out to the ranch to stay with Brandon."

"If it's a problem, let me know."

After several more phone calls in a row, Katie slapped the dust cover back on the old Remington.

CHAPTER 41

Lynn and Carol Reynolds arrived at the ranch about nine-thirty the next morning. Brandon ran into Lynn's arms and held on tight. Carol knelt down on the floor next to Jason. "You are one cute little guy. I love those boots you have on. Did Kirk buy those for you?"

He smiled and shook his head. "Yeah, and he got me a new cowboy hat too."

"I thought that would've been Kirk's doing," Carol said.

Lynn whispered to Katie, "I've got a couple of little cars for the boys. Should I wait 'til you get back?"

"No, Pops, I think it might be good for Jason to have it to take with him."

Lynn backtracked out to their Mustang and brought in two 1:18 scale die-cast cars still in their original boxes. He looked at Brandon and asked, "Okay, who gets which one?"

Brandon took one look and chose the little '66 Candy Apple red Mustang fastback. Jason's eyes lit up when he was handed the aqua and white '57 Corvette.

Kirk placed his hand on Lynn's shoulder. "I think you just made their day!"

Jason was still clutching his car as they marched into the Brimm Institute. Katie was dreading this time and wondered if Betty had informed the psychologist of Jason's situation.

Once seated, the psychologist made Jason her friend, asking about the prized little Corvette he was holding. She then got him to talk about his mother, moving from general talk to eventually approaching the dreaded subject. Katie and Kirk sat there, amazed at how the lady eased into it. Then she asked Jason if he believed a person might go to Heaven when they got old and died.

Jason looked up from his little car and said, "My grandpa went to Heaven."

"How do you know that?"

"Well, 'cause my mom told me so."

"Do you want to go to Heaven when you die?"

Jason thought for a moment, and then said, "I guess so."

From that point the psychologist eased into a conversation explaining that his mom may have gone to visit with Jason's grandpa, and she wouldn't be back. Jason sat perfectly still—stiff. The finality of the psychologist's statement hung in the air. Kirk reached over and gave him a big hug, and Katie laid her head on top of Jason's. He seemed to understand the significance of the psychologist's words, and a few tears trickled down his cheeks, but he sat statuesque, saying nothing.

While Katie dabbed his eyes with a tissue, the lady reached behind her and pulled out a large coffee table style book, turned the pages to a beautiful color picture of a garden-like setting. In the center of the picture stood an image of a person on a beautiful manicured lawn with their back turned. They appeared to be staring at the horizon beyond. It wasn't clear if the person was male or female. The psychologist scratched the surface of the open page, leaned over her desk, and held the book in front of Jason. "Smell this. What does it smell like?"

"It smells like when Kirk mowed the grass in the front yard." Still, a tear dropped onto his little yellow and navy Rugby shirt.

"That's right! Do you think your mom would have liked that smell?"

"She might—if she didn't have to mow that grass herself. She doesn't like that."

Laughter filled the room. From that point on, the psychologist made laughter the focus of the remainder of the visit. She then motioned for Kirk to take Jason out of the room. She told Katie, "There will be more tears to come in the next few weeks—even months. I'll need to see him again soon. My secretary will set up your next appointment."

Katie stood and stared. "You were amazing! Brilliant!"

She put her hand on Katie's shoulder. "It's not over. This little boy is still in for some difficult times. Just do your best with him, and I'll see him again soon."

The difficult time was sooner than expected. Kirk pushed the center console up and buckled in Jason between himself and Katie in the front seat of the truck so he wouldn't have to sit alone in the back. Jason cried most of the way home. Katie couldn't help it; she cried too.

Kirk and Katie were still very careful to keep the boys away from any local news. Jason didn't need any more details at this time. KOKY was now reporting that Bryce Collier had been charged in the strangulation death of Joyce Richards. He had been caught in Brownsville, Texas trying to buy a fake I.D. He was now being held without bond in the Oklahoma City jail.

Jason had been quiet since the meeting at the Brimm Institute. More than once, Katie had noticed a tear trickling down his face. She wanted to say something to comfort him, but each time she tried, he turned away and was gone.

"Honey, maybe he just needs time to think this through for himself," Kirk said.

"Kirk! A five-year-old boy is not capable of thinking this through for himself. This is way more than he can handle on his own."

"You're probably right, but this is what I'm gonna do. I'm gonna spend some extra time with him—just me and him. I'll not talk about his mother unless he brings up the subject. I think what he needs most is to know that we are here for him. We'll talk about what he wants to talk about, with extra hugs thrown in. I have a feeling he may have been talking to Brandon about Joyce already. I'll try to find out this evening down at the milk barn when we're alone. Jason still wants nothing to do with those nasty cows."

"Well, I don't blame him; they are pretty yucky."

After the milking machines are turned off, the milk barn can sometimes be compared to a barber shop—lots of guy talk, and most of it is pretty frivolous. But this time Brandon opened up to Kirk with some serious words. "Jason misses his mom, but he says he also misses his grandma."

"Where does his grandma live?"

"He doesn't know, but he says it is another state, like maybe Arizona or Albuquerque." Brandon snickered. "I told him Albuquerque isn't a state; it's a city. So he decided it was Arizona where she lived. He wants to go live with her."

"Does he ever ask how his mother died? Isn't he curious?"

"He thinks Bryce beat her again. He saw him throw her into the wall one time and then put his hands around her neck and almost choked her. He told me that he thought Bryce did that because his mom had sassed him—just like he had sassed Bryce."

"Brandon, the police think it was Bryce; he's in jail now and charged with her murder. If he brings it up again, it's okay if you tell him that. Tomorrow is Saturday, and I'm gonna spend some time with him—just me and him. Maybe I'll take him for a ride down to that old deer stand. Do you mind if I let him ride Puzzle?"

"He can ride Puzzle, but you might have to adjust those stirrups for him. They're almost too long for me, and his legs are shorter than mine."

After a late breakfast, Kirk and Jason headed for the horses. Jason wanted to know why Brandon wasn't coming with them. "Brandon's got some homework, and Miss Katie's gonna help him with it."

"So what horse am I going to ride?"

"You can ride Puzzle. Brandon's already said that would be okay with him. Oh, and here's an extra hat you can wear."

"I don't like that kind of hat. I wear baseball hats."

Kirk saddled up Puzzle and adjusted the stirrups. He sat Jason in the saddle to measure, and then had to adjust them again. He then saddled Dandy for himself and handed Puzzle's reins to Jason. Kirk noticed Jason's eyes, and they told him Jason was a little apprehensive about being on a horse. "This your first time?"

Jason didn't answer but nodded his head somewhat and looked down, holding the reins and grasping the saddle horn in a death grip. Kirk put his hand on Jason's shoulder. "Hey pal, loosen up. Puzzle is very, very gentle. She knows she's carrying a little boy and she'll be extra careful."

They rode side-by-side down through the big bluestem grass, with Noah running fifty feet ahead of them. Farther on, Noah spooked a covey of quail. Jason instinctively ducked as the birds flew overhead, then to the right of them. Several minutes passed and Jason said, "Kirk, Do you think my grandma knows where I am?"

"I don't know, Jason. Do you know where she is?"

"I think it's Arizona."

"Did she ever come to Oklahoma to see you?"

"She came once, but she and my mom got in an argument, and she left."

"Was your grandma good to you?"

"Yeah, she bought me some new jeans and shirts—oh, and underwear. And some shoes too."

"What's her name?"

"I don't know. I just called her Grandma, and mom called her *Mother*. But she made it sound like she didn't even like her."

Just then an unexpected flood of tears rolled down Jason's cheeks. Kirk pulled Dandy over next to Puzzle, leaned over and put his arm around the boy. With his other hand, he reached into his back pocket, pulled out a red bandana, and wiped Jason's tears. "Hey pal, it's okay to cry; it'll do you good. Someday you'll see that life is much better than you see it right now."

"Why do you think that?"

"Because I can see you—six feet tall, big and strong and with a wife and kids of your own. You will be a good husband, and you'll be a very good daddy."

Jason stared into Kirk's eyes. "Just like you?"

"Yeah, just like me—without the cowboy hat."

Jason grinned and looked ahead. "Where are we going now?"

"Come on, you'll see."

Soon they rode into the trees and Kirk pointed out the old tree stand the hunters had used in the past. "You wanna climb up a bit and peek inside?"

"NO!"

"No? Why not?"

"I got in trouble for climbing a tree in our backyard."

"Well, hey, you won't get in trouble with me. Come on, I'll be right behind you and holding you as you climb up. Just don't go inside that old shanty; it's nasty in there."

Jason hesitated, but started up when Kirk touched his back. When he got to the floor and peeked over he said, "This looks like Bryce has been here."

"Why would you say that?"

"All those beer cans and cigarette butts."

"Okay, well come on down. We don't need to see any more of that." They rode back up to the barn, unsaddled, and led the horses to the water trough.

"I wish my mom could have seen that."

"What are you talking about?"

"The quail. My mom loved birds." He looked straight at Kirk. "Do they have birds in Heaven?"

"Well, I'm sure they do—birds of all kinds, colors, and sizes."

After a long pause, Jason said, "Good."

CHAPTER 42

Denise Brewer sat in the last of six evening classes that she was required to attend after her accident. Since this was her first DWI, and with nothing else on her record, the judge gave her a short period of community service with the requirement that she attend a class designed for first offenders, as well as mandatory and regular attendance at AA meetings. The wrecked, but still drivable, old Plymouth Valiant that Bryce had bought her had been impounded after the accident. She hadn't seen him in over a month. So now she had no car, was without a job, and was being evicted from her apartment. Happy to have the boring classes behind her, she and a newfound friend from the AA meeting bounced out of the room, got in his car, and drove away.

Katie was back at her old Remington when the phone rang. Kirk answered, took the phone to Katie, held his hand over the mouthpiece, and said, "It's Betty. She's saying Denise wants another parent visit."

Before she took the handset she said, "Kirk, that is just nuts! The woman has shown no interest for several months and now she wants to see him."

"Yeah, I know. I guess we have to jump through the hoops one more time. Here, just talk to her. I'm afraid I'd be a bit rude."

After hanging up, it was clear to Katie that Betty was on the same page as Kirk. She told Katie that she couldn't believe Denise would suddenly show interest in her son after being so aloof with him during the previous visits. Nevertheless, a visit was scheduled for three o'clock the next day.

Kirk and Katie, along with both boys, were a few minutes early. Katie was visiting with Betty's petite little secretary, Jennifer. Just out of ear shot of the boys, Kirk and Betty were exchanging their mutual feelings for Denise's unexpected and impulsive interest in her son.

At exactly three o'clock, the door swung open and Denise promenaded through, looking like a model straight off a cover of *Vogue*. Her Irish red shoulder length crimped hairstyle framed her oval face that had been expertly retouched to perfection in color and shading. She was wearing a chocolate brown Valentino knit dress with a Burberry Brit double breasted peacoat slung over her right arm. She carried a leopard print handbag by Coach. Katie noticed the huge diamond solitaire on her left hand. She was followed by a man wearing a Giorgio Armani suit and a horse bit pattern silk tie by Gucci. He carried a small gift-wrapped package. Katie gawked and wondered if Denise had hired another lawyer.

Kirk whispered, "Wow! If it ain't the dude and the dame."

Denise went straight to Brandon, knelt down in front of him, and touched his shoulders. "Brandon, you are growing up so fast! You're gonna be a very tall man."

Brandon backed away a bit and stared.

Betty stood behind Katie, with a stunned look on her face. Her chin had dropped drastically, as if the jack holding it up had suddenly failed.

There was a moment of awkward silence, and then Denise introduced the man with her. "I'd like for you all to meet my husband, Martin Van Buren. We were married last month in Vegas."

Martin looked at Kirk and offered his hand. "And you must be Brandon's foster dad, Kirk Childers."

From his seat, Kirk reluctantly reached up and shook the man's hand, muttering some standard canned greeting.

Betty was still standing behind Katie, with a look on her face that said, "I'm not believing what I'm seeing and hearing." Finally she managed to direct all of them to the conference room and said, "If you don't mind, I'll come in with you this time. Denise, I've got to hear your story."

After they were all seated around the conference table in the center of the room, Denise looked around the room, taking her time to focus on each person. "First off, Martin and I have two little presents for Brandon." Martin handed the gift he had carried in to Brandon. Brandon took the gift wrapped box and laid it in his lap without opening it.

Denise got up and strolled over to Brandon, putting her hand on his shoulder. "Brandon, honey, we'd like for you to open it now. Is that okay?"

Brandon sat stiff. After his mother urged him again, he placed the gift on the table and started methodically removing the wrapping paper and ribbon. Then from the exposed cardboard box he pulled out a silver picture frame, with small engraved dice bordering the outer frame. It was a wedding picture of Denise and Martin with a small handwritten note taped toward the bottom of the glass, *Brandon, we wish you could have been here with us to be our ring bearer.* Brandon slid the picture back in the box, slapped the wrapping paper over it, and laid it back in his lap, barely looking at it. There was more silence.

Then Martin reached in the vest pocket of his jacket and pulled out the little electronic game called a PSP, handing it to Brandon. There was little hesitation this time. Brandon was quick to accept it and said, "Thanks."

Betty broke in, "Well, now that we have those nice gifts out of the way, Denise, tell us more about your recent marriage. You said you married in Vegas?"

Denise leaned back in her chair, crossed her long slender legs, and twirled the sparkling rock on her left hand. "Yes, we were married last month at the Chapel in the Clouds, on the hundred and third floor of the Stratosphere Tower Vegas."

"How did you meet?"

"That's the embarrassing part," Martin announced. "We met at the classes we both were required to attend after our separate accidents. I had met with clients one evening, had about four Harvey Wallbangers, and—you guessed it…"

Laughter erupted in the room.

"…so driving home, I did just that. I banged into the wall of a convenience store. It was very stupid of me to have allowed myself the third, much less the fourth, drink. Like Denise, I was ordered to attend the remedial classes. Although I don't recommend couples meeting like we did, it has turned out to be a blessing for both of us. As you know, Denise was down on her luck, and me—I was picking up the pieces after a very lengthy and ugly divorce with my first wife. I think both of our lives have changed—for the better. I know I'm happy and… well, you can see, Denise is smiling again! So I'd say we are good for each other."

Denise reached for Martin's hand and said, "Okay, that's enough about us." She looked across the table at Brandon. "Tell me what you've been up to?"

Brandon refused to look at his mother. Instead, he ducked his head and stammered only two words. "Nuthin' much."

"Are you in third grade now?"

He shook his head. "Yeah." But he still refused to look toward her.

"See, I have missed out on almost a whole year of your life. Honey, I'm so sorry!" The silence in the room was again awkward. She directed her question to Katie. "How have his grades been?"

Hearing her name, Katie revived from her astonishment. "Oh. Uh, Brandon is doing very well. His reading has improved dramatically. Kirk is buying him fourth and fifth grade level books to read after he's finished with his homework and chores. He's at the top of his class in math."

Martin took Denise's left hand under her downturned palm, careful to not hide the huge solitaire. "Brandon, I hear you are living on a big ranch, and you have your own horse to ride. What's his name?"

Brandon stared at the man, "You're not interested in my horse's name, and it's not a *he*!"

Martin grinned. "So does *she* ever buck you off?"

Brandon sneered. "That's a dumb question! Kirk would never buy me a horse that would buck me off!"

The laughter started with Martin and was contagious, echoing around the room, with the exception of Betty. She sat motionless and looked deep in thought. When she became aware of the laughter circling the conference table, she smiled; then she reverted to a frown. "Denise, I've said this to you previously, but you need to keep me informed of any change of address."

Denise pulled out a pen and one of Martin's business cards from her handbag. "Here, I'll just write it on the back of Martin's card. That way you'll have his cell number too."

Betty took the card and turned it over to the back. "So you're living down in the Bricktown area?"

"Yes, before we were married, Martin had a fifth floor condo overlooking the canal. I love going down to the little sidewalk cafés just below us and watching the ducks in the canal. Most weekends we have at least one band down there next to the water. Of course we're only a block from Mickey Mantle Drive, with the ball park right there. There's just so much to do down there. We're hoping Brandon will be allowed to come for a visit soon. Martin wants to take him to a RedHawk's game at the ball park."

Betty tightly squeezed the business card in her hand, almost to the point of crushing it. "Denise, it appears that this marriage has been very good for you, but we'll have to take this visitation thing one step at a time. Up until today, you had shown little or no interest in following any of the rules in an attempt to regain custody of Brandon. I am still reeling from what I have seen and heard just now. Would you and Martin step into my office for a minute? We do need to talk.

Martin interjected, "Ms. Sawyer, I believe my wife—"

"No, wait 'till we are in my office."

Betty followed them both in and closed the door. Martin began again. "…I was saying, I believe my wife had been in a state of severe depression. As you know, depression can make a person act in some strange ways. When she decided to get rid of the scum bucket she'd been dating for some time, her true personality showed up. You see, once a person gets the devil out of their life, their smile returns. They care. They look at life very differently."

Betty scowled, "Well, I'm not sure the transformation can happen quite as fast as you indicate. I'm telling you, it will take time for your wife to prove to me that she is who you say she is. I'm not a skeptic, but I believe it takes more than a weekend wedding in Vegas to change a person."

Betty looked at Denise, squinted her eyes as if she were searching deep into the chameleon soul of the woman. "If you have really made a change in your life and want to regain custody of this child, you will have to follow *my* rules. There should be no more late arrivals at visitations, as you have in the past. I will have to visit your home several times. And, more importantly, you will have to show me that you care about your son. This is not about you or any fancy attire you may acquire! It is about Brandon!"

Denise reached across the desk and touched Betty's hand. "I understand what you are saying. But please try to understand and trust me. When I came out of that awful lifestyle I had with Bryce, then after another failed attempt with a man, I met Martin. My life changed. Martin has gone with me for counseling at that big Methodist church we attend on North Robinson. I feel like a new person. Betty, I'm now ready for Brandon to be part of my life. I wasn't back then; but I am now!"

"Just the same—I like to quote Ronald Reagan, 'Trust, but verify!' I'm telling you that the verifying part will not happen overnight; it will take time."

"I understand, Betty."

"Shall we rejoin the crew in the conference room now?"

Jason was watching Brandon play on the PSP. Kirk and Katie had been exchanging silent glances at each other, as if they could read each other's minds. This was just too much, too fast. Did Denise ever once consider that she may have been the one that could have been killed at the hands of Bryce Collier? Kirk's thoughts probably were a bit more sexist. He whispered to Katie, "She may dress up in them fancy stitches, but she's still just a selfish—"

"Drop it, Kirk!"

Martin held the door for Denise. Before she was seated, she reached down and kissed Brandon on the cheek. He turned and glared at her. "Brandon, Martin and I would like to take you to a RedHawk's game some evening. Would you like that?"

"I don't like baseball; I like horses!"

"Well, how about if we go out to Remington Park and watch the races?"

"I don't *watch*—I *ride*!"

That brought another round of laughter across the table. Martin said, "Brandon, since you're gonna grow up to be too big to be a jockey, what kind of riding do you think you might want to do?"

"Well, I won't be riding horses round and round in circles on a silly race track. I have my own horse, and you wouldn't like it where I ride."

Katie leaned over and whispered in Brandon's ear, "Watch it; don't be rude."

Betty said, "Folks, I've got to close this shop. I have two more homes to visit before I can go home myself. Denise, if you would like another parent visit, you know how to reach me."

"I'll call you Wednesday." Denise stood up, picked up her Gucci bag, and Martin Van Buren ushered her out through the door.

CHAPTER 43

Three weeks after the murder of Joyce Richards, Bryce Collier was no longer in the news. A trial date had not yet been set. Katie had wondered where Joyce's death would lead for Jason. She and Kirk had talked about the possibility of adopting him. Kirk said, "Honey, he's got no one but us. We have to give him a permanent home. I don't want him tossed around to different foster homes and wind up in a group home. Think of what would happen to him when he turns eighteen! He is kicked out of the system with no home, no way to finish high school or go to college, no family to bridge him into adulthood. Those kids have it rough."

"Are we sure Jason has no relatives out there somewhere that would take him in? Remember, he mentioned a grandmother in Arizona."

"But how would she know about his situation? Betty has already told us that no one came forward to give Joyce a funeral."

"I think I'll ask Betty how long the state would be required to wait for a relative to come forward before Jason would be free to be adopted."

"Honey, however long it takes, we will wait. I cannot allow this little guy to remain in the foster care system and be turned out—on his own—into a cruel world at eighteen. At this point in his life, we are his source."

Early Wednesday morning Betty's phone rang. "Betty, this is Denise. I promised I'd call you today. Martin and I both enjoyed our last visit with Brandon. I believe it—"

"Denise, I was just about to call you. Prior to your next visit, I will need to have a home visit at your new place. When would be a good time for you?"

"I'm here most of the time and Martin often works from home, so whatever would fit into your agenda would probably be fine with us. I could see from our last visit that it may take some time to win my little boy's heart back over to me. I know he has been hurt."

"Yes, Denise, he has. Will tomorrow morning be okay?"

"Sure, remember, it's building two. Just take the elevator to the fifth floor; we'll be on your right as you exit—Five-A."

As Betty hung up the phone, Jennifer stepped into her office. "Was that Denise again?"

"Yeah, Jen, I don't know what to make of that woman! It's almost like a different person has taken over her body. I'm just trying to decide if this is real, or if she just graduated from acting school. What do you make of her latest act?"

"I think it's just that—an act! No one changes overnight like that just because they go to Vegas and marry a rich guy. I think the bigger question is what was her new hubby thinking? He may need to have his head examined even more than Denise does!"

"Yeah, but some men only look at the gift wrapping. I imagine it won't be long 'til he starts to unwrap the hyena hiding inside."

"Betty!" Jennifer looked surprised. "I don't think I've ever heard you talk like that."

"Probably not. Not until this one came across my path." Betty put her hand on her forehead. "What am I thinking? I'm sorry, Jen. I guess it's possible for a person to change. After all, that *is* what we strive for in this job—changed lives, resulting in reunited families."

"Yeah, but the change in lives needs to be more than an act. I just have a feeling the curtain has just now opened on Act Two."

"Right, and Act Three is going to depend on Act Two."

The next morning Betty parked her Buick and followed the flagstone path around to the canal side of Building Two. Honeysuckle covered a cedar portico over the path near the corner of the building. Hydrangeas adorned the side of a rock retaining wall, and a giant weeping willow draped out over the canal. The manicured lawn framed the aquamarine Endless Pool. The peaceful setting was polished by the bright yellow Bricktown Water Taxi slowly making its way up the canal with about twenty passengers enjoying the cool morning air in view of the changing Oklahoma City skyline. Betty walked into the towering atrium, decked out with windmill palms reaching for the glass ceiling above. She took the elevator to the fifth floor and stepped out onto the polished hardwood floor. On the right, Five-A welcomed her with huge oak double doors. She pressed the doorbell and was startled to hear Denise say, "Oh hi, Betty, I'll be right there." She looked in the direction of the sound to see Denise on the screen above and to her right.

There was a five second wait. The heavy oak door opened and Denise stood there in white tennis shorts, an Alexander McQueen blouse and Jimmy Choo nude patent leather flat thong sandals. Betty was speechless.

"Betty! Come on in. I was in the back guest suite. Martin is having it redone for Brandon. The painters are here now, so we will have some paint fumes to deal with."

Betty stammered, "You're having a room redecorated for Brandon?"

"Yes, it's a mess back there. There are tarps on the floor, ladders, and painters tape everywhere, but I can show you the decorator's drawings." She picked up a large decorator's portfolio. Here, flip through these pictures while I get us some coffee."

"No, that's okay. I've had my two cups already, but thanks."

The drawings were more than the typical decorator's sketches, and a little boy's dream room came alive on the contents of the full color portfolio. Every angle of the room was depicted with careful attention to tones and form. The pictures were so realistic; they almost looked to be in 3-D.

Denise returned with her own coffee and pointed out the western theme they had settled on. The walls were to be a rich mocha with a genuine cowhide wainscot, topped by a half round three inch log trim chair rail with the bark still attached. The lodge style bunk beds were made from yellow pine logs, with a log ladder to the top bunk. A large rough cut single plank oak desk gleamed under numerous coats of lacquer and angled across one corner of the room with a saddle chair that looked like it had been taken right off a horse and equipped with a five leg base with casters. A wild mustang fresco in an accurate array of colors would run the length of one wall. There were swatches of fabric attached—a triple braid horse tail design, followed by a faux leather fabric, and an unusual animal print on a Thai silk bedspread.

Denise insisted, "Oh, please come on back with me. I want you to see the door that our master carpenter has made for the room. Just ignore all of these ladders and clutter." She pushed open the top half of the two-piece door that looked as if it had just been removed from a Louisville boarding stable, sanded smooth, and layered with fifteen coats of lacquer finish, giving it a glass encased look. The bottom half remained closed. As Denise pulled the top half back again, Betty saw the deep cut hand-carved name—*Brandon*, centered between two actual horseshoes that had been left in their unfinished state and straight out of a blacksmith's shop.

"Denise! You are going to a lot of expense with this room!" As they moved back away from the workers in the bedroom, she paused. "I am still reeling from the extreme makeover in your life. What happened to the old Denise?"

"The old Denise is gone forever! I will never allow myself to go back to that sort of lifestyle again. When I met Martin, I felt that I had just awakened from a very bad dream. Martin knows about my past, and he loves me for the person I am now—not who I was."

"Can it really be that instantaneous?"

"Yes, it certainly can."

"When the right man comes along, uh?"

"No, not entirely. After my accident, I made up my mind I was not going to stay in the slums—even if I had to do it all on my own. I was determined to make something of my life and build a safe environment for Brandon."

"What brought about that change?"

"You're going to laugh. I was moaning about the predicament I'd gotten myself in—you know, with the alcohol, the resulting car wreck, and those classes I had to attend, the beatings I'd taken from Bryce, not to mention the next guy that turned out to be a married man, with a wife moving back in. I'd managed to pick up a few odd jobs, cleaning apartments, and was able to move into a small efficiency apartment in another drug-infested neighborhood. So I was sitting there on the old worn out, Duct Taped vinyl couch, surfing the channels on this little black and white TV someone had tossed in the dumpster downstairs. Nothing interested me. I wasn't even watching. I'm not even sure who it was, but some lady with a raspy voice was saying, 'Get up out of your ghetto. Make something of your life!'"

"What program was that?"

"I don't even know. I never even looked at the screen. I just got up, turned the TV off, and I started trying to figure out what I could do to change. I didn't have all the answers, but I knew I would do it.

"That evening, I met Martin at the classes we had been ordered to attend. After the class, he and I drove down here to Bricktown. We strolled along the canal, spilling the deepest secrets of our hearts to each other. I had no idea he owned one of the condos here. I just thought he'd chosen a romantic place to talk. We sat down on a park bench and must have talked for two hours. He never, ever indicated to me then that he was an heir to one of the biggest oil and gas producing companies in North America. I mean, this guy was wearing some old faded Levis with holes in the knees, a shirt that had never seen an iron, and a RedHawks baseball cap with a thread-bare bill."

"So when did you learn that he owned this condo and had more money than a sultan from Siam?"

"He kept it a secret for at least two weeks. I thought he was just a good old Joe that earned a pretty good wage somewhere. We never talked about money. He never mentioned his job. I just knew from our conversation that he was nothing like Bryce. He wasn't a bum! He had character. We talked about what we believe is important in life—family, caring for other people, doing unto others as we would have them do unto us. I told him about the horrible lifestyle I had allowed myself to fall into, and I told him about Brandon. He asked a lot of questions about him and became determined that I should get my son back."

"Well I am delighted that you have made such a transformation. I would like to visit privately with Martin. I've picked your brain today; now I'd like to hear from his heart."

"Just say when. Today, he is in Florida on a business trip. His flight is due back in about noon tomorrow."

"Have him give me a call. I want to set this up with him—him alone."

Betty walked out, and Denise quietly closed the large oak door behind her. The elevator was still there on the fifth floor. She rode down, still reeling from the complete makeover of the woman. *I have never, in my entire career, seen such an instantaneous reformation in a person—inside and out! I'm beginning to believe that was the Man Upstairs Himself, directing those words to her through that little black and white TV.*

CHAPTER 44

"Kirk, I knew this day would come. Jason is not eating, and I have found him crying in his room several times. I try to comfort him, but I've never lost a parent, not even a grandparent. I just know that he is hurting, and I don't know how to help."

"Honey, I might not be much help either, but I know one thing. If I was in his situation, I wouldn't want people around me clamming up and not talking about my loss. I think we should get him to talking about his mother. What things does he remember that were special about her? What was her favorite food? Who were her friends? And what about that grandmother in Arizona? Can he remember anything about her—her name, a phone number his mother might have kept somewhere? Would he like to see her again?"

"Kirk, you are exactly right! I was doing the opposite. I was afraid to say anything about her that might bring more tears. I can see that was probably the wrong thing to do."

"It seems to me that if people around me refuse to talk about my loss, I would take it that they just don't care. I would want them to talk, even if it brings more tears. I see tears as antibiotic; they wash away the bad stuff."

Katie rested her head against Kirk's shoulder. "How'd this cowboy get to be so wise?"

"It's the hat!"

"The hat?"

"Yeah, it keeps the brain warm. Think about it—do you feel very smart after eating ice cream too fast, and you have a brain freeze? That's when I feel pretty stupid. The old brain needs something to blanket in the warmth. Then the wisdom will come."

"Well that hat must also make you silly."

"Where is Jason now? In his room?"

"Yes, you wanna go try out your theory and talk about his mother?"

Kirk found Jason on his bed, under the covers, sobbing. He sat down on the side of the bed, pulled back the cover a bit, and put his face down to Jason's, feeling the warmth of his recently released tears. He told Jason that tears were a good thing. "They clean out all the bad memories and replace them with good memories."

Two, three minutes passed with no words. Then Kirk asked him to tell him some of the things about his mom that was very special to him. In no time the river of tears and sobbing had turned to an occasional trickle. Jason started opening up, and Kirk learned more about Jason's mother than he ever dreamed possible. His grandmother in Arizona suddenly had a name, and he knew she lived in a big city. Kirk suggested Phoenix, and Jason said he thought that was right. Jason told Kirk that his mother was a dancer. Kirk only said, "I'll bet she was a beautiful dancer."

Equipped with new information about Joyce Richards, Katie relayed everything they had learned to Betty. Betty thanked her. "This may just be what we need to contact that grandmother. She probably hasn't even heard about her daughter's murder."

A gravelly baritone voice bounced Jennifer from her thoughts. "Hi… Martin Van Buren. I have an appointment with Betty Sawyer."

The tall lanky guy was standing at her desk in Carhartt work dungarees, a Duluth Trading Post Fire Hose presentation jacket, and was wearing some badly scuffed work boots. Jennifer almost didn't recognize him.

"Mr. Van Buren, I'll let Betty know you're here."

When Martin appeared in Betty's office, she was just as surprised as Jennifer. "Good morning, Mr. Van Buren. It's good to see you again, although—I have to admit—I hardly recognize you."

He looked down at his clothes. "Oh, sorry. My plane just arrived back from the Louisiana Gulf. I've been on an off-shore rig that my company just purchased."

"Have a chair, Mr. Van Buren."

Martin sat, crossed his legs, and continued. "This one incorporates some of the latest technology in directional drilling."

"Excuse my ignorance, but what is directional drilling?"

"Directional drilling has been around for many years. It's the technique of increasing the exposed section length through the reservoir by drilling through it at an angle."

"Why would that be advantageous?"

"Because it allows more wellheads to be grouped together on one surface location, allowing for fewer rig moves and thereby costing less to produce the wells. Several wells can be grouped together, fanning out from the one offshore platform. The concept is also being applied to land wells, allowing multiple subsurface locations to be reached from one pad with less surface area disturbance. And— you know— the green people like that. This rig that we just bought incorporates some of the latest technology in the directional drilling process, so I'm excited about some of the things that can be done with it."

"Well, it sounds complicated. But let's discuss a complication that I'm dealing with now—the future of your wife's son. Denise has told me that you are aware of her previous situation."

"Yes, we hold nothing back. We believe in being very honest with each other."

"Mr. Van Buren—"

"Please, it's Martin."

"Martin, I believe you when you say the two of you are being honest with each other now, but I have to tell you, that has not always been the case with Denise. Over the months that I've been dealing with her, I've realized that almost everything she told me was in fact, a lie."

"Betty, I know Denise is past that stage of —"

"Sir, you may know that, but I don't. How can I trust her when she has done nothing but lie to me all this time?"

"Denise has suffered at the hands of several men—men that she should have never allowed in her life. They dragged her into a pit of despair. She saw no way out, so she conformed to their way of life. But she awoke and decided that she'd had enough and decided to crawl out of that pit. That's when we met. I trust Denise. I have never caught her in a lie—ever!"

"I have to ask you this question, Martin. Do you see yourself being married to this woman when you are eighty?"

"Absolutely!"

"Do you honestly believe she will stay with you and not take off with any old Joe that comes across her path?" Betty had said it, although she realized that probably wasn't a licit question she should ask.

Martin laughed. "Denise knows when she's sitting on a gold mine."

Betty shot back immediately. "Hey, money is not always everything."

"Betty, I'm not talking strictly about money here. Denise and I have a love that goes way deeper than any form of financial prosperity. It's a love that incorporates respect, friendship, trust, and—last of all—physical attraction. Hey, it just doesn't get any better than that."

Betty looked deep into Martin's eyes and hesitated before continuing. "Tell me, Martin, do you believe you can be a good father figure for Brandon?"

"Absolutely."

"Do you have children by a previous marriage?"

"No, I believe God saw the final chapter of my previous marriage way before I did, and He said no to me fathering a child at that time. I think He knew what was best for me back then. Children would have been an unnecessary complication when it came to our divorce."

"Martin, you've only seen Brandon one time. How can you be sure that he will meet your expectations as a permanent fixture in your home? Brandon already seems quite different from you. I'm not convinced you will ever have anything in common with that boy. He loves the farm and ranch life; you seem to be more of a jetsetter. How's that going to work for you?"

"Does any man get that chance prior to fathering a son? Hey, I'm already one up on any birth father—I've seen this fine-looking young man first."

"Well, you're right about that. We don't get to pick and choose our offspring. We take what we are given, and then it's our job to mold that child into a very special part of the human race."

"Denise and I look forward to doing just that."

"Yes, but I'm afraid Brandon is already taking a definite shape at the hands of his potters—the foster parents that have nurtured and loved him now for the past two years. Let me ask you this, Martin. If the Department were to return custody to Denise, where would Brandon go to school? Have you thought about that?"

"We've already got that covered. It will be one of the best private Christian schools Oklahoma City has to offer."

"What activities do you see Brandon being involved in?"

"I think Denise mentioned that he wants to learn the guitar. I will see to it that he will have that opportunity. He will also be encouraged to find a team sport—I'm hoping for baseball."

"Martin, you do realize that Brandon adores his foster father. While it is always the goal of the Department to reunite these children with their biological parents, you should understand that it will be very difficult breaking him away from Kirk and Katie Childers. Those two have worked miracles with that child. I hope that you and Denise would respect Brandon's feelings for them. The kid loves them dearly."

"You got it! I know that we'll be walking on thin ice for a while."

"Sir, that ice *will* break at some point. The question will be who goes under; you or Brandon?"

"If it's Brandon, I've got a very long arm. I'll be there for him."

"Well, just *being there for him* is quite different from holding him—and encouraging him—when he comes across life's problems. You've got to be willing to give up some of your own time and spend it doing what he wants to do. You will no longer be allowed the luxury of selfish fulfillment on your part. It will be all about Brandon, not you and Denise. Your preferred types of entertainment will change. You will now be participating in the entertainment of this child."

"Yes."

"Martin! Did you hear what I just said? You will now be participating in the entertainment of this child. Your own entertainment has to be secondary!"

"Betty, I think we're prepared to do just that."

"And another thing … Brandon's education should be very high on your list of priorities. I'm not just talking about getting him into the most expensive private schools. A parent should never transfer all of the responsibility of educating a child to the schools anyway. That's only half of the educational equation. Parental involvement at home is of utmost importance. Brandon has gotten to where he is now academically because his foster mother has been willing to give up things she wants for herself, and instead has tutored this child daily now for over two years. His foster father has made Brandon his full-time sidekick. Brandon will need you and Denise more than he'll need designer sneakers, five-hundred dollar skate boards, and a two-thousand dollar a month private school. He will need your time more than anything else."

"Betty, we are fortunate in that we will be able to give Brandon many material things as well as what you've just mentioned that is most important—our time."

"Okay, Martin, you've been very helpful. I'll want to visit with Denise again. It takes a lot to convince me, but I think I know where I'm headed with this. I'll want to bring Brandon to your home for a couple of short trial runs prior to any final decision. You should understand I want to make sure I'm doing what is best for the child, not your teeter-tottering wife."

That last adjective for Denise suddenly chilled the air. Martin Van Buren stood and started toward the door. "Brandon's room will be waiting for him—and so will we."

CHAPTER 45

It was a Saturday and branding time on the Childers Ranch. The boys had already been told they could help Kirk and a hired hand with the annual branding of the cattle. Brandon was excited to get to help, but Jason wasn't buying in. Brandon had told him how they stick a hot iron to the cow's hide and it burns a brand in. Jason had decided he wanted no part of such a cruel treatment of the animals.

Kirk told the boys this year they would be using a new process called *freeze branding*. "We won't be sticking a hot iron to them this year. Freeze branding uses a branding iron to freeze a mark on the hide of an animal. We use extreme cold to kill the cells in the animal's skin that produce pigmentation—or color. So a freeze branded animal will have white hair reappear where the branding iron has touched the skin. Since all our cattle are black, that white hair, caused by the freeze branding, will show up really well. Another good thing about freeze branding is it is more difficult to alter than hot branding. Thieves don't normally have access to this process; they just use a hot iron."

"That's cool!" Brandon said. "I like that better than sticking a hot poker to a cow's hide like we did last fall."

"We're lucky our cattle are all black. It doesn't work very well on a Charolais. Remember, a Charolais cow is all white, so if the freeze branding leaves hair white, that won't show up on an already white animal.'"

"I'm gonna tell my bus driver about this. Mr. Simpson runs Limousins. Will it work on them?"

Jason looked confused. "On a limousine? Why would anyone want to put a brand on a limousine?"

Kirk laughed. "No, not like a stretch limo. He's talkin' about the Limousin breed of cattle. And yes, it ought to work well on a Limousin since they're somewhat of a creamy coffee color.

The boys jumped in the pickup with Kirk and headed for the corral. Kirk's helper had already rounded up the young heifers and bulls that missed last year's branding. A chute was used to trap the animal while being branded. Brandon had dozens of questions. "How is this gonna work? Do we have to put the branding iron in a freezer first?"

"Good question, Brandon! But no, we won't be doing that. We use liquid nitrogen. Here's what we'll do. You boys will stand on the outside of the chute. First I'll have Brandon reach through the bars of the chute and shave the hair off the animal where the brand will go. Then Jason will use a sponge to soak the area with alcohol. I'll take the branding iron from the liquid nitrogen and place it on the shaved area. I'll have to hold it in place there for several seconds before we open the chute's gate and let the animal go free."

Jason asked, "Will this hurt the cow?"

"No, not like a hot branding iron does. The hair will soon grow back, but it will be white hair where this special branding iron was held to it."

Brandon was wowed. "Who thought of that?"

Kirk told him the method had been around for some time, but most ranchers used the hot iron because it was cheaper than the liquid nitrogen method. "My very generous Uncle Carl believes we ought to have the best here on this ranch. He loves these black beauties as much as I do."

Brandon felt of his head and realized he had forgotten his cowboy hat. "Kirk, you gotta take me back so I can get my hat."

Kirk agreed to do that for Brandon since they weren't quite ready to run the first cow into the chute. A spare hat was offered to Jason, but he didn't want it. When they returned, Ronnie, Kirk's helper, was ready to start moving the first cow into the chute. With a great deal of anticipation, Brandon shaved the area on the first animal. Kirk said, "Good job, buddy! Now, Jason, take this sponge and dip it in the alcohol and wipe that spot down really well."

The boys didn't seem to tire of their jobs. Before lunchtime a total of ninety-six heifers and bulls had been branded. When Kirk herded the boys back into the truck he asked, "You guys think you'll be up to helping with doctoring the cattle next time that's being done?"

Again, Jason was confused. "How do you *doctor* a cow?"

"We vaccinate them, just like you get vaccinated for diseases."

"You mean we have to stick them with a needle?"

"Yep, that's part of it."

"That ain't all they do." Brandon's face was plastered with an obvious smirk. "I watched them one time."

"What else do we do, cowboy?"

Brandon grinned and said, "Well, I'm just gonna say, if I was one of them bulls, I'd run as fast as I could to the far pasture!"

"Don't blame you, buddy! Now, let's go see what Mamma Katie's got for lunch."

Betty had warned Katie that the Department might have to return custody of Brandon to his mother. The phone rang, and when she heard Betty's voice, she froze. *No, please, God, don't let it be now.* She opened her mouth, but no sound came out.

"Katie, are you there?"

"Yes, Betty, I'm here."

"Katie, I've got news. We've located Jason's grandmother in Phoenix. That name Jason remembered was right. I just talked to her and had the unfortunate job of telling her about her daughter. She knew nothing of Joyce's murder."

"So how does she feel about Jason?"

"She didn't hesitate. She wants Jason to come live with her."

Katie admitted to herself that she was relieved that the call wasn't about Brandon, but she also hated to see Jason leave them. She felt that they were just now getting the little guy to open up a bit. There were still occasional tears, but he seemed to be handling it as well as could be expected. "So is she coming to Oklahoma City to pick him up?"

"Yes, but we are required to do some checking on her first. Assuming our investigation goes as expected, he will most likely be leaving us in a couple of weeks. She told me that Jason is her only grandchild so she is looking forward to getting to know him better. She indicated that her relationship with Joyce had been cool at best."

Katie told her that she was a bit relieved that the call wasn't about Brandon.

"Oh that's the other thing we need to talk about."

Katie's heart stopped. "No, don't tell me."

"Well, I'm afraid I must. Katie, I've visited with Denise in her home. I've also had a private consultation with her new husband, and I can tell you Denise is a different person! I believe she is ready for Brandon."

"Well, I'm not convinced," Katie's cynicism became a bit caustic. "Those fancy clothes and the big diamond ring isn't what it takes to be a good mother."

Betty agreed with her and then described the room she and Martin were decorating for Brandon. "Katie, they're not only preparing for him with a room any boy would love, they are planning for his education and extra-curricular activities. Both of them are most agreeable with what I suggest."

There was silence, and then Katie asked, "What are you suggest-ing?"

"I have told them I will want to bring Brandon into their home for a couple of short visits before finalizing anything."

Katie's heart jumped up into her throat. She knew she didn't have the courage to continue the conversation, so she abruptly said, "Okay, let us know." She brought the phone back to its cradle to disconnect.

ን

CHAPTER 46

It was Thursday when Betty called Katie again. "Katie, I'll need to pick up Brandon after school tomorrow for a weekend visit with Denise. Can you have a couple of changes of clothes ready for him?"

"Yes, Betty, I'll have it ready for him. But I've gotta tell you, that woman is nothing but a hyena, dressed in a mink's hide. I will never trust her!"

Friday afternoon Brandon and Jason exited the school bus and took their seats in the pickup. Kirk stared straight ahead, saying nothing. Brandon reclined his seat a bit and was also silent the whole way to the ranch house. Katie had a couple of PB and J sandwiches ready for the boys. No one said a word. Jason looked around, first at Brandon and then at Kirk. Then at Katie. The silence was broken by the door bell ringing.

Kirk opened the door for Betty. He stood there, deep in thought and unable to greet her. Noah's wagging tail was her only welcome. She saw the boys at the table. "Whatcha got there, guys—PB and Js?"

Still with a mouthful of the sticky stuff, Brandon finally managed, "Yep."

"Brandon, while you're finishing up there, Katie and I will go to your room and get your things."

Katie opened the door to Brandon's room. Both of his little die cast Mustangs were on the floor in front of the bookcase. Several books were scattered around the room and his hat was setting on the bed upside down. Katie stood there staring at the gym bag she'd packed for him. When she turned back to face Betty, there was a tear sneaking out of the corner of her eye. But with no mascara to smear, it just made a little opaque trail down her cheek.

Betty noticed it. "Katie, we both knew this would be a possibility two years ago when I first brought Brandon to the ranch."

"I know, but we had gotten our hopes up when Denise continued to show no interest in her son. Brandon has captured Kirk's heart to the point that the two of them are bonded like Super Glue. Kirk can do no wrong in Brandon's eyes." Another part of the story was written in Katie's eyes. "This ranch will not be the same without our Brandon."

"Katie, I think this is probably the hardest part of my job, maybe even harder than removing a child from his own birth mother. I hate doing this."

For a moment there was total silence again. Katie stood there in her jeans and OSU sweatshirt, with her long light auburn hair trailing over her drooping shoulders. Finally she wiped at her eyes, picked up the gym bag and said, "Let's see if he's finished with his sandwich."

Brandon had taken his last bite and was about to finish off the glass of milk. "Miss Betty, sometimes I wish I could lie."

"What?"

"Yeah, I wish I could just play sick and tell you I have to stay here in my bed."

"Well, Brandon, I'm glad you don't lie. I think you are going to be surprised when we get there. Your mom and Martin have made a special room, designed just for you. It's even got a desk chair made from a real saddle! Oh and there's a swimming pool just outside the building. Are you bringing some swimming trunks?"

"I don't have swimming trunks. When I swim in the pond, I just wear some cutoffs."

Betty looked over at Jason. "And how are you doing today, Mr. Jason?"

"I don't want Brandon to go."

"Well, he'll be back Sunday evening. You two have school Monday morning."

Kirk excused himself, placed his hand on the back of his head in an attempt to ease the tension headache, and headed toward the back door. Katie hugged Brandon and told him to be a good boy. "We'll see you Sunday evening."

The trip to downtown Oklahoma City was limited to a one-sided conversation. Betty tried every trick she knew to get him talking. She described the canal just outside Denise's condo. She talked about the mamma duck leading her little ones on the water's edge. She described the wild Mustang fresco covering an entire wall of his room like giant gift wrapping. He glared at her, pursed his lips, and said, "She won't get away with this!"

CHAPTER 47

Denise opened the huge door and wrapped her arms around her son. "Brandon! Every time I see you, I think you have grown a couple of inches. You're gonna be one tall dude." She put one hand on Betty's shoulder. "Come on back with us, and have a look at Brandon's finished room."

Everything in the room was completed as she had seen in the decorator's portfolio. The enormous wall-to-wall mustang fresco was striking. The four beautiful animals energized the atmosphere of the room with their powerful gallop across the entire length of the wall. Betty looked at Brandon and said, "This is what I wanted you to see first. Aren't they beautiful?"

"I wish it was Puzzle and Dandy."

Denise saw the disappointment and moved on to the desk and saddle chair. "Hop up here big guy. See how this fits your bottom."

Brandon climbed on, looked down at his boots and said, "Where are the stirrups?"

Denise laughed and said, "Brandon, you won't need stirrups on this horse. Your feet touch the floor."

"This is silly, sitting in a saddle with no horse under it."

Denise pointed back to the personalized door. "I'll bet you didn't see the special door to your room, with your name carved in the upper half."

Brandon glanced toward the door, turned and stared at the cabin style log bunk beds. "Which one do I sleep in?"

"You can sleep in whichever one you want. The other one can be for a friend."

"Can Jason come with me next time?"

Denise looked at Betty for an answer, but Betty was still staring at the mural. A few seconds later she said, "Sure, if that's okay with Betty."

The question had finally registered with Betty and, replying to Denise, she said that it wouldn't be possible for Jason to come next time. Not wanting to say that it would be against Department rules, she just said, "Jason will be going to live with his grandmother in Arizona soon." As soon as she said it, she knew she'd made a mistake. *We've never told Brandon about that.* She saw the hurt in his eyes. He went over to the bed, sat down, covered both knees with his hands, and dipped his head into his chest. Betty went to him and tried to soothe him by telling him that Jason's grandmother was going to give him a good home in Phoenix, and he would be very happy there. It didn't work. Realizing she'd opened up a brand new problem, Betty said she needed to get back to the office. Denise showed her to the front door.

"I'm sorry," Betty said. "I screwed up by springing that on him. I guess I thought his foster parents would have told him that Jason would be leaving."

"We'll work on him." Denise leaned against the open door. "I've got some tricks up my sleeve that might bring him out of his mulligrubs."

Betty summoned the elevator. The door opened and Martin Van Buren exited. "Hello, Mrs. Sawyer. Good to see you again. Is Brandon here?"

"Yes, but I'm afraid I'm leaving him in a sad frame of mind. He has just learned that his little foster brother will be moving to Arizona to live with his grandmother. You might see what you can do to perk him up."

Martin went on back to Brandon's room. "Hey partner, I thought I might find you here. Have you had a chance to look around at your new digs?"

"My what?"

"You know, your digs—your room."

"Oh."

"Well, Brandon," Denise said, "we were hoping you would like what we've done to make you a cool room. Most cowboys would be proud of this kind of bunkhouse. We thought you would fit right in here, surrounded by wild Mustangs, a saddle, and a big bear rug in the middle of the room—have you even noticed the cool rug?"

Brandon swiped one boot over the edge of the rug, making the course animal hair stand on end. Martin cringed.

Brandon stood up, turned his back to them and was silent. They were getting nowhere with him. Martin reached down and gently slapped Brandon's knee. "Hey, let's you and I go down and see the ducks. One Mamma duck down there has about eight babies trailing her. We'll take some bread down and you can feed them."

After only a short walk along the canal, they spotted the little family of ducks on the other side of the canal, making their way toward them. Martin handed him the bread. "Go ahead; throw a couple of pieces out to them."

Brandon stood there with his hands in his pocket. "Where I live, we don't *feed* ducks—we *shoot* 'em."

Martin rubbed his own forehead. "Well, these are special city ducks. You'd have all the neighbors mad at you if you tried to shoot these ducks."

Brandon kept his hands in his pockets, turned, and headed back to the condo. Once they were back upstairs, Martin whispered to Denise, "Well, I bombed out. He didn't wanna feed the ducks—said where he lived, they shoot ducks, not feed them."

Denise grinned, "Yep, the kid's gonna have some adjusting to do here. Maybe if we get some food in his belly, he'll snap out of it."

"Where do you suggest?"

"How about Trolley's? We can have a steak and order pizza for him."

Brandon had retreated to his quarters and perched on the saddle chair, staring out the corner windows onto the black expanse of parking lot below. While the guys were down by the canal discussing the ducks, Denise had opened Brandon's gym bag and put away his things. She grabbed the windbreaker Katie had put in and handed it to Brandon. "We're going to go grab a bite to eat. Take this with you; it'll be a little chilly before we get back."

The three of them walked down to the restaurant, about a block away. After they were seated, both Denise and Martin tried to engage Brandon in conversation, asking several questions—most were answered with short contrived sentences. "What kind of pizza do you like?"

"Homemade, like Katie makes."

"Okay, well what does Katie put on your pizza?"

"Pepperoni and cheese."

Denise looked up at the tall teen looming over them. "Waiter, let's get this boy a large pepperoni pizza with extra cheese. Martin and I will have your sirloin and shrimp special. Hold the baked potato on mine, but bring me your strawberry-mango mesclun salad with an extra-virgin olive oil and sherry vinegar dressing on the side. Martin would like the fully loaded baked potato."

Brandon only ate part of a couple of pieces of the pizza. Denise had the waiter box up the rest to take home. Their short power-walk back was a little brisk. "Don't you guys have a car?" Brandon asked.

"Yes, in fact we have two," Martin said, "but we knew it was only a block, so why bother with the car on a beautiful moonlit evening like this? Come on, I'll take you around to the garage and show you what we have. Brandon watched with a cunning eye as Martin tapped in the combination on the garage door keypad. I just bought your mother this little Mercedes SLK. You know red is her favorite color—it matches her hair. The big black H3 Hummer is what I drive when I'm not in the air in my company jet."

"You have a jet?"

"Well, yes, my company does. It's what I use to get down to the rigs off the coast of Louisiana and Texas in a hurry."

"You own an oil well?"

"No, my company owns several oil and gas wells. We also own several drilling rigs. Most of the time we lease these out and other speculators do the drilling. But I do own one rig personally down there. Right now I'm using it to drill for myself. I've named this rig *The Denise*."

"I guess you'll be mega rich if you strike oil, uh?"

Martin laughed. "Brandon, it takes a lot of money to drill for oil. Let's hope we hit it big. My geologists tell me it should be a good one."

"Can you take me with you sometime so I can see it?"

Martin glanced at Denise and back to Brandon. "Maybe when you're a little older."

"Hey, you pulled it off!" she whispered back to him. "You got him to talking." But neither of them seemed to notice the disappointment in Brandon's eyes. Martin probably had no idea that he had just thrown away his one chance of bonding with the boy. A trip—just the two of them—in a company jet to an offshore oil rig might have provided the adhesive for the beginnings of a relationship.

Sunday was uneventful. Denise tried to get Brandon to go for a swim. She had even bought him some swim trunks, but he wasn't interested. He walked alone down to the canal, picked up a few small rocks and was skipping them across the canal like he'd done hundreds of times on the big pond on the ranch. Just as he counted six bounces on the last one, some blue-haired lady saw him and screeched, "You can't do that; it's not allowed here!"

He went back up to his room and looked all around for some books to read. *Kirk could build a bookcase for this silly make-believe room—to hold all of these books they don't have!* Then he laughed at that thought. He sat down at the empty desk. *Not even paper or a pencil!* With nothing else to do, he laid down on the bottom bunk, atop the tiger skin pattern Thai silk bedspread. He was on his back with one leg crossed over the other.

There was a slight knock at the door and Martin appeared, looked at Brandon lying there with his boots still on. "Brandon, you should remove your boots before lying down on that bedspread. That is very expensive Thai silk."

Without a word, Brandon swung his feet off the side of the bed, got up and slunk back to the kitch— — was pulling the leftover —. on was a drag. He went nly the ducks traipsing r at one of the ground that didn't like it when corched deep into him

Martin & Denise tried their hardest to win Brandon over with material items but it didn't work. He was bored & uninterested

The doorbell resonated throughout the condo with an extended eight-note cathedral chime. He was standing by the front door, his gym bag packed and in his hand. Brandon never dreamed that he'd be so glad to see his caseworker. She took her time visiting with Denise and Martin. Brandon remained by the door with his hand on the over-sized door knob while Denise filled the caseworker's ears with stories of their wonderful weekend adventures.

Finally, Betty walked over toward the door. "You ready, Brandon?"

Brandon wasted no time in opening the big door and shot out toward the elevator. There were no *goodbyes* or *see you next time*—not a word.

CHAPTER 48

The big room was quiet, except for the clack, clack, clack of Katie's steady keystrokes on the old black Remington. Her fingers recorded the story with amazing accuracy and speed. She paused. *Why would I ever want an electric? Or even a computer?* She jumped when she felt two big arms envelope her. "Kirk! That had better be you!"

"Who else would it be?" He bent down, pulled her face around toward him and kissed her. "I thought you were supposed to substitute for that new kindergarten teacher today."

"She called me first thing this morning and said her doctor appointment had been cancelled, so she didn't need me to come in."

Kirk touched the paper from the top of the typewriter. "So you still workin' on your story?"

"I was, until this big ranch foreman dude came in and about scared the bejeebers out of me. I thought you had gone into town to buy a part for that old tractor."

"I did, but it didn't take me all morning. Kate, it's past noon. You really are wrapped up in that story."

Katie looked at her watch. "You mean I've been sitting here at this desk for four hours?"

"Looks like it," Kirk grinned. "How many pages you typed?"

"I haven't kept count. I'm just writing what comes to mind. And right now, my mind is saying I need to get us some lunch started." She pulled her chair out from the desk, stood and stretched her fingers.

"Hey, let's just throw some quick sandwiches together. I've got a guy comin' to look at a bull." He took both her hands in his. "That way you can get these hands flying back over that typewriter again. How fast you figure you type now—sixty, maybe seventy words a minute?"

"I don't know, Kirk, and I don't think you care. All you want is some lunch. Come on, I'll slice a tomato and you grab the deli meat from the fridge." She followed her six-foot-two man around to the kitchen.

"This milk any good? I forgot to bring a fresh gallon up from the fridge in the dairy barn."

"Yes, it's just two days old. While you're there, get the lettuce from the crisper drawer and the mayo… if you think you've just got to have it."

Kirk set the gallon jar of milk on the table, turned, and reached for the lettuce. "So, I gotta ask you something, Miss Writer. I saw a big stack of paper by your typewriter. That looks like a lot of words to me."

"So what's your point?"

"Where are you getting all your info? I mean… you're writing about our kids, right?"

"Yes, I think I told you that earlier."

"How do you know that much about them? Their backgrounds— you know—before they came to us. You obviously know a lot more about them than I do."

"Good observation, Mr. Childers. I like it when my students ask questions."

Kirk ducked his chin and looked at her under his big thick eyebrows. "Since when did I become your student, Miss Childers?"

Katie set two glasses on the table and poured both their milks. Then she opened the bread sack, took out a couple of slices for Kirk and one for herself. Taking her time to answer had become her trademark.

Kirk knew better than to push for a quick reply. Always when he did, it led to a snappy comeback that never really answered his question.

"If you're curious enough to ask questions about my work, then you are my student." That brought a smile to both of them.

Just as he liked it, Katie slathered an abundance of mayonnaise on Kirk's slices of bread. "Here's the deal." She lifted the knife in the air to make a point. "I don't know every detail of their past. I just have to fill in the blanks to make it readable. I've learned a lot from caseworkers, birth parents, even grandparents. The kids themselves. But there's a lot that I don't know. I just have to imagine."

"So it's like you're writing all this as fiction?"

"No... Yes... I mean, I guess you'd say it is fiction but based on a lot of facts. Most of it is non-fiction, but I've had to fictionalize the non-fiction."

Kirk grinned. "Man! I'd like to see you explain that to a publisher."

"I don't have to explain it to any publisher. I'm writing it for myself—it's therapy." She paused. "And right now I'm feeling the need of some therapy."

"Okay, babe, you go back to your therapy. I'm gonna try to sell that bull."

A bewildered look flashed on Katie's face, and Kirk burst out laughing. "Oops, I didn't mean your writing. I meant the Angus bull."

Katies book

CHAPTER 49

Tuesday morning, Betty called Denise to see if she wanted to have Brandon back over the following weekend. Denise answered her cell phone from Grand Bahama Island. "Betty, Martin and I will be down here for another week; how about the following weekend?"

Betty still wasn't sure she could believe Denise, "I didn't realize you could get cell coverage from the Bahamas."

"Yes, Martin says it's quite expensive, but it is available through our regular cell carrier."

"Okay, I'll make sure the following weekend will work with the Childers. Enjoy your vacation."

"Oh, it's not really a vacation. Martin has a condo down here and this happens to be a business trip for him. But you're right—for me, it is a little mini vacation in the sun."

Knowing that both boys might not be with them much longer, Kirk had been spending a lot of time with them. He wanted to be as much of an influence as possible for the little time he had left. Katie had still been spending evenings helping with their homework. Kirk knew he got to do the fun stuff with them on weekends.

It was Saturday morning. He had promised the boys he would take them rabbit hunting. At first light, Brandon bounded into the master bedroom. "Come on Kirk; get your lazy self out of bed. You promised we'd go hunt some rabbits this morning."

After a quick breakfast of Cheerios and milk, they headed toward the pasture where Kirk had seen rabbits scampering through the short grass earlier in the week. Equipped with a Crosman Quest .22 break barrel carbine and a Gamo Big Cat .22, the guys were off to their big hunt. The Crosman Quest had an ambidextrous design and a two-stage, adjustable trigger—perfect for Brandon, the lefty in the family.

Kirk told the boys that if their hunt was successful, they would be eating hasenpfeffer for supper.

Brandon frowned. "What's that?"

"Rabbit stew! It's a recipe my grandmother used to make when we boys would come home with a rabbit or two. It has bacon, shallots, and several different spices. Let me tell you, that was some good eating."

"Sounds awful!"

The early morning dew was still on the grass. The sun was just beginning to peep through the trees on the horizon. "Okay guys, before we see any rabbits, I need to go over some safety rules again with you." He instructed them on how they were to hold their weapons. "First of all, make sure the safety is on. You *never* carry a gun with the safety off. You might trip and the gun fires. Look at me Jason—this is important. Before you aim at a rabbit, you make sure there is nothing in your line of fire except that rabbit. Make sure there are no cattle ahead. And for sure, make sure one of us isn't standing in your line of fire. It is only then that you take the safety off, aim, and pull the trigger. Okay, now you guys tell me the order you do this in. I wanna make sure you understand the precautions you have to take to hunt. A gun is a deadly weapon. You better make sure you know what you're doing."

Brandon repeated back the safety measures. Kirk handed him the Crosman. Jason couldn't repeat back the safety instructions, so Kirk told him he wouldn't be allowed to handle the gun until he did. He repeated them a couple of times until Jason was able to echo the rules. Kirk was watching both boys closely, making sure they were carrying their guns right and the safety was on. As soon as they entered the pasture south of the barn, a rabbit jumped up, ran about ten yards away, and turned and stared at them. Kirk said, "Brandon, this one's yours. You remember what you're to do?"

Brandon looked ahead of the rabbit to make sure there were no cattle in his view, brought the gun up, released the safety, aimed, and fired. He missed.

"Don't worry buddy, we'll catch up with him or his brothers later, and you'll have another chance."

Three hours later, Kirk found himself carrying three cottontails. Brandon had killed two and, with a little help from Kirk, Jason shot the third. "Now we gotta get them back to the barn, skin and clean them."

Jason looked at Kirk, "How do we skin them?"

"Just wait, I'll show you. We'll make one cut, hold them up by their hind legs and the skin will peel right off."

Wide eyed, Jason said, "Wow!"

Before they started back, Kirk told the boys to unload their guns. "You can't be too careful."

That evening the boys filled up on hasenpfeffer, Kirk's grandmother's recipe from the old country. Katie's homemade bread straight from the oven, with home churned butter, and honey from their bee hives down by the creek topped off the one meal they boys would never forget.

The adventure club for the boys at the little community church had never materialized, but Kirk's friend, Jack Newton, had come out to the ranch a couple of times with his boys for an evening of fishing in the big pond. Kirk knew that Brandon was scheduled to spend the following weekend at Denise's, so he was glad when Jack called and wanted to bring the boys out to fish on Thursday evening. He knew it might be the last time he got to take Brandon fishing. Jason would be going soon too. It was a good evening, and each boy caught at least one fish. Brandon topped everyone with his four. A stringer of nice bass was shared with Jack to take home with him.

Later that evening Kirk went to Brandon's room. "Hey buddy, you up to reading me a chapter out of that book you're holding there?"

"Naw. It's not a very good book."

"What's wrong, man? You look like you've lost your best friend."

Brandon looked down at the book, and a tiny tear oozed out of the corner of his eye. "I'm about to."

"What?"

"I'm about to lose my best friend."

"Who? Jason?"

"No—you."

Kirk swallowed hard. After a long silence he managed to say, "Hey, buddy, we will always be friends; nothin's ever gonna change that!"

"Oh yeah? Miss Betty will."

"No, Brandon, she can't destroy our friendship, even if she sends you back to your mother. No one can keep me from calling you, and Katie and I will write to you often."

"Will you wait for me?"

"What? Wait for you?"

"Yeah, will you not forget about me 'til I get eighteen? Cause I'll come back and visit you then, even if I have to walk all the way. Yeah, and then…." Brandon sniffled. "And then, we can go fishin' again, and we can go rabbit huntin' again, and I'll help you with the milking. I'll even help you when you make them bulls into steers." A full river of tears spilled over onto his cheeks and dripped onto his shirt.

"Oh, Brandon—Brandon! Of course I'll wait for you. You will never, ever be out of my thoughts. Buddy, this won't be the end—I promise you! But we can't get Denise mad at me. I gotta stay on the good side of her so she'll let me call and write to you."

"I don't wanna go live with her. She doesn't care about me. She only cares about whatever man she's with at the time. She will do whatever it takes to make him happy—including leaving me alone in a stupid bedroom with no books, no TV, and not even a dog to play with. And Martin don't want me either. He was afraid I was gonna get that expensive bedspread dirty with my boots. They are in love with their fancy stuff, not a boy like me. I'm not fancy enough for them!"

"Brandon, I think you're a little bit wrong about this. They are doing their best to make sure you get to live with them."

"She didn't even want me this last weekend. I heard what Betty said."

"What did Betty say?"

"She said Denise and Martin couldn't have me this weekend because they were gonna be in the Bahamas—or somethin' like that."

"How did you hear that?"

"I was listenin' on the other phone. That's what she said. See, she would rather be gone so she wouldn't have to have me there."

"Hey, buddy, I don't think that's the case at all. The way I heard it, Martin was there on a business trip, and Denise was with him. She's looking forward to you being back with her this next weekend."

"Well I know Martin doesn't want me!"

"Oh yeah? Then why did he spend so much money on that fancy room for you?"

"That room's not for me. It just makes him look good."

"Brandon, that's crazy! Of course the room is for you. You should be thankful. I mean, what little boy wouldn't like a room like you described to me?" Kirk grinned. "But, hey, if you don't want that cool saddle chair, I'll take it."

"You can have it! All I want is the room I got right here. I don't need that goofy chair. I don't need that big bear rug staring me in the face when I get out of bed, and I sure don't need that fancy tie-sick bedspread he's so proud of!"

"Hey, your room will be waiting here for you when you turn eighteen. Maybe you could live here and go to college close by."

Kirk took his bandana from his back pocket and wiped Brandon's eyes and cheeks. But the truth was he knew he'd also need that bandana for his own tears later. He turned and saw Katie standing just outside the door, wiping her eyes on the sleeve of her sweatshirt.

"Brandon, you've got school tomorrow. You'd better get some shut-eye now." He leaned down and kissed him on the forehead, took the not-so-interesting book and laid it on the night stand, got up and took Katie's hand in his. Together they walked down the hall and peaked in on Jason. He was sound asleep.

CHAPTER 50

Friday afternoon Betty called and told Katie she wouldn't be able to come and pick up Brandon for his weekend visit. "Do you think you and Kirk might be able to drive him over to her place?" The silence was a bit embarrassing for a couple of seconds. "Bricktown is a beautiful little downtown area. If you've never been there, I think you'd enjoy it. You guys could take a ride on the Water Taxi while you're there. You can catch it just outside Denise's condo."

Katie was a little hesitant but told her they could deliver Brandon to Denise. Getting Brandon to agree to go would be the next step— probably the more difficult one.

She had an afternoon snack ready for the boys when they got in from school. As expected, Brandon was uncooperative and tried to delay everything from finishing his snack to changing out of the jeans he'd managed to get mud on while playing in the school yard. Katie had called her mom to see if they could drop off Jason at their house while they delivered Brandon. Carol agreed and said, "It won't even be out of your way."

Bricktown was new to Kirk and Katie. As they pulled into the parking lot behind the condos, Kirk said, "Wow! This is quite an improvement from just a few years ago. This is the area where the homeless people and bums hung out. It sure wasn't the most desirable neighborhood back then. I wonder where they moved all those homeless people."

Building Two was easy to find. Kirk parked, and they took the flagstone path around to the front of the building. The huge windmill palms greeted them just inside the towering atrium. Brandon pointed the way to the elevator. Once inside, he told them he had forgotten his homework. "Maybe we should go back."

"Nice try, Brandon, but you're not getting by with that little tactic," Katie said, "I've got your homework packed in your bag."

He looked down, snapped his fingers and said, "Man!"

Martin met them at the door. "Hey guys! Good to see you again. Denise is back in Brandon's room tidying up for him. Let's go on back. I'd like for you to see where he'll be hanging his hat."

The room was just as had been described to Katie—beautifully decorated, but sterile. Denise was smoothing out any wrinkle that she might have seen on that Thai silk bedspread. She immediately started small talk with Katie, but never acknowledged Brandon.

Katie stopped her mid-sentence. "Denise you do see your son standing here, don't you?" As she was starting to reply, Katie continued, "I think it was Toni Morrison that asked the question, 'When a child walks in the room, do your eyes light up?'" She whispered in Denise's ear, "I don't see the excitement in your eyes. Honey, your son is waiting!"

The silence was as thick as fog. Totally ignoring Katie's remarks, Denise slipped past her and into the hallway. "Brandon, you can put your bag on that little table by the closet."

Martin tried to change the mood by asking if they had any problem finding the place. Before either Kirk or Katie could answer that, he immediately started talking about all the amenities they enjoyed living in their special little secluded community. "We've got the ballpark, just a block or so away, and Denise loves all the little dress boutiques within walking distance. And there are a dozen or so sidewalk cafes and coffee bars lining the front of the canal. We're both hooked on espressos now."

Kirk ignored the braggadocio chatter and asked Brandon what he would like to do before they left the area.

"You can take me for a ride on that yellow boat out in the canal." Brandon said.

Denise spoke up. "That's a great idea!"

Brandon's eyes glared at her. "Well, you guys have already done that, so we'll be back in a little bit." He grabbed Kirk's arm and headed for the door.

The ride only took about twenty minutes, but Brandon wasn't ready to go back up to the Denise and Martin Van Buren Museum. He pulled Kirk in the opposite direction.

"What's down here?" Kirk said.

"I don't know. Let's just check it out."

"Actually, Brandon, we probably should get you back up to your mother. I don't think she was any too happy the way you excluded her and Martin from our little float trip. You might try being a little more congenial."

"Why? So I can get to sit on that fancy saddle chair and stare out the window into the parking lot below? Whop-tee-do!"

"Brandon! That's uncalled for. Just stop it right now."

As they stepped back into the atrium, Brandon didn't say a word. He punched the up arrow button and then tapped the LED light inside for the fifth floor. Kirk watched him as he turned to lean his head against the wall of the elevator.

Katie told Kirk she didn't want to visit any more with Denise. "I'll just stay outside and hold the elevator. She doesn't want to hear anything further from this lowly farm girl."

When Denise opened the door for them to come in, Kirk told her they needed to get back to the ranch. "We'll be back to pick him up Sunday evening about seven."

On the drive back over to Katie's parent's home to pick up Jason, Kirk asked Katie if she wasn't a bit rough on Denise. "I understand the woman should have greeted Brandon with a big hug. She was way too concerned about showing off her impressive digs to us, but still, we can't afford to get on that wildcat's blacklist. We have to think of our future relationship with Brandon—assuming that will even be a possibility with her."

"That was just my point! She valued that fancy condo of theirs more than she did her own son! That, I find, is very disgusting!"

"Katie, she's been living in the slums so long that she probably thinks she has a right to want to show off her new lifestyle."

Katie was livid now. "She has *no right* to ignore her son like that! What a fool she is! No wonder he doesn't want to see her. She's given him no reason to."

"Honey, your eyes are beginning to match your red hair. Settle down. She'll get it together soon. She hasn't had a child in her house now for a couple of years—probably has forgotten all about nurturing. Give her some time."

He looked over at her, staring out her passenger window. He knew Katie—knew she had more to say.

She turned back toward him. He saw her pursed lips. Then she said, "Brandon can't wait on *her* to grow up."

Lynn and Carol Reynolds were playing a game of Old Maid with Jason when Kirk and Katie arrived. Katie turned to Kirk. "Now that's how a parent is supposed to treat a child. Denise could learn a few lessons from my mom and dad!"

Carol tried to hide a grin. "I take it your visit didn't go all that well?"

"Mom, his so-called *mother* was more interested in showing off her fancy condo with all its fabulous amenities than acknowledging that her son had arrived on her planet. He was standing there staring her in the face. She didn't even bother to say hello to him."

Kirk rolled his eyes but said nothing.

Jason was eager to let them know that he had won two games of Old Maid.

"I didn't know you even knew how to play that game," Kirk said.

"Grandpa taught me. And he said I can have this deck of cards. He'll buy himself another one."

"Wow! You did alright. I hope you remembered to thank him."

Katie had moved to the kitchen with her mother, and Kirk could hear the discussion of Denise continuing. "Mom, it's just not fair that she's gonna get Brandon back! What kind of system do we have that would place a child back with an uncaring mother like that? She won't have him two weeks 'til she's ready to ditch him. Her newest man and her fancy designer clothes is all she cares about!"

Kirk looked at his father-in-law and shook his head. "Katie's not taking this good—neither am I."

Brandon visits his mom again & Katie gets pissed when Denise ignores him to brag about her new lifestyle

CHAPTER 51

Sunday evening Kirk drove in to the city and picked up Brandon. Katie refused to go. On the way back, Brandon filled Kirk's ears with some of the same bitterness toward Denise that he'd heard from Katie on Friday evening. "Kirk, she spent the whole weekend in bed watching TV! I heard them planning another trip to some island in the Pacific—or someplace. That was all they talked about the whole time I was there. They don't have any books in my room, and I had to watch a stupid baseball game with Martin. I was bored, and I was hungry. I looked in the fridge to find something to eat. Martin gave me a dirty look—like I had no business snooping in their fridge; so then he took me down to a café to eat."

"What did you eat there at the café?"

"It was awful! A hamburger that tasted like cardboard with slimy cooked onions and mushrooms on it"

"Why didn't you tell him you didn't like onions and mushrooms?"

"He didn't give me a choice; he just ordered for me!"

"Well it sounds like you could use one of our good old Angus burgers with lots of pickles and ketchup, just the way you like 'em. Just tell Miss Katie that's what you want next."

It was the following Tuesday when Betty called to tell Katie that Jason's grandmother had obtained custody and would be taking him back to Arizona with her. "She is flying in tomorrow. I'll come out and pick him up tomorrow afternoon. You'll need to have his things ready then."

While the boys were still in school, Katie went through Jason's closet and gathered up his clothes. She looked around the room, saw the little die cast Corvette her dad had given him, and she placed it in the extra suitcase she found in the attic. Then she picked out a dozen first-grade level books that she knew Jason had liked and slipped them in beside the little Corvette. When Kirk came in, she told him she just had to send Jason away with something he would remember them by.

Kirk said, "Take some pictures of him and Brandon when they get in from school. I'll even have the horses saddled up for them. That should make for some good pictures and memories." Then it hit him. "I guess we'll have to mail them—no—I'll run them in and get them developed at Walgreens this evening. They're open late."

"Kirk, I want him to have a picture of you and me too. We could have Brandon take a picture of us. Oh, and he should have one of all four of us. Our camera has a time feature on it. He needs to be able to remember the time he spent here with us in our special little part of the world." A tiny tear was trickling down one of her cheeks. "I worry about him."

"Honey, he'll be fine."

"I just hope that grandmother will be good to him. He's a very special little boy with a very tender heart."

"Katie, we've done all we can do. I believe we've made an impact on his life."

Kirk had the horses saddled up when the boys got in from school. After a glass of milk and some homemade oatmeal cookies, they all headed to the stable. Kirk took a timed picture of all four of them, and Katie took pictures as the three guys took their mounts. Kirk offered

Dandy to Katie, but she said she just wanted to watch the three guys ride off toward the east end of the ranch. With the camera still in her hand, she snapped a couple more shots and then watched until they were out of sight.

The next morning she was preparing a good hearty breakfast for her three boys. Brandon was dressing for school and Jason was bragging that he didn't have to go to school today. Kirk grabbed the remote and turned to the morning news.

The jury in the Bryce Collier murder trial has returned a verdict of guilty of first degree murder in the death of the southwest Oklahoma City woman, Joyce Richards. Sentencing is expected to follow tomorrow with life in prison without possibility of parole.

Kirk whooped! "Kate, did you hear that? That means he won't have a chance to beat another child or murder their mother."

"Should we tell the boys?"

"Well, sure! They need to know he can't get to them ever again."

At two o'clock Betty rolled up in her Buick to pick up Jason. "Did you hear the news? Katie asked. "Bryce was found guilty of first degree murder."

"Yes, I did. And I know Jason's grandmother will be relieved. She mentioned her concerns to me that Brice might try to find Jason for revenge."

"Betty, I have to ask you. Do you believe she will be good to Jason? I mean, he is such a tender-hearted little boy. I don't want him to be hurt."

"Katie, I've talked to her several times by phone, and I do believe she will be good for little Jason. She has already contacted the school he will be attending and talked to his teacher. The teacher knows that Jason's mother was murdered so she'll be sensitive to that. Grandmother says there are several kids in her neighborhood and they seem to be good kids. I'm not worried about him."

Kirk went back to Jason's room. "Hey, pal, are you ready to go meet your grandmother?"

"I guess."

"Well, Miss Betty is waiting on you. I'll get your suitcase; you get that other little bag."

Back in the big room, Jason asked Katie if she had put in his little car. "Yes, Jason, I wouldn't forget that. That was a present to you from my dad."

After the hugs and a couple of tears, Katie handed Jason over to Betty. She took his hand and said, "Come on big guy, you and your grandmother have a plane to catch." Katie watched from the front yard as they drove down the gravel lane toward the front gate.

The ranch house was quieter than usual. Even Brandon had few words. Kirk watched him through the kitchen window petting Noah. The usual romp between the two was absent. Katie sat at the table nibbling on the last oatmeal cookie. "Kirk, my heart is aching for little Jason, and now I'm overcome with fear that we are about to lose Brandon too."

Kirk turned and headed toward the couch. "Honey, you're hurting, I'm hurting, and I know Brandon is hurting and fearful, but it hurts even more to talk about it, so I just need to drop the subject for now. Okay?"

"You know, we all need a change of pace. Why don't we take Brandon to the National Cowboy and Western Heritage Museum? It's practically here at our back door, and we've never bothered to go."

"Good idea, Kate! I think I remember hearing that there is free admission on Wednesdays, now that school has started. Do you think it would be okay if we picked up Brandon a little early Wednesday?"

"Oh I'm sure it'll be okay, but I'll check with Mrs. Dalton and let her know."

Brandon was ecstatic! He told everyone in his class that he was getting to go. "They even have a real cowboy town and a frontier military fort. And all of the rodeo stars are featured there."

Mrs. Dalton asked him if he would tell the class all about it after his visit. Brandon beamed!

But Wednesday never came.

Brandon complained that martin was rude. Also, Jason was taken away to go live with his grandma in Arizona. Every 1 was sad.

CHAPTER 52

It was the phone call that Katie had feared the most. As soon as she heard Betty's voice, she shrank down into a ball on the sofa.

"Katie, this is Betty. I know this is going to be hard on you and Kirk, but Denise has regained custody of Brandon. I'll be out to pick him up tomorrow. You'll need to check him out of school in the morning. I'll be heading your way in the early afternoon."

A river of tears followed Katie's silence. "Betty, I—I can't… I can't talk about it right now." Finally, she somehow managed to say, "I'll have him ready."

A steady stream of tears cascaded onto her shirt and onto the leather sofa. Her world had just imploded. She saw nothing around her, only felt her own arms wrapped tightly around herself. The only sound came from within. Heavy sobs followed bellows of excruciating grief. The pain permeated her inner soul. She longed for her husband to hold her, but dreaded to have to tell him.

An hour passed as she curled there on the couch. Then she heard a Northern cardinal just outside the window—*what-cheer, what-cheer, what-cheer.* Then its mate—*purdy, purdy, purdy,* followed by a *chip.* And all was silent again. The path of light from the window had relocated farther to the east on the hardwood floor. Katie wanted to pray, but couldn't find words—any words.

CHAPTER 53

The clack of the keys on my old Remington typewriter was the only sound in the enormous room. This big house is barren. Kirk says the entire ranch seems vacant. I've always wanted to write; now I have the time, but I'd much rather be in Brandon's room, reading with him or preparing his favorite meal. I miss driving him up to meet the bus in the mornings and meeting him there in the afternoons. Kirk hasn't been fishing since he left. Noah is quite lethargic—just lies around looking sad. The next day after Betty came and picked up Brandon, I was busy changing the sheets on his bed and giving the room a spring cleaning in *November*. Noah was sacked out on the floor by the empty bookcase. I told him he was lazy. He opened one eye and stared at me, as if to say *it wasn't my ancestors that ate that apple, so you just go on working, and let me be*. Kirk had offered to let Brandon take Noah with him, but Denise said no way; Martin would never allow that.

So now I have the time to write, and write I will! I'm going to pour out my heart on paper. For many years, I've dreamed of writing children's books. Now I'm just going to write about *our* children, our foster children—and one very special foster child that has touched my heart in a way that I never dreamed possible. My memories of this extraordinary child will forever be etched in my mind.

Brandon's leaving us may have been the hardest thing Kirk and I have ever had to endure. We went into this fostering program knowing full well that we would get attached to one or more of the children left to our care. Everyone had warned us that one day our hearts would be broken—they were so right! Now there is nothing left but emptiness. I've cried a gallon of tears, and Kirk is always quiet. He does his job, but I can see the joy is gone. I can see it in his drab gray eyes. I swear they were once blue.

I've argued with God, telling Him this is just not right. Brandon hated everything about Denise's new life, and he loved everything about the time he spent with us. It's just not fair. These kids have no rights of their own. It doesn't matter what they want or even what might be best for them.

Just because a woman gives birth to a child, that doesn't make her a mother. I prayed—no, I argued.

But God was silent…

The unfinished page was still rolled into the old Remington. Kirk clicked on the TV. It was a KOKY reporter that abruptly halted my typing.

CHAPTER 54

The evening news was just starting:

Take a look at this video just in: Oklahoma Highway Patrol followed this black Hummer on I-Thirty-Five for several miles this morning. The vehicle wasn't speeding, and no apparent moving violations had occurred. But take a closer look at the driver. It looks as if the driver is very young, barely seeing over the steering wheel. So even though everything else seemed normal, cops questioned the age of the driver. Lights flashing and sirens blaring, the driver finally decided to pull over. Yeah, you guessed it. It was a very young boy—said he was nine years old.

After being questioned, the young boy said he just wanted to go see Kirk and Katie. Apparently this couple had been his foster parents until his mother had recently regained custody. When asked how he got the vehicle, he told them he memorized the combination to his step father's garage, and the keys were in the Hummer.

Highway Patrol commended him for being a safe driver, but told him they had to take him back to his parents. One officer drove the Hummer, while the other followed in the patrol car. This all happened with busy traffic heading north on Interstate Thirty-Five. His mother has not responded to our request for an interview.

Of course Kirk hooted, "Good job, Brandon!" Kirk gave a two-thumbs up sign. "See Kate, I taught him well. Told you a boy needed to learn how to drive a truck—okay, so it was a Hummer—same thing.

But Katie cried. She secretly wished he'd made it all the way back to the ranch, even though his visit would have been short lived. If she could just see him again! After the report, she turned to Kirk. "I wish they would have shown a close up of his face."

✑

The next day Betty called and asked if they were ready to accept another foster child. Katie told her that she knew that would be the best therapy for them now, but she just wanted to wait a while. "I know it sounds crazy, but I really want to have myself a big pity party. I somehow feel that if we bring another child into our home, it will be like we are forgetting Brandon."

Betty listened. She knew her friend needed to talk.

"No child can take the place of that little guy. Even though it was less than two years, I feel like Kirk and I invested a lifetime in that kid. When he came to us, he was a very scared little boy. He wanted to go back to the only mother he'd known, even though it meant being beaten by her abusive boyfriend. He'd been bounced around from one school to another and missed so many days that it seemed inevitable that he would be retained." She paused, not sure Betty was still on the line.

"Go ahead, Katie."

"Kirk bought him books—even built that bookcase for his room. We read to him when he couldn't read. Then gradually he began to recognize the words. This grew into a real love of books. He couldn't get enough. We bought books instead of eating out or going to the movies. The money we spent on those books! But it was worth it. I wonder— would Denise have spent that kind of time teaching him how to read?"

"I don't think so," Betty conceded.

"Would she have spent evenings using math and spelling flash cards with him?" The tears were flowing now. "Would she take him to the pound and let him pick out a dog to be his own? Kirk says every time he looks in the tack room and sees Brandon's saddle, a tear tries to escape his eye. I've watched as the school bus drives by without stopping, and I cry." There was another gap in the monologue.

"Katie, please go on. This is good for you. I'm listening."

"I've picked up the phone several times, wanting to call you to see if you've heard how he's doing. I guess I'm not supposed to do that, so I slowly lower the phone back to its cradle."

"Honey, you pick up that phone and call me anytime. I may not have any news, but I'd like to visit with you just the same."

"Thanks, Betty. I appreciate that. And thanks for listening to me ramble on. I think I know how a person feels when their spouse or their child has battled a long disease—and lost."

"Katie, I'm going to leave it up to you to let me know when you think you and Kirk are ready to invite another child into your home. But in the meantime, you call me anytime you want to talk. I'll have my hearing aid on and ready."

"I will. Bye."

Three days later, Katie had started pecking out her woes again on the old Remington. The phone rang and rattled her thoughts. She ripped out the paper and tossed it in the trash before answering the phone.

"Katie, this is Betty. How're you and Kirk doing?"

"I don't think you want to know. I'll just say this ranch is like a tomb."

"Well, the reason I'm calling is Denise has contacted me and tells me that Brandon is terribly depressed.

"Oh, I forgot to ask you the other day, when we talked on the phone. Did you hear about him taking Martin's Hummer and driving north on I-Thirty-Five when he was pulled over by the HP?"

"Yes, we saw that on KOKY. Wasn't that something?"

"Well, the reason Denise contacted me was to see if you and Kirk would be okay with Brandon visiting you some weekend. She didn't know what else to do. She told me he doesn't eat, and he just sits and stares at his books you sent him."

"Oh, Betty! My heart is racing right now. Of course we want to see him, but do you think that would be a good thing to do? Would it just prolong the time of hurt for Brandon?"

"Katie, I think it might help. But you have to understand, the Department can't be involved in this in any way. You would have to work out the details with Denise."

"Denise may not be very receptive to talking to me. I pretty much scolded her the last time we took him for a visit. She didn't even greet him or acknowledge that he was there. All she was interested in was showing off the professional decorating in that stinking million dollar condo of theirs."

"Katie, she sounded pretty much at wits end. I think she would be more than happy to visit with you now."

Friday afternoon, they drove over to Bricktown once again. Brandon was still in school. Kirk and Martin found common ground and managed a decent conversation down by the canal. Katie sat down with Denise at her kitchen table—she with espresso fresh from her fancy new espresso machine, Katie with a plain cup of coffee—black.

"Katie, I just don't know what to do with Brandon. It's like he is depressed all the time. His teacher has called and talked to me about his lack of attention in class. Martin has wanted to take him to a Red-Hawk's game down at the ballpark here in Bricktown, but he's not interested. We take him to the nice restaurants here in our little neighborhood, and he nibbles at best. I can't get him to eat. I've never seen a kid that won't watch TV, but he doesn't."

"Denise, he never was interested much in TV. I spent a lot of time with Brandon teaching him to read, and he developed a real love of books."

"Yes, I know. And I appreciate you sending all of those books, but the truth is he just sits and stares at them. I can't even get him to read them."

"Denise, have you sat down with him and read to him or asked him to read to you?" It was obvious she hadn't.

"I guess you heard the news about him taking Martin's Hummer and heading your way?"

"Yes, we saw it on the news."

Denise burst out with a loud cackle. When Katie sat unfazed by any humor, Denise's raspy cackle dropped off suddenly to a forged snigger, and then an awkward silence before she managed to go on.

"Well, it was then that I decided I had to do something. I know he misses you and Kirk, so I thought if he could just come for a visit that might help."

"Denise, of course we would be thrilled to have him visit. Kirk will have lots of plans for him throughout the entire weekend. But I have to ask, do you think that will be any long term help? I mean, what do you plan to do for him after we return him to you again?"

"Katie, we've tried!"

"Yes, but have you asked him what *he wants to do*? You've got to let him be part of the planning. You can't just tell him you're taking him to a baseball game—which he hates—and expect him to be happy about it. Find out what he wants to do. The main thing is to spend time with him. Do you ever eat any of your meals at home?"

"Hey, I don't cook. Martin knew that when he asked me to marry him, and he's okay with that."

"Denise, it's not about Martin. It's about your son. If you don't cook, ask Brandon where he'd like to go eat. He told us that Martin ordered a fancy hamburger at one of your restaurants down here. He said it had 'slimy cooked onions and mushrooms' on it. He hates both."

"So what are you saying?"

"I'm saying let him make some decisions for himself. Most of the time, I would ask him what he would like me to fix for dinner. He always loved one of our good old Angus burgers with nothing but pickles and ketchup. This kid has grown to be a regular farm boy. He's not going to like most of the food in those fancy restaurants down there."

"Phew! I thought I knew my kid!"

"Denise, you've been away a long time. It'll take time to renew your bond with him. Just make sure you make him the center of your world. He deserves it after all he's been through."

"Katie, you've seen that room we decorated for him. We've given him a beautiful—and safe—place to live. I've bought him designer sneakers, jeans, and tee shirts from the most popular brands. You know, Abercrombie—"

"Stop it! You've given him all of these *things*! That's not what Brandon wants. He wants your time. Get out of your world; get into his! Kirk and I made sure we spent several hours with him each day. We ate our meals together. We read books to him or listened to him read to us. We took him to shop for books and let him pick them out himself. We tried to take him to the zoo..."

"Oh, don't remind me. Bryce! That scum bucket! He is where he belongs now. I hope he rots in his stinking cell!"

"I'm just saying don't exclude Brandon in your life. I saw the look on his face that time that he asked Martin if he'd take him with him to one of his offshore rigs. Martin said no, he'd have to wait until he was older. Denise, your husband lost a perfect opportunity to bond with the kid. So what if it's a little extra trouble? Brandon is worth it!"

"You're probably right. Here come the guys. Would you want to go with me to pick up Brandon from school?"

"I'd love to."

Katie wasn't sure if she did any good talking to Denise. She went with her and got to see Brandon's school—a very exclusive private school, one of Oklahoma City's finest. He literally jumped into her arms, and when they got back to the condo, he did the same thing with Kirk.

The weekend went by way too fast. They took him to the National Cowboy and Western Heritage Museum and gladly paid the full weekend admission. He wanted to go horseback riding again, so the three of them rode all over the ranch. Katie was on Lilly, Kirk on Dandy, and Brandon rode Puzzle—just like they'd done dozens of times before.

Kirk grilled some good old Angus burgers. Katie made French fries. Brandon was right there with Kirk helping with the milking. He gathered the eggs and washed them before putting them in the fridge. He had his romp with Noah. The dog's tail was slapping from side to side at supersonic speed.

She later told Kirk, "I feel like this weekend was just a small Band-Aid on a giant weeping wound in my heart."

As promised, they returned Brandon back to Denise Sunday evening about eight o'clock. The drive downtown to the Van Buren condo was quiet. After saying goodbye to Brandon, Kirk reluctantly rang the doorbell. Denise opened the door and Kirk and Katie turned and walked back to their truck.

By nine p.m. they were back to an empty house in the middle of eighteen hundred acres of darkening shadows. Katie stared at her old Remington. With the wind just outside the window howling a tune in a minor key, she wondered what the next chapter would contain.

CHAPTR 55

Denise tried to recall everything Katie had suggested. She remembered one thing she had said. *When a child walks in the room, do your eyes light up?* But she couldn't remember who Katie had attributed that quote to—some famous person, maybe a poet. She thought about what Katie had said about spending time with Brandon, making him the center of her life. She told Martin, "I think Brandon *was* their life! They seemed to do nothing that didn't involve Brandon. We could do that too!"

Martin appeared to be thinking about what Denise had said. "Yeah, but we don't live on a ranch out in the boonies. There's life here in the city, and I've got obligations all over the world. I need to be in China in January. We sure can't take Brandon with us; he's got school!"

"What do you mean we can't take Brandon with us! We most certainly will!"

"Honey, you know that won't work for us! We don't live the kind of life that Kirk and Katie do. Our life is complicated."

"You're right. It's complicated for us. Katie and Kirk live a simple life, with no obligations other than doting on their foster children. I know we can't do that, but we've somehow got to find a way to bond with my son."

"What do you want me to do? Maybe I should buy some cowboy boots and a hat and take up bronco busting. You could learn to—what's that called—barrel racing? I could forget about my company, sit by the fire, and read books to him, and you could bake cookies and cook beans and cornbread. Come on, Denise! You know that won't happen! We've got a life to live."

"I know, but we have to do something."

"Hey, Brandon's just gonna have to conform to our way of life. We can't give up our lifestyle for a nine-year-old. Kids are resilient; he'll get used to it."

Denise picked up Brandon from school. The weather was unusually warm for November, and she had the top down on the Mercedes. When Brandon got in the car, he buckled up and was quiet. Denise didn't know what to make of it, so she just let him remain in his silent world. Later in the evening she went to his room, knocked slightly, and peeked in. He was lying on his bed, staring at the bottom of the top bunk. "Brandon, you are awfully quiet. Tell me what's wrong."

"You wouldn't understand."

"Maybe not, but I'd like to hear about it anyway."

"Naw. I don't think so."

"Well, we've not had dinner yet. Where would you like to go for dinner tonight?"

"Nowhere around here."

"Well, where?"

Brandon perked up. "Can we go to Chuck E. Cheese? Kirk took me there once when we came to the city. But I don't know where it was."

Denise looked up Chuck E. Cheese in the yellow pages. When she told Martin where they would eat, he looked at her like she'd just walked on the ceiling. "You've gotta be kidding—Chuck E. Cheese? You can't be suggesting that you and I eat there."

"Yes, that is exactly what I'm suggesting. That's where Brandon wants to go for dinner, and that's where we are going!" Her brown eyes bore a hole straight through him with an agonizing pause before she said, "And you and I will sit down and eat with him there at *Chuck E. Cheese!*"

Thanksgiving was just around the corner and Denise asked Martin what they should do for the holiday. "I have an aunt in Boston," Martin said. "I haven't seen her in a few years. I'd like to take you there to meet her."

"What? Just like that—no invitation from her?"

"No, it's not like that. This aunt practically raised me. She would love to have us visit. Maybe you could ask Kirk and Katie to keep Brandon while we're gone."

"Why would I do that? He should go with us!"

"Honey, you don't know my aunt. She's got all these little expensive things setting around her house. If Brandon broke something, she'd never want us to come back."

"Well, if that's the case, then we probably shouldn't go in the first place. I want to spend the holidays with my son. It's been a long time since I've had that privilege."

"So what do you suggest we do for Thanksgiving? You don't cook."

"I can have a turkey and all the trimmings catered in for us. Let's have a family meal around our dining table, which we've never used. You and Brandon can watch a football game, and I'll lose myself in a good mystery novel."

"Honey, just give Katie a call and see if they'll keep him. I'm anxious for you to meet my aunt. She needs to see what a gorgeous wife I have now."

"Martin, I am not calling Katie! We are his parents, not them. It is our responsibility."

The day before Thanksgiving, Martin and Denise Van Buren boarded a plane to Boston. Martin had found a nanny to come to their apartment and stay with Brandon. Denise knew it was wrong, but she also knew she had to think about her marriage. She knew she could have done a lot worse when it came to men—and had! He was definitely a catch. She knew she had to keep him on the hook.

Thanksgiving quickly rolled right into Christmas. This time Denise knew better than to ask Martin what he wanted to do for Christmas. She called Martin's travel agent for three tickets to Aspen. This time she would stand up to him.

The ski lodge was beautiful. Their suite had its own river rock fireplace. There was a beautiful kitchen, complete with granite countertops, the latest stainless steel appliances, and a beautiful wet bar separating the kitchen from the living room. Massive windows in the large room allowed for a full view out onto the powdery white slopes, filled with people swooshing downward, as a chair lift delivered dozens of others upward.

A ski instructor was hired for Brandon for four hours on the slopes while Martin and Denise enjoyed mature beverages in the lounge below. A beautiful white Christmas in Aspen, Colorado! What could be better? The ski instructor delivered an exhausted Brandon back to their suite. Martin was watching a game on TV while Denise was down on the streets shopping in the winter wonderland of Aspen. Fresh snow had fallen overnight, and a few flakes continued to parachute down through the crisp mountain air throughout the morning. Denise set her four shopping bags down on the king-size bed. *This is exactly what we've needed—a family vacation for the three of us.*

After arriving back at Will Rogers World Airport in Oklahoma City, Martin started discussing his plans for their trip to China. Denise had been dreading this. Martin had already adamantly stated his opinion that Brandon should remain in school in Oklahoma. She knew the dilemma she was facing. Finally she spoke up. "Martin, I'll just stay here with Brandon. I am not going to have a nanny stay with him for several months."

"Denise, you are my wife. You will go with me!"

"Look, if I go, Brandon goes too!"

"Honey, you know that won't work. Where would he go to school?"

"I'll home school him. But I'm not leaving him here!"

"Ha! You—without even a high school diploma—you think you can homeschool him?"

"Shut up, Martin!"

"You keep telling me how Katie recommended that you start letting Brandon make decisions for himself. Why don't you ask him what he wants to do?"

"Martin, don't be ridiculous! A nine-year-old can't make a decision like that!"

"Well, then you need to make a decision. About him, as well as yourself!"

"What exactly is that supposed to mean?"

"Take it however you want, Denise."

Denise had hoped the holiday in Aspen would bring her little family closer. She knew Martin and Brandon needed desperately to bond with each other. Martin's attitude, instead, seemed to be headed in the opposite direction. It appeared that he now saw Brandon as a huge intrusion into his life, inhibiting his ability to conduct the business of his company as he should and obstructing the leisure time he needed to share with Denise. Any suggestion of the three of them spending a

Saturday or Sunday together in family activities was always met with disparagement. Usually Denise would hear Martin say, "Honey, you know I have to be gone quite a bit throughout the week. I just need the two of us to be able to spend some quality time together—just the two of us."

Denise remembered it well. It was the morning of December 31ˢᵗ. She had wanted to spend a quiet evening by the fire, playing Brandon's favorite game—Monopoly. She had ordered an overabundance of snacks catered and delivered to the condo. A huge silver tray filled with jumbo shrimp, imported cheeses, caviar and crackers, cinnamon and sugar coated pecans and almonds was delivered about six in the evening, along with two bottles of <u>Philipponnat Brut Clos des Goisses</u>, the very best champagne available from her caterer. Each room of the condo was filled with the spicy vanilla aroma of candles imported from France. Martin had spent the day betting on the horse races at Remington Park. Denise thought about that. *What a perfect opportunity that would have been for some good father and son bonding.* Instead, Brandon was stuck in his room again with his video games and books. Denise was determined the evening would be different. As she looked over the enormous tray of food she'd ordered, she knew this evening would be the precursor to the family connection she'd been hoping for. A quiet evening at home for her little family—that's what Katie would have done.

At eight-thirty that evening, Martin marched in the door, hugged his wife, and topped it off with a lingering kiss. "Hey, babe, you smell wonderful! I'll give you a couple of hours to change while I make a few phone calls. I've got an evening planned for the two of us that you'll never forget." He slapped her on the bottom and said, "Now go do your magic with that beautiful body of yours. That black dress you bought in Boston would be perfect. Oh, and you'll want to grab that coyote fur coat—five thousand dollar coat—you picked up in Aspen last week. That thing is drop-dead gorgeous on you!

Denise protested. "Martin! I thought we'd spend a nice quiet evening here at home with Brandon. I've ordered all this food, and I had planned for us to play a game of Monopoly right here by the fire. I've even got a couple of bottles of the very best champagne my caterer could find for you and me. I've just been waiting for you to get in."

Martin pulled Denise to his side and wrapped his arm around her waist. "Honey, this is New Year's Eve! We are not going to spend our first New Year's Eve together cooped up in this condo, playing Monopoly!"

"Well you didn't mind spending the day at the race track without us!"

"Honey, Remington Park is not a place for a nine-year-old. There's gambling, old men sloshing beer all over the place, and language not fit for a child."

"Oh, so you'd rather spend your day with old men sloshing beer on one another and cursing like sailors, than to spend it with me and Brandon?"

"Denise, you are trying to excavate the Grand Canyon! You should step back and enjoy the beauty. There is nothing wrong with me spending a day at the races and then taking my beautiful wife out on the town for the evening. I'll bet you haven't even called the nanny."

"No, I haven't called the nanny! Brandon is my son, not hers! You never think of Brandon; you're always leaving him out of the picture. It's no wonder he hates you!"

"Oh yeah? I guess he also hates the private school I pay for—where he doesn't have to put up with a classroom full of good-for-nothing-kids from the hood. And I guess he hates being the best dressed kid in town. And you're not even thinking about this expensive condo I've provided for him with his own special bedroom designed by the very best interior designers the city has to offer. Denise, you need to consider what you and Brandon have got here."

"Martin Van Buren, what we've got here is a man that thinks only of himself. You are not still single..."

"Oh yeah? Well, I've considered that. Maybe I should be!"

Denise thought about that last statement. She dropped down in the big leather chair by the fireplace, thinking back about her life with Bryce in that roach infested twelve by sixty foot trailer smack in the middle of Oklahoma City's cornucopia of drugs. She thought about the summer she'd spent broiling in that hot and humid motel laundry room, with sweat drenching the pants and shirt she'd gotten at Goodwill. *No, I will never go back to that—never!*

Earlier in the day, Martin had tried to call the nanny. Unable to reach the one they had used before, he'd made a few calls and then found a nanny that his accountant had suggested. Denise slung the coyote coat over her left arm and followed Martin out through the massive oak front door. She looked back and saw the squatty little seventy-year-old nanny sitting by the fire, starting to munch on the copious culinary creations from the three foot diameter silver tray sitting on the large leather ottoman in front of the couch. Brandon was alone, staring at the mustang fresco stretching across the wall in his twelve-thousand dollar designer room.

As the p.m. stretched into the a.m., Martin had introduced his wife to dozens of his business associates and friends. There were several comments, similar in content. "You two make a good-looking couple." Or, "Martin, you've picked a beauty this time." Or, "Where did you find this beauty queen?" It was all very flattering to Denise, but also a bit repulsive. It was obvious they thought of her as *Martin's trophy wife.* With two other couples crowding around their small two-foot cocktail table, chattering about nothing of any substance, Denise thought about herself as Martin's so called trophy wife. *A trophy is supposed to be something you earn; not something you buy!* She was in her own world, totally unaware of those packed around the small table. Her thoughts were anywhere but in that smoke filled sanctum of jet setters. *Have I sold my soul for a life of prosperity and abundance?*

CHAPTER 56

In less than four weeks Martin was scheduled to be in China. The Nanpu block in Bohai Bay's Jidong oil field in northern China had proven disappointing after the much touted first estimates. Martin's high technology rigs were seen to be an answer to the lackluster production.

Denise realized it was decision time for her. She could move Brandon to a boarding school, if there was such in Oklahoma, and accompany Martin to China. Or, she could refuse to go without him and hope that she would be able to homeschool him in a country that she knew nothing about. There was a third alternative—one which she simply couldn't imagine. If she refused to go with Martin, it would be the end of their marriage. She watched from their fifth floor window as a few snowflakes began to trickle down to the ground below. A male cardinal landed on the window ledge outside. Her thoughts were racing. *I wish I had someone to confide in. My mom's gone; my sister in LA won't speak to me. I have no friends here—not much different than the solitary confinement Bryce Collier is in, after attacking his cell mate and almost killing him.* Twice she picked up the phone intending to call Katie to see if she would talk to her. *Katie would have an answer—she has all the answers.* But each time she slammed the phone down. *What am I thinking? I just can't see Katie Childers as being on my side!*

It was time to pick up Brandon from school. She was hoping Martin would have left her the Hummer since the roads were icing over.

ELDON REED

She tapped in the code to the garage door. The Hummer was gone and her Mercedes sat there with the top still down. Yesterday when she picked up Brandon, the temperature had been in the sixties with plenty of sun. She'd driven on snow before, but ice was a different thing entirely—especially with a rear wheel drive lightweight little car. She tapped the button to extend the convertible top and pulled out of the garage. Brandon's school was only about two miles from their condo. Two blocks from home, the digital temperature on her dash showed twenty-six degrees. *That's Oklahoma weather for you. One minute I'm basking in the sun. The next I'm driving on ice!*

Brandon came barreling out from the school, minus a coat. "Hey! Where's your coat?"

"I couldn't find it. I put it in my locker when I got to school this morning."

"Brandon! That was a North Face Nuptse down jacket. I just bought that for you at Nordstrom's. I paid a hundred and forty bucks for that!" Still staring at her son, she pulled out of the line of cars, into an oncoming Cadillac. Both frontal air bags burst into action. Brandon hadn't buckled up yet. He screamed! The impact drove the middle of the left door of the Mercedes into Denise's ribs, in spite of the side curtain air bag. Dazed, she sat there with the now deflated air bag in her lap, unable to think what to do next. Finally, Brandon's screaming jolted her back to reality. She turned and looked at her son. He was shaken but seemed to be unscathed. Then she noticed the blood oozing through the left sleeve of her shirt. Brandon was staring at her.

"Denise, are you okay?"

Had she heard him right? That wasn't the first time he'd called her Denise. And come to think of it, she couldn't remember him calling her *Mom* since he was taken from her over two years ago. Her pain was stabbing. She handed the cell phone to Brandon. "Honey, you better call nine-one-one."

Less than two minutes later, she heard the sirens. First, an ambulance pulled up beside her; then a police car pulled in behind the ambulance. It was only then that she thought about the Cadillac she'd rammed. *God, please don't let me have killed another person!*

Brandon took over and called Martin's cell phone. Denise's injuries were thought to be pretty superficial. It didn't appear that any ribs were broken and her left hip seemed to be okay. She had a minor cut in her left side where the door had punched her. The lady driving the Cadillac was unhurt. Denise had rammed the unoccupied right side of her car.

Ten minutes later, Martin drove up in the Hummer, got out, took one look at the smashed left side of the Mercedes, and swore. Then swore again. He walked completely around the car before going to Denise. "Denise, what in the world have you done now?"

"Honey, I was getting on to Brandon about losing his coa—"

"Look what you've done to this car! This thing's gonna be totaled out!"

Her brown eyes penetrated deep into his irritated face. "So go buy another one, Mr. Van Buren!"

CHAPTER 57

Denise's wound was healing nicely; her heart was not. Martin was pushing her for a decision. "Denise, I've got to buy our airline tickets soon. You've gotta decide what you're gonna do."

It wasn't as if she hadn't been thinking about her dilemma. The fact was she couldn't get it off her mind. She talked to Brandon's teacher about homeschooling him from China. Where could she get the necessary books and materials? She went online to see what she could find out about the area in northern China where they would be staying. She wondered if Martin had even considered their housing arrangements there. Was it a rural area, or would they be living in a city? Without speaking the language, she knew life would be a prison cell for Brandon and her as well. Three times she'd asked Martin why he would need to be there for so many months. He'd never given her a satisfactory answer. All he would say was that it would probably take about six months to make all the arrangements, get the three high tech rigs they now owned delivered, hire a willing crew, and make sure drilling was on schedule.

When she asked why he couldn't go over for a week or so, return, then go again later, all he would say was, "Denise, you just don't understand."

Martin came home late one evening. It was clear he'd fallen off the wagon—liquefied. "Okay, Deneeese!" He even slurred her name. "I want an answer now!"

As if she didn't know, she smarted back at him, "An answer to what?"

"Hey! You know exactly what I'm talkin' about! Are you goin' with me or not?"

"I don't think you're giving me much of a choice."

He was in her face and his breath was reeking, "Oh yeah? I think I could say that about you too!"

She knew her alternatives weren't good. "Of course, I'll go live on the other side of the world in a godforsaken part of China, where no one speaks our language. And I *will* bring my son with me."

Martin drew back away from her face. "Denise, you shou... you should leave the kid here!"

"Tell me, just how many drinks have you had?"

"Shut up, Denise!"

"Yeah, I think I've heard those words before. That bad boy's sittin' in a federal prison in solitary confinement. I will not have *any* man tell me to shut up, ever again! You got that?"

He stepped closer again, reached for her hand, "Honey, I'm sorry. I shouldn't have—"

"Are you sorry enough that you will sober up and stay that way? I won't have an alcoholic, abusive, and controlling husband! I've already been through that."

"Babe, I said I'm sorry. And yes, I promise to stay sober. It's just that I was so depressed over your indecision about our future—"

She stopped him mid-sentence. "So you decided to go and guzzle some more depression, uh?"

"I'm sorry, babe."

"Give me the keys to the Hummer. I've gotta go pick up Brandon. I hope you didn't drive in your condition."

"No, I was just down at the sports bar less than a block away. I just warked…walked home."

"You mean you stumbled home."

On the way to pick up Brandon, Denise made up her mind. She knew what she had to do. When she got back to the condo, she told Martin to just buy one ticket for himself. "Brandon and I will come as soon as I can get together the items I need for homeschooling."

"Honey, you sure?"

"Yeah, I'm sure. It'll take me a week or so to tie up all the loose ends here. Brandon's teacher has agreed to help me with the things I'll need for his lessons."

"Okay, I hate to push my luck, but I'd hoped it would be just you and me. I had dreams of us doing the tourist thing—maybe hiking the Great Wall together, you know."

"Martin, the Great Wall is not even in that part of China. You haven't researched this thing out enough to even know what you're getting into."

"And you have?"

"Yes, I have! I know we will be going to an area very unlike the major cities of Hong Kong or Beijing. This is a very primitive area, Martin. There will be nothing for us to do there—no corner coffee shops, no sports stadiums, no shopping as we know it here."

"And just how did you learn about the area? You don't even know how to turn on that thirty-five hundred dollar laptop, and you wouldn't have a clue where the local library is. I'm sure of that." Martin's alcohol reddened face glowed under the crystal chandelier. "…probably wouldn't be able to read the words anyway."

"Oh yeah? Well tell me then just how would I know about those—should I be tactful and just call them *questionable*—sites you've been visiting on that fancy laptop?"

"That's none of your business, Denise! What I do on that laptop is *my* business."

Denise plopped down in the Regina Andrew gray wool tufted tub chair and started picking at her nail polish. She could feel Martin's impatient glazed stare. "I'm going with you, but I am telling you right now, I'm coming back home in six months—with or without you!"

"Fair enough."

"Well, I'm glad we've got that settled."

"Honey, I did locate a boarding school in Tulsa. Would you consid—"

"Martin, you knew my answer to that before your lips even tried to form the words. What a stupid question!"

"Okay; okay! Geeze!"

Denise watched Brandon over the next several days. She was aware he knew Martin didn't want him. His grades were still dropping even more, and he had become a bit lethargic. She'd had three consultations with his teacher recently. The teacher appeared to be a very intelligent and caring person, but she just simply didn't understand their family situation. How could she tell her that she was married to a man that would rather Brandon drop off the face of the earth.

She decided to try some of Katie's tactics. She bought a cookbook, gathered all the ingredients for homemade lasagna. She remembered Katie telling her that Brandon couldn't get enough of her lasagna. She pulled the different cheeses from the fridge, got out the big wide noodles from the pantry, and reread the recipe about preparing the sauce. She stared at the big six-burner Viking range. *Now, how in the world do I turn this monstrosity on?*

The lasagna was pretty good. Brandon seemed to like it. Martin's take was a bit different. "Honey," he said, "let's just go out to a nice Italian restaurant next time. Maggiano's Little Italy can do lasagna the way lasagna's supposed to be done—and their wine selection is superb."

Denise crossed her slender and tanned legs, still picking at her nails. "Well, next time, you just go on down to your stinkin' Maggiano's. Brandon and I will dig into *my* lasagna here in our own dining room."

The evening before Martin's plane was to leave the next day, Denise wanted desperately to gather her family together for a time of relationship mending—no, it would be more like a major overhaul. She remembered Katie telling her how Brandon had been so disappointed that Martin wouldn't take him to one of the offshore rigs. So that was part of her after-dinner plan. She figured she'd get her family used to the cuisine of the country they would be spending the next six months, so she had her caterer prepare a variety of Chinese dishes to be delivered around seven that evening. There was egg foo yung for starters, followed by mu shu pork with fried rice, zong zi dumplings, which is a bamboo wrapped dumpling, and Peking roasted duck. All of the traditional condiments were accompanying the food, including special hot mustard, unlike what's in those little packets at the typical Chinese restaurant. She had even ordered a special colorful floral arrangement with tiny red fans scattered through the several shades of hibiscus and white and pink Chinese lotus for the dining table.

Brandon looked at the arrangement displayed in the center of the table. "Are we gonna eat here?"

Martin had showered and dressed for an evening out. When he came into the dining room and saw what Denise had done, he said, "Wow! You're really getting into the swing of this Chinese thing early, uh?" He pulled her chair out for her to be seated and leaned down to kiss her cheek.

"Wait guys, I forgot the candles!"

Brandon looked at his plate with the chopsticks lying beside it. "What am I supposed to do with these?"

"Those are chopsticks," Denise said. "Here let me show you how to use them."

You might as well have given that nine-year-old farm boy a pair of hay hooks and told him to eat his food with them. On his first try with the strange sticks, he flipped a dumpling across the table, landing in Martin's plate. Denise laughed. Brandon froze, and Martin scolded him severely. On the second try, Brandon knocked over his egg foo yung, with the liquid spilling across the table toward Martin. He jumped up, threw his linin napkin down on the table and said, "Okay, that does it, Denise! Get that kid a fork and a spoon, or get him outta here!"

"Martin! He's just a kid! Can't you have any patience?"

Brandon jumped up from his chair, excused himself, and went to his room. Martin glared at Denise. "Honey, we can't have him spoiling a dinner night out with strangers in a strange country. You need to think seriously about that boarding school I found for him in Tulsa."

Denise again considered her options. "Honey, let's not botch this special dinner for us too. Let's just enjoy this scrumptious food. It's your last night here with us. I don't want to spoil it for you."

After dinner, she coaxed Brandon back into the family room with her and Martin. She sat down next to Martin and put her hand on his leg. "Honey, would you explain how your fancy rigs work to Brandon? You know when he first came back to us he really was interested in them. Remember, he even wanted to go with you sometime down to the Gulf so he could see it all."

"Honey, now really! Do you actually think a nine-year-old could comprehend the workings of a multi-million dollar oil or gas rig?"

Brandon stared at Martin in disbelief. He jumped up and said, "That's okay. We all know a *nine-year-old*—no, a ten-year-old—you forgot about my birthday yesterday... Anyway, we know a ten-year-old isn't even capable of discussing those kinds of things!" As he stomped out, he turned and stared at Martin, then said, "Maybe someday I'll figure out what I'm smart enough to discuss!"

"Get back in here, Brandon!" Martin started to get up. "You little …"

"Martin, let him be. You really blew that one!"

"Oh yeah? Well, it looks like you really blew it too! You didn't even remember his birthday yesterday? What kind of mother forgets her own son's birthday?"

CHAPTER 58

Denise drove Martin to the airport for his six o'clock take off. Brandon slept in the backseat of the Hummer. At the security check-through, she kissed her husband and told him she'd meet him in China in a couple of weeks or so. She winked and said, "Don't you latch onto some cute little thing before I get over there."

"Honey, I've got my cute little thing right here, and I'm lookin' forward to having you with me in a few." He pecked her on the cheek. "You got nothin' to worry about, babe."

"Oh crap!" She turned and started to run back toward the parking lot.

Martin turned and hollered at her, "What's wrong, honey?"

Without slowing down she shouted back to him, "Martin! I forgot Brandon! He's asleep in the Hummer!"

The last thing she heard as she was barreling out the door was, "Denise! Don't I get a goodbye kiss? The kid will be okay. For crying out loud, he's asleep!"

When she got in sight of the Hummer, she knew she shouldn't use the remote to open the door until she was right by the door. *Who knows who's lurking out here? It's not even daylight yet.* The parking lot lights were still on.

She ran to the vehicle, punched the remote, grabbed the door handle, and with the force of a hefty pair of Vice-Grips, jerked the door open. Brandon wasn't there in the back seat where she'd left him. She closed her eyes and screamed! Dropping to her knees there by the open door, she shouted, "No, God, NO!" She knelt there sobbing for a few seconds, then reached for her cell phone and opened her eyes. It was then that she saw Brandon climbing over the back seat from the cargo area.

"Where'd you go?" he asked, wiping at his sleepy eyes.

Denise looked up toward the sky and silently mouthed, *Thank you, God!*

Brandon repeated his question, "Denise, where'd you go?"

"Oh, honey! I'm so sorry! I totally forgot that you were back there sleeping. Are you okay?"

"Yeah, but I don't think you are."

"Baby, I'm just shook up. When I opened the door and didn't see you in the back seat where we left you, I freaked out!"

"Well, you'd better get up off that ground. Someone's gotta drive us home." He laughed. "And it probably shouldn't be me."

For several days, Denise questioned herself. *What kind of mother am I? Who leaves their child in an airport parking lot? And what mother forgets her son's birthday? I don't deserve to be a mother!* She knew she should be getting prepared for their trip to go half way around the world, but something was holding her back. Ever since Brandon came back to live with her, she knew he was miserable. To tell the truth, she knew she was also miserable. *God, all I wanted was to raise my son in a good safe home with a father—okay, stepfather—that was like... Yes, I'll admit it—like Kirk Childers!* There was an ache in her stomach that seemed to be unrelenting. *God, you know this is not working. You must know I've tried!*

She drove Brandon to school and walked in with him, with the full intention of asking his teacher for some materials she could use for homeschooling. At his classroom door, she bent down and kissed him on the forehead, turned and walked back to the Hummer.

Back at Bricktown, she parked inside the garage, closed the door, and headed for her favorite coffee shop. A double espresso might just be the thing to ease her pain. As usual, the waiter tried to flirt with her. Without a word to him, she took the cup of double dark roasted liquid and headed outside. She sat down at a patio table, grasping the cup with both hands in the freezing air, staring off into the nothingness beyond. Her head was spinning. *God, will you send me to Hell for doing what I'm about to do?*

CHAPTER 59

Denise stood staring at the phone on the nightstand in the master bedroom. Eventually she picked up the courage and reached for it. She knew the number well. She tapped it into the handset; then immediately pressed the end button and slammed the phone down. She dropped to her knees there beside the bed.

When she opened her eyes and looked at the clock on the nightstand, an hour had passed. She sat down on the floor by the bed, ran her fingers through her dense red curls, picked up the phone, and hit the recall button. "Jennifer, can… can you put Betty on the phone?" And after a long pause, she managed to say, "This is Denise."

Jennifer held her hand over the mouthpiece of the phone. "Betty, Denise is on the phone and wants to talk to you."

"What's that all about?"

"I have no idea. She seemed hesitant, almost scared."

Betty picked up the phone. "Denise?"

"Betty." There was a long pause. "Betty, we need to talk."

"What's wrong, Denise?"

Denise wiped her mascara streaked eyes. "Betty, I'm… I'm no good for Brandon."

"What? What are you talking about?"

"I'm not the kind of mother Brandon needs."

"Honey, whatever makes you say that?"

I'm telling you, I am no good for Brandon. He no longer sees me as his mother. He even calls me Denise."

"Hey, a lot of kids are doing that nowadays. I wouldn't worry about that."

"No, you don't understand. Listen… listen to me. I am not the kind of mother he needs."

"Well, what child gets to pick his parents? Come on, he just needs some time."

"Betty, Brandon deserves better than me. I'm no good for him. I took Martin to the airport and left Brandon sleeping in the Hummer—in the airport parking lot, for crying out loud! I even forgot his birthday! I can't cook meals for him. We have nothing in common. He's just stuck with this pretty woman with a fancy condo by the river. I don't know what he wants. His grades have tumbled and he hates Martin. I thought I was giving him a father when I married Martin, but what I've given him is a stranger that can't be bothered with a nine-year-old—oh yeah, I guess he's ten years old now!" She was sobbing freely. "I would have never known if Brandon hadn't told me!"

"Denise, you are his mother. You have a responsibility to that child. Pull yourself up out of the mulligrubs and start loving that child again."

"Oh, I love him. I just can't be his mother."

"Why not?"

"Betty, it is complicated. You know what my life was like when you picked up Brandon over two years ago. Well, when I met Martin, I wanted out of my drug infested neighborhood. I was determined to make something out of my life. Remember, I told you about some raspy voiced woman on TV saying, 'Get up out of your ghetto. Make something of your life.' Well, Betty, I had good intentions, but I failed! What I made myself into is a *trophy wife* for a wealthy jetsetter that hates kids."

"Denise, I think you're being too rough on yourself."

"No, I'm telling you, I'm no good for him. I'm a total failure in the parenting game. He needs to be with a family that knows how to love and care for him."

"Well, don't you think it's a little too late for that, sister?"

There were a few moments of uncontrolled sobbing. Denise dropped the phone in her lap. She put her hand over her eyes and slowly slid it back over her forehead.

"Denise, Denise. Are you there?"

She took the phone from her lap, leaned back against the side of the bed, "Yeah, Betty, I'm here—for now."

"Denise, are you alone?"

There was a full minute of silence. "Yeah, why?"

"You're not thinking about harming yourself, are you?"

"I don't know what I'm thinking. That might be the easy way out."

"Honey, don't talk like that! Would you let me call and get you some professional help? You can well afford some good professional counseling."

"No, Betty, it's too late for that."

"Denise, are you home now?"

"Yes."

"Honey, I'm heading your way right now. Don't do anything. I'll be there in ten minutes tops."

The elevator was stuck on the fifth floor. Betty panicked! After tackling a hundred and thirty-five stairs, she reached the fifth floor, out of breath and unable to gather her thoughts into any acceptable scenario. She pressed the bell and waited. She pressed it again. Now she was really starting to panic! She stood there for more than a minute, wondering if she should call nine-one-one. Then a disheveled Denise opened the door. Betty stared at a very pitiful looking woman. "Honey, you scared me half to death!"

"Sorry."

"Can I come in so we can talk?"

"Betty, I'm sorry you thought you had to come here to talk.

"It's okay, you got any coffee? I sure could use a good strong cup about now."

Denise pointed to the cold Styrofoam cup of espresso she'd carried back from the coffee shop. "Sorry, that's the closest thing I've got right now. It's cold by now. I never touched it this morning. In fact, I don't even remember bringing it back up here from the coffee shop down by the canal."

After the two had settled down on the big leather couch facing the fireplace, Betty quizzed the reedy, but disheveled, woman beside her. "Where is Martin?"

Denise giggled, "Oh, I sent him down under."

"What!"

"Martin Van Buren is half way to China by now."

"Denise! Talk to me. What is going on here? What have you done?"

"That's part of the problem." Denise managed to compose herself a bit. "Martin is on his way to China to set up some of our rigs there in an oilfield that isn't producing as expected. He thinks he can solve their problem with his rigs. He says he'll be there for at least six months. He wants—no—he *expects* me to go with him. But there is a big problem; he doesn't want Brandon to come. In fact, he doesn't want Brandon— period!"

"Denise, I thought Martin was happy that he was going to have a son."

"Yeah, until he learned that Brandon wasn't a Martin Van Buren clone! You see, he expects his son to like what he likes, eat what he eats, dress like him, but stay out of the way when it comes to his jet setting lifestyle."

"That's pretty unrealistic—and selfish!"

"Yeah, I know. I think I have even said those exact words to him."

"So why don't you just stay here with Brandon?"

Denise dropped her head. "Betty, I have to go with Martin. If I don't, I won't have a husband when—and if—he returns."

"So you have to choose between your husband and your son, right?"

"That's about it. I don't have any other choice."

"Denise, you said this is only for six months or so?"

"Yes, but it's not just a matter of these six months I have to get past. Martin will never accept Brandon. Brandon hates him, and really—I think he hates me too."

"Honey, I'm sure you guys can resolve this…"

"No, I've made up my mind. I want you to call and see if Kirk and Katie still want to adopt Brandon."

"You have got to be kidding! You're not even going to *try* to work this out?"

"Oh, I've tried. Believe me. I have no choice! I am nothing but a trophy wife for Martin—and there is no room for Brandon on that trophy shelf."

"Well, of course, I want nothing to do with this plan. If you are determined to carry this out, you'll just have to do that on your own, girl."

"Can you give me Katie's number? I had it at one time."

"Denise! I can't do that either! You're trying to put me in a place that I don't want to be. But if you're sure this is what you want, I'll give Katie a call and have her contact you. But I'm not going to tell her about this absurd plan of yours! You will have to do that yourself."

"Fair enough."

Betty got up and showed herself to the door. As she opened the giant door, she turned and shot Denise a grimacing look.

She didn't wait until she got back to the office; she called on her way. "Katie, this is Betty. You're not going to believe this!"

"What!"

"Denise wants you to call her. I'm not going to say what it's all about. Do you still have her number?"

"I think so—yes, here it is, if it hasn't changed."

"As of today, it is still the same. I can't say how long you'll be able to reach her there. She will soon be heading to China."

"China! Good grief! What's that all about?"

"Katie, just call her. You probably should call as soon as we hang up."

CHAPTER 60

This is February 20th. I'm sitting here at my typewriter, looking out the window at the falling snow—flakes as big as half dollars. But it's not the snow that's brought new life to the landscape here on this ranch. Brandon outshines any winter snow or any summer sun. He is an all-encompassing beam of light to us, and this entire ranch! Kirk's new fulltime helper, Ronnie, says Brandon makes his day with the positive attitude he exhibits freely and naturally. He and Kirk built the fire in the fireplace this morning. Brandon is eager to take that job on full time. He watched Kirk place the kindling and firewood just right, and he says he can build a fire every bit as good as Kirk.

Our attorney finalized the adoption papers and we went to court just two days ago. The courtroom was packed with family and friends in a child custody case. The judge told them he was requiring them to remain seated for the next case. When we entered the courtroom, we didn't know what to expect. Kirk whispered to me, "Where did all these people come from?"

The judge directed us to come forward and stand before the bench, Kirk on one side of Brandon, and I was on the other side. He looked at our petition for adoption, laid it down, removed his bifocals, and directed his question to Brandon. "Young man, I understand you want this couple to adopt you; is that right?"

Loud enough for the entire courtroom to hear, Brandon belted out, "Yes Sir! I sure do!" Laughing broke out in the unexpected crowd.

We gave Denise limited visitation rights, with Brandon having final say with each visit. We will cooperate with her regarding visits, providing Brandon agrees each time.

The judge continued, "Mr. and Mrs. Childers, I see that you two have fostered this child, as well as—what—four other children in the last couple of years? You have an excellent recommendation from two caseworkers, Betty Sawyer and Bob Murphy. In light of those recommendations, I'm inclined to waive the six month waiting period that is normally required in adoption cases."

The judge looked down at Brandon and said, "Young man, I am now declaring you to be the legal son of Kirk and Katie Childers. You may hug your new parents!"

The crowd was standing, clapping, and hooting! Someone broke out with an ear-splitting two-finger whistle. We were shocked!

When they had quieted down a bit, I asked the judge who those people were. In an intentional loud voice he said, "It's a typical child custody case. Mom is accusing Dad, and Dad is accusing Mom." That silenced the room immediately.

Kirk and I walked out, with one happy little boy between us. I looked down at him as we exited and saw a big grin dominating his sweet face. Then, as he was bouncing along between us, he started whistling a familiar tune I'd heard before. A thought occurred to me. *Yes, Andy Griffith knew how to be a real dad too.*

Mom and Dad followed us out the door. Dad asked Brandon if he still wanted a little Mustang one day. Brandon looked confused. "You already gave me two!"

"No, you don't understand. My grandson is going to have a *real* one when he graduates from high school and starts college. What color do you want?"

"Blue! Just like yours!"

The End

Although this is a work of fiction and no people or incidents in the story are real, the setting for the book was real. Here are some pictures of that actual ranch:

Entrance to the ranch

Milking barn and corrals

ABOUT THE AUTHOR:

While this is a work of fiction, some of the settings are borrowed from real places. I had the privilege of living on this beautiful ranch with my parents, John and Lorene Reed. It is northeast of Oklahoma City, near the little town of Luther, Oklahoma, where I graduated high school. The big solid rock ranch house we lived in was much the same as what I've described in this piece of fiction. The milking barn, horse stalls, white fences, and big hay barn were all there. Memories of life on that ranch are still very dear to me. Many happy holidays were spent with my cousins down in that hay barn. Fortunately none of us ever got trapped in between the hay bales. However, I do recall someone losing a shoe in there. We didn't find it 'til the next spring, when the barn was fairly empty. It was a country place that everyone loved to visit—and were welcomed.

My parents fostered dozens of children while living there. Most of these kids came from troubled homes and some even bore the scars of hardships they had endured there, but with the excellent nurturing they received from my parents, it didn't take long to see them develop into beautiful and loving children with bright smiles. Each one was special. As was the case in this novel, it was difficult saying goodbye to these children. Some were returned to their biological parents; some were adopted, but each one still holds a special place in my heart. I've had the privilege of reuniting with some after they reached adulthood.

I wish I could see them all now. One thing I am sure of; they will all remember the loving foster parents who nurtured and loved them at a critical time in their life.

My wife and I have tried to carry on that tradition. We have fostered children and adopted two of our three children. It is my hope that the readers of this book will be inspired to foster a child. You will be forever changed. So come on, put your own special brand of love on a child. There are so many waiting!

Eldon Reed

Look for the sequel coming soon, *The Branding of Thorne Barrow.* This story maintains the foster parent characters of Kirk and Katie Childers and is set on the same eighteen hundred acre ranch in central Oklahoma. Thorne Barrow comes from a horrific environment and is placed in the Childers home. Will this child receive the same *brand* of nurturing that Brandon did in the first book? Is there ever a chance of reuniting him with his birth family?

A third novel in the sequel is already in the works.

If you've enjoyed this book, please tell a friend.

I love to hear from my readers and enjoy your comments.

Feel free to E-mail me at: eldon@eldonreed.com

My web address is: www.eldonreed.com

Catch me on Facebook at: https://www.facebook.com/EldonReed

Follow my blog at: http://eldonreedbooks.blogspot.com

In my blog, I discuss the publishing industry and current trends in faith-based fiction. I also do a few book reviews of some of my favorite Christian novels. We are blessed with a variety of wonderful Christian authors, writing in most genres, from romance, mystery, the Amish novels, Western, legal thrillers, and my favorite—Southern fiction.

READING GROUP GUIDE

1. What gave you the first clue that Denise may have been negligent in caring for her son?

2. After Brandon's father committed suicide, what caused Denise to choose the type of men she did?

3. Use your imagination for a bit of back history, not revealed in the story. What in Bryce Collier's past may have contributed to his horrible methods of disciplining a child?

4. Did he really mean it to be discipline, or was it something else? If so, what?

5. Kirk and Katie Childers led a simple life. What affect does that type of life have on a child?

6. Clearly, that country home was a happier place than the million-dollar luxury condo was for Denise. What are the essentials in life for happiness?

7. Think about Brandon's demeanor when he was first brought to the Childers Ranch. How did he change over the three years he was with Kirk and Katie?

8. Was the Department of Family Services to blame in any way for the failed mother/son reunion?

9. Did Denise make the right decision in the end?

CPSIA information can be obtained at www.ICGtesting.com
Printed in the USA
BVOW04s0849030714

358105BV00010B/139/P